A. L. O. E.

Sheer Off

A Tale

A. L. O. E.

Sheer Off
A Tale

ISBN/EAN: 9783337242558

Printed in Europe, USA, Canada, Australia, Japan

Cover: Foto ©Andreas Hilbeck / pixelio.de

More available books at **www.hansebooks.com**

SHEER OFF.

"Franks had but an instant to try to save him by catching at the rein, as the maddened hunter rushed like a whirlwind by."
FRONTISPIECE.

Sheer off.

A Tale.

BY

A. L. O. E.

AUTHOR OF "CLAREMONT TALES," "GIANT-KILLER, AND SEQUEL," ETC.

NEW YORK:
ROBERT CARTER & BROTHERS,
530 BROADWAY.
1870.

CONTENTS.

SHEER OFF.

I.

The First-Born.

"WHY, there are the church bells a-ringing! as if it wasn't enough to have all the school-boys going in procession with their garlands, and nosegays, and nonsense!" exclaimed Nancy Sands, the wife of the Clerk of Colme, as she stood in the shop of Ben Stone the carpenter, with her arms a-kimbo, and an expression anything but amiable upon her flushed face. "One might fancy that our new young baronet was a-coming home, or bringing a bride, or that the queen and all the royal family were a-visiting Colme, instead of this fuss being for nothing but the christening of a school-master's brat!"

"Ned Franks is a prime favorite with all the village," observed the stout, good-humored carpenter, as he went on with his occupation of planing a bit of mahogany, which his visitor wanted for a shelf in her cottage.

"A broken-down sailor, with only one arm!" exclaimed Nancy, with a snort of disdain.

"But with a good head and a better heart," observed the carpenter. "Ned Franks manages so well to keep his lads in order without thrashing them, that one arm is one too many for all that they need in that way. Not but that the wooden affair which I knocked up for him myself, with an iron hook for fingers and thumb, might serve well enough on a pinch to knock a little wit into a blockhead, if that were Ned Franks's fashion of teaching," added Ben Stone with a little chuckle.

"Teaching! he has no more learning in him than my mangle," muttered the scornful Nancy.

"But, like your mangle, he has a wonderful knack of getting things smooth and straight. I don't know what we'd have done in Colme without him, now our poor vicar has been tied up so long; it's Ned as has kept everything going like clockwork. Of course the young curate isn't just at once up to the ways of the place, letting alone that he looks as young as a boy, and as shy as a girl; he does his best, no doubt, but he couldn't get on without Ned Franks showing him the ins and outs of everything."

Nancy gave another contemptuous snort, but without specifying for whom it was intended. Ben Stone went on with his planing of the shelf and his praise of the school-master, his hand having a very different effect from his tongue; for the more he planed, the smoother grew the wood; while the more he praised, the rougher grew the temper of Nancy. Ben Stone saw this, and took a little malicious pleasure in stirring up the envy and jealousy of his customer; for, though he was not one to break the peace himself, and had never been known to be either out of spirits or out of temper, Ben Stone was certainly not a man to be reckoned amongst the peacemakers. He rather enjoyed " poking the fire in a neighbor's grate," as he once jestingly observed to his wife, and there was always plenty of dry fuel in Nancy's.

But why should praise of Ned Franks be as gall and wormwood to the clerk's wife, seeing that the one-armed sailor, now school-master at Colme, had never willingly wronged a person in his life, but was, on the contrary, ready to do a good turn for any one? Nancy had never forgiven Ned for having been given the place of school-master, to which she thought her own husband better entitled.

Ned's appointment was, in her eyes, a standing grievance, a shameful injustice, a cause for quarrelling, not only with him, but with all the world. "As if a fellow who has been accustomed to nothing but tarring old ropes, and running like a cat up the rigging, could be compared for one moment with a man like John Sands, who has been clerk for ten years in the parish, next to a parson, one might say, and who can draw out a certificate of baptism or marriage in the neatest and clearest of hands." Not that Nancy had herself much veneration for her husband, or, if report spoke truly, treated him with any kind of respect; but she did not choose that any one should be put over his head, least of all "that canting tar with a wooden arm," as she scornfully termed Ned Franks. Whenever Nancy met the school-master, she scowled at him under her black brows, as if he had done her a wrong. And she was never tired of speaking against him whenever she could get a listener. Now she spoke of the arts with which he had wheedled himself into the favor of Mr. Curtis, the vicar, though every one knew that Ned was simple and straightforward as a child; then she spoke of his violent temper, pitied his wife, " poor unlucky soul ! " from the bottom of her heart, though all in the village were aware that Persis Franks was one of the happiest wives in the world, and that if ever a young couple deserved the famous Dunmow flitch, she and Ned might have claimed it. The happiness of Persis was now as complete as earthly happiness can be; for after nearly three years of wedded life, the desire and prayer of her heart had been granted, — she had presented her first-born babe to his father. But this seemed a new grievance to Nancy Sands. Had not she, too, once had a son? and was he not lying under the shadow of the church-yard wall? Why should these Franks be so happy when she was childless? Why should all be sunshine with them when her sky was clouded with gloom? Nancy did not attempt to answer the question, but it soured her spirit; and the sound of the merry church-bells, chiming for the baptism of Franks's little son made her feel as gloomy and wretched as when she had heard the knell tolled at the funeral of her own.

But we will not linger with Nancy Sands, but rather turn towards him who is at once the object of her outward scorn and her secret envy, — the one-armed school-master of Colne. A very gay scene meets our eyes on the green in front of the school-house, which is full of groups of village children seated on the grass, enjoying a simple feast of oranges, nuts, and home-made cakes; for, on the occasion of the christening of the first-born, Ned Franks entertains, in his homely fashion, all his scholars and their little sisters; he feels in his joy as if he should like to feast all the world. Every guest has a bunch of wild flowers, — the violets, cowslips, and primroses of spring; and merry is the sound of the prattle of nearly a hundred young voices, the ringing laugh, the snatches of song. Persis Franks, quiet and serene in her happiness, moves from group to group with her child in her arms, receiving the congratulations of all, and, with a mother's fond pride, drinking in the praises of her little treasure. Of course there was never such a beauty, at least in her eyes, as her little pink-faced babe, with his downy head and dimpled fingers. Ned is less calm than his wife; being of a temperament naturally impetuous and warm, with rather more of the sailor than of the school-master in his manner, he shows the keen enjoyment of a boy. To the great amusement of his scholars, Ned displays his skill, maimed as he is, in dandling a baby three weeks old; and Persis, who, despite her confidence in her husband, feels a little nervous on account of her fragile treasure, is not sorry when the infant is once more resting upon her own gentle breast.

But the buoyant mirth of the young father is calmed down, and his sunburnt face, though still bright with happiness, wears a graver and more earnest expression when he stands up to address a few words to his guests. As he raises his right hand a little, all the murmur of merry voices is hushed at once, and for some seconds there is no sound heard but the soft breeze stirring the young leaves budding on the elms. Then Franks speaks a few earnest words; for, whether in sorrow or in joy, the teacher at Colme never forgets the office to which he has been appointed by his heavenly Master,—that of feeding, as far as he has power to do so, the lambs committed to his charge.

"My children," thus the sailor began, "this is a very joyful, a very thankful, and also a very solemn day to me and my wife. We have seen, as it were, a little boat freighted with an immortal soul, launched on the wide sea, bound for the port of Heaven. If I did not trust that He who gave it will guide it, I should have many fears when I think of all the storms that it may meet on its course, the rocks and the shoals on which many a poor bark has been wrecked. But I have given my boy to God, and whether the voyage be a long or a short one, a rough or a smooth one, I trust that the little boat will drop anchor in the harbor of glory at last!" Ned paused a little, and Persis, as she bent down and pressed a long, fond kiss on her sleeping infant, left a tear on his soft cheek, but not a tear of sorrow; no feeling of misgiving dimmed the bright hope of the mother's heart.

"And now," continued Franks to his pupils, "let me just add a few words to yourselves. You also have all been launched on the great voyage, and I trust that you all have Faith for your compass, the Bible for your chart,

and heaven for your port; but I must remind
you that you have need to keep a good look-
out for breakers ahead, that you must steer
warily, and mind your soundings. There's
danger of running on the sandbank of the love
of money, or of being drawn into the whirlpool of intemperance; there's the iceberg of
falsehood on the one hand, the sunken rock
of self-righteousness on the other. When
temptation would, like a strong current, draw
you near any dangerous place, don't trust
your own seamanship, boys, to sail close under a rock and yet not strike it; give it as
wide a berth as you can; sheer off, I would
say, sheer off! And, above all, look straight
up to Him whose wind alone can fill your
sails, and bear you onwards in your course;
look to him in storm and in calm, in gloom
and in sunshine, praying that he may guide
you here by his grace, and afterwards receive
you to glory!"

The address of Ned Franks was simple and
homely, characteristic of the speaker, and
suited to the hearers, who were well accustomed to his sea-phrases. Franks had once
compared himself to a buoy anchored down
to warn vessels where navigation is danger-

ous; and not only his pupils, but many a tempted one who came in his wandering course nigh to the school-master of Colme, had cause to thank God for the buoy. If the account of such a life of lowly usefulness as that of Ned Franks have any attraction for the reader; if, in his own voyage over life's perilous sea, while he blesses the beacon, he despises not the buoy; while honoring God's gifted ministers, if he feels that there is spiritual work also for those who have little eloquence but that of a consistent Christian life,—he may find in these pages something to interest him, and possibly, if God bless my humble labors, to help him to "sheer off" from some of the dangerous points where hopes have too often been wrecked, and promising barks have gone down.

II.

The Falling Almshouses.

"I'm afraid, Ned, that there were but poor collections in church to-day," observed Persis to her husband, as they sat together by the fire on the evening of the following Sunday.

"I'm not afraid, but I'm certain of it," replied Ned Franks. "Sands told me this afternoon that the whole collections after the two sermons only came up to four pound three, and when our poor vicar's bank-note was added, there were not ten pounds altogether. What are ten pounds to repair seven almshouses that have scarcely been touched for the last hundred years, and to build up another that has fallen down through sheer old age! The state of those cottages is a disgrace to the village. I wish that Queen Anne's old counsellor, when he built these eight almshouses for our poor, had left something for keeping the places in repair. Those still standing are hardly safe, and as for comfort—one would almost as lief live in an open boat as in one of them; they let in the wind from all the four quarters of the compass, and the rain too, for the matter of that."

"Poor old Mrs. Mills tells me that she is in fear every windy night of her chimney coming down through the roof, or of her casement being blown right in," observed Persis; "and Sarah Mason's wall leans over so to one side, that if it is not propped up soon, the whole cottage will be coming down with a crash, and burying the old dame under its ruins!"

"I must see to that propping myself to-morrow after lessons are over," said the school-master, rather to himself than to his wife; "Ben Stone will give us a beam or two, like a good-natured fellow as he is; the worthy old woman shall not be buried alive if we can hinder it."

Propping Mrs. Mason's tumble-down wall would not be the first piece of work done by the one-armed school-master of Colme for the old almshouses in Wild Rose Hollow. Many a time had Ned clambered up to the top of one or other of the wretched dwellings, as actively as he would have made his way up into the shrouds of a vessel, to replace thatch blown away, or in winter to clear off the heavy masses of snow that threatened to crush in the roofs by their weight. Scarcely a day passed without some aged inmate of one of the almshouses hobbling to the school to ask Ned Franks if nothing could be done to mend a chimney that would smoke, or a window that would rattle, or whether there were no way of keeping the rain from making little ponds in the floor. Ned, with his one hand, was more clever at "stopping a leak" or "splicing a brace" than most men with two hands, for he worked with a will; but when he had done all that he could for the counsellor's tumble-down almshouses, he was wont to say that no caulking of his could make such crazy old hulks seaworthy. "They need to be hauled into a dry dock, and rigged out new:" such was the one-armed sailor's oft expressed opinion, and it was one which no one could contradict.

"Everything seemed against our having a good collection to-day," remarked Persis; "our old baronet dead, and his lady away, dear Mrs. Lane absent in France, and, worst of all, our vicar still so ill, and unable to preach the sermon himself. His nephew the curate is very nice, but—but of course it is not the same thing."

"I'm afraid that half the people did not hear Mr. Leyton, and half of those who did would not understand him," observed Ned Franks; "yet he gave us true gospel sermons; there was nothing to find fault with in the matter, and one shouldn't be too nice about the manner."

"Mr. Leyton is so young and shy," said

Persis, "he cannot speak with authority like his uncle, and then he scarcely knows any of us yet; but I dare say that when he gets courage—"

"I'll be bound you're talking of our young parson," exclaimed a jovial voice, as the door of the school-master's little room was thrown open, and Ben Stone, the stout carpenter, entered. Ben Stone always considered himself a privileged person, and usually omitted tapping for admittance. "I never care to knock," quoth the jovial carpenter, "unless I've a hammer in my hand, and a nail to drive in, and then there's a knocking and no mistake." Stone came in, nodded a good-evening to Persis, and taking possession of a chair by the fire, as if he felt perfectly at home, he stretched out his broad hands to the cheerful blaze, for the weather was rather cold.

"You were talking of the young parson," he continued; "he's not one to conjure money out of folks' pockets. Did you ever hear such a sermon? What had all the silver and gold, and shittim wood, and precious onyx-stones, that he talked of, to do with repairing a set of old almshouses? Our people might open their eyes wide at his grand words, but they kept their purses close shut, I take it."

"The sermon had plenty of meaning; there had been much study spent upon it," observed Franks, who disliked criticism on preachers, and who had besides a kindly feeling towards the young Curate of Colme.

"Meaning! Oh, I dare say, if one could get at it," laughed the carpenter; "but when one wants to give a loaf of bread to a hungry man, one does not generally stick it at the top of a pole; there's not every one as can climb as you do, Ned Franks, or bring down onyx-stones and shittim wood to patch up rotten deal timbers. Why, there was but one little bit of gold to-day in the plate, and a scanty sprinkling of silver, though one might have thought the state of those wretched cottages would have preached loud enough of itself."

Persis and Ned could have told where that one little bit of gold had come from, and why it was that a certain hearth-rug with a pattern of lilies and roses which had taken the fancy of the school-master's wife, and was to have been a present from her husband on the anniversary of their wedding, still hung up in Grant's shop, while their old one, faded and patched, still kept its place in front of their fire. But these family matters were things which the Franks never cared to talk of to others; they had given the gold with cheerful hearts, as a joint-offering to the Lord; and though it was more from them than a thousand pounds would have been from Sir Lacy Barton, they never thought that there was any merit in the little sacrifice which they had made.

"I dare say," continued Ben Stone, "that Mr. Claudius Leyton is a fine scholar, but he's no more fitted for parish work than a gimlet is to saw through a plank." While the carpenter was picking holes in the curate's preaching, he was at the same time, unconsciously of course, picking another with the end of his stick in Persis's unfortunate rug. "Why, he's afraid of the sound of his own voice, and can't so much as touch his hat to you, without blushing up to his eyes. It was rare fun to see him yesterday. He came to my workshop in the morning, to ask me where he could find Mrs. Sands, the wife of our clerk. 'Now,' thinks I, 'I know well enough why you want to visit Nancy. She showed in the face of half the village yesterday, that she had had a drop too much, and you think that it's a parson's business to reprove as well as to teach. But if you ever screw up your courage to rebuke Nancy Sands, I'll give my new hatchet for a two-penny nail!' I told the young parson where Sands's cottage lay, just in sight of my own, and I watched him as he slowly walked towards it. I'd half a mind to go after him, and see how such a lamb of a shepherd would manage such a vixen of a sheep. I marked him shaking his head slightly as he walked, as if he were conning over what he should say; and though I could only see his back, I could just fancy the anxious, uneasy look on his smooth young face."

"Poor young clergyman!" said Persis. "He was about the most painful of all a minister's duties. I should be very sorry myself to have to rebuke Nancy Sands."

"Something like having to pull out a tigress's teeth!" laughed Ben Stone, who had succeeded in making a large hole out of a very little one in the old rug. "But Mr. Leyton never got so far as the pulling! I watched him, would you believe it, walk three times up and down before the gate of Nancy's little garden; it was clear he couldn't screw up his courage to go in. Then she chanced to come out of her door. Maybe she was wondering why the parson took that bit of road for his quarter-deck walk, or she guessed what he was after, and thought she would brave out the business."

"Do you know what passed between the two?" inquired Franks.

"I saw Mr. Leyton raise his hat a bit, in his very polite way, and Nancy drop a little saucy bob of a courtesy, as who should say, 'What have you come here for?' and almost immediately afterwards the parson walked away a good deal quicker than he had walked to the place. I was curious to know what had passed, so I put down my saw, and went up the road to Nancy, who was still in her garden, pulling up groundsel; she has a rare crop of it there, and little besides. 'What said the young parson to you, Nancy?' says I. 'Oh!' says she, 'he hummed and hawed a bit, and then told me — as if I didn't know it afore — that as his uncle is ill he has come to this here place to do duty for him, and that I must remember;' and at that he stuck and stammered and blushed, so I took him up sharp, and I says, — says I (Ben Stone mimicked the insolent toss of Nancy's head as he repeated her words), 'Yes, I remember this aint the first time as you've been at Colme; your mother brought you to the vicarage afore you was out of petticoats; that aint so very long ago.'"

"How could she?" exclaimed Persis Franks; but Ben went on with his story.

"'And so,' continued Nancy, 'he was put down in a moment and took himself off. I guessed what he'd come after, and I wasn't going to be lectured and preached to by a smooth-faced boy like that!'" Ben burst into a hoarse laugh, as if he thought the discomfiture of the youthful minister a very good jest; neither of his hearers joined in his mirth.

"Why, you don't seem to see the fun of it," cried Ben Stone; "but if you'd heard Nancy Sands, you'd have laughed as I do. The old tigress is more than a match for the shy young blushing boy of a parson."

Ben stopped suddenly short, for there was a knock at the outer door, and he was aware that whoever gave it must have overheard his last sentence, for Ben habitually spoke very loudly. Moreover, there was something peculiar in the knock : it was unlike what would have been given by the knuckles of any rustic. The three in the school-master's parlor intuitively rose from their seats, even before the door was opened, and Mr. Claudius Leyton appeared.

The curate did indeed look extremely youthful. A small frame, delicate features, and a complexion like a maiden's, with smooth, fine, flaxen hair parted down the middle, gave the impression that the curate might be five or six years younger than he really was, and that a student's cap and gown would have suited him better than the dress which he wore. Notwithstanding his shy, nervous manner, however, Claudius Leyton was thoroughly the gentleman, and Ben Stone felt more awkward than he would have cared to own at his slighting observations having been overheard. The burly carpenter first made matters worse by a muttered " Beg pardon, didn't know who was there ; " and suddenly becoming aware that an apology was a blunder, he said something about his old woman wanting him at home, and, in his hurry to make his escape, first dropped his stick, then, in recovering it, stumbled over the cradle which was at the side of Mrs. Franks, and awoke the baby.

The cry of the infant effected a seasonable diversion; it covered the retreat of the carpenter, and gave Persis an opportunity of soon quitting the room and carrying the child upstairs, that the curate might have an undisturbed conversation with her husband. Franks placed a chair for Mr. Leyton with more of courteous respect than he would have shown to his cousin, Sir Lacy, the lord of the manor, while Ben Stone went home and made his wife merry with the account of what had occurred, wondering, between his explosive bursts of laughter, how the curate had liked to hear himself called "a blushing boy of a parson."

No one knows how often Claudius Leyton had repeated to himself, as if the words haunted him, the exhortation to Timothy, *Let no man despise thy youth;* nor what a burden the want of self-confidence, added to natural shyness, was to the Curate of Colme. Mr. Leyton lacked neither talent nor zeal, but he was painfully aware that as yet he had not the weight and influence with his flock

which every faithful pastor should have ; and
the young clergyman sometimes seriously
contemplated wearing spectacles, although
his sight was perfect, in order to take away
that boyishness of appearance which marred
his usefulness so much.

———

III.

The Curate's Visit.

"I HAVE many apologies to make, Mr.
Franks, for calling so late, and on a Sunday
evening," said Mr. Leyton, after nervously
motioning to the school-master to take a seat
opposite to him; "and I'm afraid that I've
disturbed Mrs. Franks."

"You are welcome, sir, at any hour, and on
any day," replied Ned, "for I am sure that
you come on your Master's business. My
noisy little man will be better upstairs."

"I'm anxious to consult you, Mr. Franks,"
said the curate, sitting forward in his chair,
and speaking faintly, for his voice was weak,
and two full services had almost exhausted
his powers. "The proceeds of the collections

to-day are, as you are probably aware, insufficient — sadly insufficient for the purpose for which they are required. It is most unfortunate that the illness of my uncle prevented his preaching himself."

Franks could not speak a flattering untruth even to soothe the evident mortification of the poor young clergyman, who had spared no pains in preparing his unsuccessful appeals. There was a little pause, which was broken by Mr. Leyton.

"My aunt, Mrs. Curtis, wrote last week about the state of the almshouses to Mrs. Lane, and I sent a letter to Sir Lacy" (Mr. Leyton was related on the mother's side to the lord of the manor, as he was on the father's to the wife of the Vicar of Colme); "these are the only large proprietors in the parish. Neither my aunt nor I have as yet received any reply."

"You are never likely to get any from our new baronet," thought Franks, who knew well that the money of Sir Lacy was far more likely to go on the race-course, than in relieving the wants of the poor. He, however, only remarked aloud, "The silver and the gold is the Lord's, sir; and, as the need is great, 1 trust and believe that he will send the supplies."

"The illness of Mr. Curtis prevents our being able to trouble him with anything like business," continued Mr. Leyton, "and my aunt scarcely quits his bedside. She and I have, however, been anxiously revolving what can be done ; for if the almshouses be not soon put under thorough repair, not one of them will be standing next year, and their poor old inmates will have no home but the Union."

"That would fall especially hard on one like Sarah Mason," remarked Franks ; "she has lived in her little cottage as wife and widow for twenty years, and her one earthly wish is to die in it. 'Twould well-nigh break her heart to be forced to turn out of the place."

"My aunt was suggesting to me that Bat Bell, the miller, is one to whom an appeal might be made. He has given nothing as yet to the cause."

"Nor is likely to give, I fear," said the sailor.

"He is rich, as I hear," observed Mr. Leyton.

"He has a thriving business at the mill, sir, and some hundred acres of land besides, which he lets to advantage. Bat Bell has but one child, for whom it is supposed that he is saving; for, if reports be true, Bat never spends one-half of what he gets, and must have put by enough of money to rebuild all the almshouses, if he choose to do so. But it is not always those who make most who are found most ready to part with their cash. If the heavily freighted vessel runs on the sand-bank, the more she has in her the deeper she sinks; and if a man has passed half his life in getting, without giving, it needs a strong cable indeed, and a mighty power, to draw him off that sandbank, — the love of money."

"I have heard from my aunt something of the character of the close-fisted miller," said the curate; "yet, in our necessity, she thinks that a strong personal appeal ought to be made. The almshouses of Wild Rose Hollow can be seen from the mill; the object for which we plead is directly before the eyes of this Bell."

Franks smiled and shook his head: "Had mere pity been enough to draw him out, the money would have been forthcoming long ere this, sir," said he. "Bat Bell has seen those cottages gradually falling to pieces year after year, and has talked with the old folks in them; yet I've good reason to know that not so much as a wisp of straw for thatching has ever come from the mill. Pity isn't a cable strong enough to move a nature like that of Bat Bell."

The young minister looked perplexed, and passed his hand across his forehead.

"But, sir," continued Franks, "we know that the shortest road to every man's heart is through Heaven, and it's not for us to give up any work for God as hopeless. No doubt the lady is right; there had better be a personal appeal."

A light flush suffused the countenance of the clergyman. He avoided looking at Franks, and played uneasily with the light cane which he held as he said, speaking with evident effort, "I came to consult you about it. I am a comparative stranger here; the parishioners scarcely yet know me, and — and it's a new thing to me to ask for money. I thought that if you were to speak instead of me, Mr. Franks, the appeal would have better chance of being successful."

Full before the mind of Claudius Leyton was his late encounter with Nancy Sands, and perhaps it was also remembered by the sailor, as he simply replied, " I can but try, sir."

An expression of relief passed over the face of the youthful clergyman. His thanks were brief; but when he almost instantly rose to take leave, he held out his hand to the school-master, and his fair small fingers closed on Ned's strong sunburnt hand with a kindly pressure, which told more than his words. When the door had closed behind Mr. Leyton, Ned Franks thought, with a smile," That poor, shy young minister will sleep more soundly to-night from knowing that he is not to be the one to board Bat Bell. A gentleman like that feels it so awkward to play the beggar, even for the holiest cause."

On hearing the outer door close, Persis returned to her husband, and the babe, who had again fallen asleep, was gently replaced in his cradle.

' Persis," said the school-master, gayly," I'm to go and try to draw money from the miller. I believe I might as well try to draw money from the millstone. I doubt whether Bell would put down half-a-crown to-day, to save all the seven remaining almshouses from being pulled down to-morrow. But I could not refuse speaking to him, Mr. Leyton was so anxious about it."

" I wish you success," said Persis.

" Your wishes are stronger than your hopes, I take it. Bell is a thoroughly selfish man, except as regards love for his child, — sunk in the love of gold. It seems to me, wife, that we might almost divide the world into two classes, — those whose motto is ' Get, get,' and the other whose motto is ' Give, give ; ' those of the closed fist, and those of the open palm. The one set make money their idol ; the other make money their servant. Now, we know that *the love of money is the root of all evil;* that is written in the Word of Truth ; and if one sees the root in a man, what can one look for but evil fruits? Remember what our Lord himself said, *How hardly shall they who trust in riches enter the kingdom of God!* "

" But let us likewise remember what our Lord also said on the subject, dear Ned : *With man it is impossible, but not with God, for with God all things are possible.* Think of Zaccheus ; he who had been covetous and an extortioner, — the publican, who had clearly made money by false accusation, or he would never have spoken of restoring it fourfold."

"Ay, ay," replied Ned Franks, thoughtfully; "there was a vessel sunk over hulk — over bulwarks — deep in the sand, only the masts seen above it; and yet it could be drawn out, and cleansed, and righted, and floated, and sent on with a favoring breeze, as goodly and fair as if it had never grounded upon that dangerous bank. But it was the power of the Master that did this, and the love of Christ was the mighty chain that drew the publican from his old habits and evil ways, and made the covetous man give half of his goods to the poor."

"That power still can work — that love still can constrain," said Persis.

"So let us ask for a blessing on my visit," cried Franks. "I'll be up to-morrow before sunrise, to see to the propping of old Sarah's wall, and after the morning's lessons, I'll be off to the mill. Don't you wait dinner for me, Persis; maybe I'll not manage to get back till the boys meet for lessons again."

IV.

Joyous and Free.

NED FRANKS took down his cap from its peg, as soon as his merry young scholars, like a swarm of bees from the hive, had poured out from the low-browed porch of the school-house. But before he had time to start for the mill, Persis, baby in arms, was at his side, with a sandwich neatly put up in paper for her husband to eat on his way.

"No fear of my being put on half rations while wifie has charge of the stores," said Ned Franks.

He only lingered to kiss the soft little face of his babe, fragrant and sweet as a rosebud, and then set off for his visit to Bat Bell, though not very hopeful as to its result. The sun was shining brightly, the trees bursting into leaf; the lark in the blue sky, the thrush from its bough, were pouring forth songs of joy. Every sight, scent, and sound was a source of pleasure to Ned Franks.

"Those merry little fellows are piping aloft," thought he, "to cheer their mates in their nests. Well may my heart sing, too, for who has such a home, and such a mate, and such a nestling as mine? The birds carol merrily, for they cannot look forward, the pleasure of the day is enough for them; but far more cause have I to sing, for I *can* look forward and think, — the spring-time is bright, but the harvest will be brighter; there is joy now, but the *fulness of joy* is to come! Ay, I can look forward and upward, too, and see what the birds cannot see, — the hand that scatters the blessings over my path, the Father's hand that filleth all things with plenteousness! And even like his free bounty should be that of his children; *freely ye have received, freely give!*"

A thin, weary wayfarer was sitting on the side of the path; his patched coat, his half-worn-out shoes, and sunken cheek told of need, although the man was no beggar. Following simply the impulse of his heart, Franks pulled out his sandwich and courteously offered it to the stranger. The smile and hearty blessing with which it was received sent the one-armed school-master on his way with a heart even more joyous than it had been a few minutes before. To give is a godlike pleasure, and he who does not know what it is to do so *with delight* has missed one of the richest luxuries which man can enjoy below.

As Ned Franks passed along the high road, he could see in a neighboring field a man engaged in sowing.

"To bury seed is not to lose seed," thought Ned, "though it seem for a while to disappear, like money which is given to the Lord, or to the poor for his sake. A man who spends all that he has on himself or his family alone seems to me like one who grinds and bakes and eats all his seed-corn. He gains some present advantage, no doubt, but he will find want and dearth in the end, for he has not sown for the future. And the man who lays by and hoards what ought to be given in charity is like one who locks up his seed-corn in a chest until it grows mouldy and worthless. It neither feeds him nor grows for him; it is worse than good for nothing. While *he that gives to the poor lends to the Lord*, and the Lord will give him rich increase, not because of the man's deserts, but because of our heavenly Father's own free bounty towards those who seek to please him."

Ned, walking on with quick, active step, overtook Ben Stone, who, carrying his basket of carpenter's tools, was proceeding at a more leisurely pace in the same direction.

"Whither bound, messmate?" cried Franks, as he came up with the burly carpenter.

"I've a job at the Hall," replied Stone; "the new baronet will be coming down to the old house one of these days, and will want to find everything right there. Where are you going, Ned Franks?"

"I'm going to see if Bat Bell won't add something to the collection for the tumble-down cottages in Wild Rose Hollow. He was not at church yesterday."

Ben Stone burst out laughing, as he had a habit of doing upon the slightest occasion. "Going to ask Bat Bell for money! Going to try how much meal you can scrape off an old knife-board! ha! ha! ha! I put my shilling in the plate yesterday;"—the carpenter said this with a self-satisfied air, as one who felt conscious of having done the handsome thing;—"but I don't mind promising to double whatever you manage to squeeze out of Bat Bell; only, of course he mustn't know that I've said so."

"Don't make a rash engagement, mess-mate," said Ned Franks, with a smile; "I may come down upon you for some ready rhino."

"Well, and if you do," answered the good-humored carpenter, "I'll not flinch from my word. I've enough and to spare, and what one gives away, as we all know, goes to our good account in the end."

"That depends on the spirit in which we give," said Franks, more gravely, for he had good reason for suspecting that his companion held very mistaken views on the subject. "One can't keep a debtor and creditor account in heaven. We know from the Bible that a man might give all his goods to feed the poor, and yet that it might profit him nothing to do so."

"That's one of the texts as I never can make out the meaning of," said the carpenter. "To give is to give, and money is money; and why, when two men do exactly the same thing, one should have a blessing, and another none, quite passes my poor understanding."

"If one could suppose that all money given in charity could be put to a test, that only what is really offered for the Lord's sake should remain money, and all the rest be turned into withered leaves, don't you think we should have heaps of dry leaves, as in autumn, to be scattered about by the wind? Consider all that's given for mere show, all that's given from natural pity, all that's given because it would be thought strange and mean to do less than others; *none* of that money is given to God, so we must not expect that God will accept it."

"Well, I grant ye this," said the carpenter, "if every man's almsgiving could be known only to himself and to God, there's many a one as gives now would keep his money snug in his pocket. But I'm not one of those, my good friend. I know, as we can carry nothing out of the world, that it's best to have something laid up in the bank above. But here your way divides from my way, — you go down the dell, I keep to the road. Good-day to you, Ned Franks, let me know what you get from Bat Bell; I'll be bound 'twill be nothing to ruin me. I've not much to do at the Hall to-day, but measuring and fitting, so maybe I'll be back before you return; just drop in at my shop and tell me what's your success;" and with a friendly nod and complacent smile, the carpenter went along the high road, while the school-master turned down the little wooded lane which led to the mill.

"I should have liked to have had a little longer talk with Ben Stone," thought Franks. "I'm afraid that he thinks that he is actually *buying* God's favor, and *earning* heaven, by the little kind acts that he does! That's a kind of error which so many people run foul of. The sunken rock of self-righteousness is, maybe, just as dangerous as the sandbank of love of money. I must have a care that I don't take to judging others, and so split on it myself. I spoke very hardly yester-evening of Bat Bell the miller, yet, when I consider what a poor wretched sinner I am, receiving so much from God, and showing my gratitude in such a poor way, I'm scarce likely to run on that rock. When one measures one's little drop of charity, and even that not pure, with the great unfathomable ocean of love of Him who gave his life-blood for us, one is far more inclined to ask forgiveness for doing so little, than to expect reward for doing so much. There's nothing that *can* give the best of us any claim to the least of God's mercies, but the merits of Christ.

That is a truth that I see the more plainly the longer I live. To attempt to hold by one's own merits would be like trying to go to sea in a bark made of gossamer threads. The gossamer web looks goodly enough when the sunbeams are glinting upon it, and the dew-drops are nestling in it, but no man in his senses would trust his life to its power to bear up his weight. It would be a madder thing still for him to trust his soul's salvation to his own merits. If any mortal had anything in himself to boast of or to trust to, that mortal was St. Paul, who was ready to spend and to be spent; who had *suffered the loss of all things for God*, — a very different kind of self-denial from what we dare to call by that name, — and yet what was the feeling of St. Paul? Did he think thus he had earned heaven? Did he not say, *God forbid that I should glory save in the cross of our Lord Jesus Christ?* If we were to strip ourselves of all that we have, if we were to give away health and time and life itself for God's service, we should never get beyond that verse, we should have nothing whereof to boast, nothing (out of Christ) whereon to rest."

Ned had now descended to the bottom of a

beautiful little dell, through which gushed a rapid stream of water, turning the large wheel of Bell's mill. The wheel was, however, at this time still, and its monotonous clack did not mingle with the gurgle of the brook and the song of the birds. Franks had many delightful associations connected with that wooded dell; for there stood the cottage in which Persis, as a maiden, had dwelt with her aged grandfather; it was there that he had wooed and won her; from that little ivy-man tled nest he had, three years before, taken his bride to church. The cottage had now other inhabitants, but Franks could not pass the spot without stooping to pluck a violet to carry back to his wife.

"I'll give this to Persis," he said to himself; "she'll like a flower from the old home, though, thank God, I believe that she has never regretted leaving it for the new one. This much I can answer for, leastways, that every day since that happy one on which God gave her to me has made me prize his gift more dearly."

V.

An Appeal.

BAT BELL was a particular man, regular and precise in all his ways, who had, as it were, stiffened into his own mould, especially since the death of his wife, and who did not choose, as he often said, "to be put out for nobody." Bell hated a visitor at work-time, and he was so keen after making money that his work-time began early and ended late. He hated a visitor at meal-time, probably because he did not wish any one to share his meal. Franks was aware of this, and tried so to time his visit to the mill that he should catch Bell in that half-hour of rest which usually followed his early dinner.

"He'll be playing with his Bessy," thought Franks, "and there's nothing on earth that softens and opens a man's heart like hearing the voice of his own little child, or dancing it on his knee." Such was the conclusion to which the school-master came after his four weeks' experience of the feelings of a father.

Franks, however, found little Bessy, not

with her parent, but amusing herself in the
lane close by the mill. She ran up to him
with open arms, and held up her little face
for a kiss, for Ned was a prime favorite with
every child who knew him, and, during her
mother's last illness, Bessy had spent a week
at a time under the care of the Franks. She
was a plump, rosy-cheeked, merry little girl,
of about five years of age.

"Is father at home, my little lass?" asked
Ned.

"Yes; father's in there," replied Bessy,
nodding in the direction of the door of the
cottage attached to the mill; "but he lets me
be here to look for the flowers."

"Mind you don't go near the water, little
one," said Franks; "keep to the primroses
under the hedge;" and, smiling a good-by to
the child, he proceeded to the dwelling of
her father.

But Bell was alone in his parlor, seated on
his high-backed wooden chair before the
solid deal table, on which appeared the remains of some bread and cheese, and the
empty pewter pot which had held his beer.
Bell was a tall, bony man, naturally of rather
a dark complexion, but skin, hair, and dress

were all powdered with the flour which showed what was his daily occupation, his shaggy black brows especially having formed a resting-place for the white dust, as the thatched eaves of a dwelling for snow.

"Good-day to you, Ned Franks, glad to see you; what brings you this way?" asked the miller, holding out his bony, whitened hand to his visitor, with as much of a smile on his face as the stiffness of the leathery skin would allow.

Franks was not one to approach any subject in a roundabout way; if there was any difficulty before him, he usually took what he called "a header" into the very middle of it. He did not say he had just looked in to see an old friend, or to ask if little Bessy would come and look at his baby, or utter any remark about the weather, or express any hope that business was brisk; he said what he had come to say the moment after he had taken a seat.

"I've called, neighbor, to talk to you about the almshouses yonder in Wild Rose Hollow;" through the window towards which Ned glanced as he spoke, the chimney of the nearest one could be seen. "I was up at

Sarah Mason's early this morning, to try what I could do for her wall; but no patching of mine can make the place fit for a human being to live in, let alone a rheumatic old woman. You know well the state of the cottages; something must be done for them without much delay, or the old hulks will soon fall to pieces."

Every symptom of a smile had disappeared from the hard face of Bat Bell as soon as his visitor had mentioned Wild Rose Hollow; and when Ned paused, the miller's only reply was a "humph," uttered in a very discouraging tone.

"Don't you think that it would be a shame and disgrace to Colme, if dwellings that have afforded shelter for two hundred and fifty years to the aged respectable poor of our village were all suffered to go to utter decay from neglect, as one of them already has done?"

"Why don't young Sir Lacy mend 'em? He has money enough," said the miller, "and flings it away right and left, they say, in ways that are little to his credit."

"If he does not come forward, is his backwardness an example to be followed?" asked Franks.

"Let the clergy see to it; it's their business," said Bell, with a little disagreeable twitch of the nostril, which with him was always a sign that something was "putting him out."

"Mr. Leyton preached twice yesterday in aid of the work, but the collections made were wretched, — not one tenth of what is absolutely required."

"The parish overseers must do something."

"They refuse to stir a finger," said Franks; "they say it's no business of theirs."

"Then I'm sure that it's no business of mine," interrupted the miller.

"Is it no business of ours," said the schoolmaster, earnestly, "that they whom we have known for years, they who have lived amongst us, and hoped to die amongst us, should be deprived of the comfort, the quiet, the independence which they so dearly prize?"

"I'm sorry for them," said the miller, carelessly; "the founder should have left something to keep the wheel going."

"What is wanted is the full stream of Christian love," observed Franks. "There are scores of charities in London kept constantly working by nothing but that stream."

The miller did not look as if he had a drop of such love within him. "It is clear," thought Franks, "that I'm not in the right tack yet. Let me try him on that of conscience. Why," he continued, aloud, "there's no plainer command in the Bible than *To do good and to distribute, forget not; let us do good unto all men, and specially unto them that are of the household of faith.*"

"I know something of the Bible, too," replied Bat Bell, coldly, and the twitch was more unpleasant than before. "I'm a father, and I don't forget that it's written that *He who provideth not for his own is worse than an infidel.*"

"Never let that text be repeated to justify hoarding!" exclaimed Franks, with some warmth, for it flashed across his mind how the devil himself can quote Scripture. "If we are to be content with food and raiment for ourselves, shall we not be content with them also for our children, without gathering up for them gold and silver, which may only prove a snare, as has happened in thousands of cases? I am a father, too," Ned added more mildly, for he saw on the countenance of Bell that he had spoken too warmly; "I am a father, and love my little one as much as a father can love; but if thoughts of saving for him made me close my hand and heart against the claims of God's poor, I should feel, that whatever else I might leave him, I dared not expect to leave him that blessing which alone giveth true riches. I should feel that my babe was coming between my soul and my God, and that I must look for God to punish me in him. Of whatever we make our idol, the Lord is wont to make his rod."

"I've no such superstitious feers!" cried Bat Bell, rising from his seat with a gesture of impatience. Had his visitor been any one but Ned Franks, from whom he had received kindness in time of sorrow, he would have given his guest a broader hint to depart.

"Let us not talk of fear, then, neighbor," said Franks, also rising, but with no intention of yet giving up his attempt to move that cold, hard heart. "Have patience with me a few moments more, while I speak of a nobler motive, — the love of God. Look around you, Bat Bell, look at this comfortable home, where want is unknown; you were ill last

winter; look at the health and strength restored you now; listen to the merry voice of
your child," — a joyous carol was heard from
without, — "and then ask yourself from whom
came all these blessings, the loss of any one
of which would throw you into sore distress.
The goods that you have you owe " —

"To hard work, the labor of my hands in
the sweat of my brow," interrupted the
miller.

" Who gave the hand strength and the mind
reason? whose power made the stream which
turns your mill? whose sunshine ripens the
corn on your fields? But why speak only of
earthly blessings, — we have more, far more
to thank God for! We have not only bodies
but souls to care for; we have not only time
but eternity to live for. Can we be content
to sit still and do nothing for others, when
we know what God's Son hath done for us;
when we think at what a price he bought our
salvation; how, though he was rich, yet for
our sakes he became poor? He calls us to
make no sacrifice for him that he has not
first made a thousand-fold for us; and when
he would teach us what charity should be, the

Lord sums up all in the words, *Love one an-other as I have loved you.*"

Ned Franks's appeal was interrupted by the door being thrown suddenly open, and little Bessy's running into the room. The white pinafore of the child, held up by one chubby hand, formed a receptacle for a number of wild flowers which she had been gathering in the lane. With her blue eyes sparkling with pleasure, the child ran up to her father.

"See, I've plucked 'em for you, every one!" she cried, emptying her pinafore on the chair from which Bat Bell had lately risen; "no, — all but this dead primrose, — it's withered and bad, it's not fit to give father!" Bessy threw the faded flower away. "I've brought you the *first* I could find; now, I'll run and get more for myself."

Bell caught up his girl, lifted her up high, and then kissed her again and again before he set her again on the floor. Bessy nodded merrily at Ned.

"You shall have some, too," she said; "but the *first* are always for father;" and away ran the happy child, leaving her spring flowers behind her.

And Bessy left something besides. The

visit of the little one had seemed to bring sunshine with it. The hard lines on the parent's face were softened, every feature relaxed, the cold, money-making man was a parent, and a fond parent still. Franks felt that the unconscious Bessy had acted the part of a little ally; that she was helping to stir the deeply-imbedded vessel which he had been trying to move.

"Will that dear little girl enjoy her flowers less because the *first* are always for her father?" said Franks, as soon as the sound of the pattering feet was heard no longer. "Would that God's children were more like her, bringing their gifts with readiness, with joy, and not like too many of us, offering only the withered thing, the dead thing, that which we will not miss, to him whose goodness towards us has been greater than that of any father on earth!"

Bat Bell's hand approached his pocket, though he did not actually put it in. "Ned Franks," said the miller, "I tell you honestly, that I wouldn't stand this kind of talk from any man but yourself; but I know that your practice is better than your preaching; so, as you've set your heart on getting something for these cottages, just as a matter of favor to you"—Bell stopped short; he could not make up his mind either to finish his sentence, or to draw out his purse.

"I do not want you to give as a matter of favor to me," cried Franks, "nor is the state of the cottages what is uppermost now in my mind. I came here, indeed, anxious to get something for *them*, but I am a hundred-fold more anxious to get something for you!" The miller raised his dusty eyebrows with surprise, but Franks went on, without giving him time to interrupt the earnest flow of his speech. "If we knew that our Lord and Master had come down again to this earth, that he was in our land, our country, our village, nay, that he was deigning to dwell in one of these cottages, which, wretched as they are, are better than the Bethlehem stable, would we not deem it the first of honors to be allowed to bring gifts to him? Would not you and I be ready to pull down our own dwellings to get beams and rafters for his, and think the best that we have, yea, *all* that we have, too little to offer to our King? And it is all the same, Bat Bell: what we give to the poor for his sake, Christ receives as given to himself. *Inasmuch as ye did it unto the least of these, my brethren, ye did it unto me.* Yes, my friend, I want help for the cottages, but I much more want something for *you*, — the joy of hearing at the last day the Saviour's welcome, *Come, ye blessed of my Father.*"

VI.

The Return.

THE fervent appeal, coming as it did from the very heart of the pleader, had stirred the stubborn hearer a little, though but a little way from his first position. Bat Bell could not help remembering that there was a reverse to the blessing, a "*Depart ye cursed,*" for those of whom Christ would witness, "*Ye did it not unto me.*" Bell feared that he might have lived all his life under the shadow of that curse ; so, anxious to justify himself to his own conscience even more than to Franks, he took refuge in the remembrance of what he deemed a good deed.

"I can give, — I *have* given, and largely,

too," said the miller, leaning his head against the wall. "There's my nephew, Rob Gates; did I not pay fifty pounds to 'prentice him out, — *fifty pounds*," repeated the miller emphatically, "of which I have not had one penny back, though the ungrateful dog has been in business these three years?"

Upon this one act of generosity Bell always fell back when any call on his charity was made, as if he considered that the lent fifty pounds covered every claim which could be made on his purse by religion or by humanity. It always gave him an opportunity of declaiming against the ingratitude of mankind; because his nephew had not repaid his loan, all who needed aid from the miller became in his eyes covetous and thankless, if not dishonest. Bat Bell tried to believe that in hazarding fifty pounds he had already given enough to God; it would have startled him to have been told that not one farthing of the money could be reckoned as real charity. Bell had helped his nephew from *natural affection*, and from *family pride*. The miller had acted exactly as he would have acted if he had been a Turk or an Infidel, — exactly as he would have acted had he never heard the name of the

Lord. Tried by this test, of how small a part of our alms, alas! will the Master be able to say, *Ye did it unto me!*

"That miserable fifty pounds," thought Ned, who had heard of it often before, and who knew too well that the miller used its loss as a perpetual argument to silence conscience, and excuse his neglect of the poor.

"You see, Ned Franks," continued the miller, "a man who has once made sacrifices for others, and has only met with ingratitude; who has spent upon a good-for-nothing scapegrace of a nephew —"

The miller suddenly stopped and started. Ned, whose back was towards the open door, only knew by the change on the face of Bell, the look of surprise that flashed across it, that a third party had unexpectedly joined them. Turning round he saw a stout young man, in a shaggy coat, with a knapsack on his shoulders, and a broad grin on his good-humored face, who advanced with both hands extended to the miller, exclaiming in a loud, hearty tone, "Here's the good-for-nothing scapegrace to answer for himself."

Bell gave his nephew a cordial welcome both with hand and voice, and Franks was so

" Here's the good-for-nothing scape-grace to answer for himself."
p. 58.

glad to see the hearty greeting, that he did not ask himself whether it were possible that the uncle's pleasure at seeing the young man might partly be owing to the hope of his now having the old debt cleared off.

"So you were giving me a pretty character, uncle," cried Rob Gates, after he had thrown himself on a chair; "well, I can't grumble at that, as you've neither seen nor heard from me for many a long year; but I never was much of a scribe, and don't trouble the postman from January to December. I don't care to write till I've something to say, so I waited till I could play the postman myself, and bring a kind of notes that are easily read, and will tell more of gratitude, duty, and that sort of thing, than reams of foolscap scribbled all over."

With a look of honest satisfaction, the young man pulled a large leathern pocket-book from his breast-pocket. His movements were watched with keen interest by the miller, as Rob opened the clasp, and then slowly drew out, one after another, unfolding and smoothing out each as he did so, ten five-pound notes of the Bank of England. He spread them with his broad, rough hands over the table, as if he took a boyish pleasure in making the greatest possible show of his wealth.

"Uncle, here's the fifty pounds which I owe you," said Rob; "you're not sorry now, I hope, that you lent a helping hand to your scapegrace of a nephew? I can't believe that a fellow ever has cause to be sorry for doing a kindness; it always in one way or other comes back."

Franks glanced at the miller, and fancied that he saw his thin lip quiver a little, and that something like moisture rose in the usually dark, cold eye. Ned could not tell what was passing in the mind of that man, as he laid his hand on one of the notes. Slowly, half reluctantly, the miller raised it, and then, as if moved by an impulse, which even his selfish nature could not withstand, Bell handed that note to the sailor, saying, "You came at a lucky time; take that, — it's for Wild Rose Hollow."

Ned stood amazed at success so far beyond all his hopes. He had indeed been led to that dwelling in a happy moment, when Bell's hard heart had been softened and touched, or, to use his own simile, "when a spring-tide had set in so strongly as to help the stranded craft off the shoal." His words of thanks were hearty, and while the miller set about preparing a meal for his hungry guest, the one-armed sailor joyously started on his homeward way.

Merrily Franks sped up the glen, his blithe whistle mingling with the chord of the lark that hung quivering over his head. Ben Stone, the carpenter, who had just returned from the hall, was standing at the door of his shop, on the lookout for Ned Franks.

"Why, he looks as gladsome as if he'd just come in for a fortune himself," muttered the carpenter, "and he's whistling away like a bird! But all that jollity must be put on to cover disappointment, for if he got more than a crooked four-penny bit from that miserly miller, I'm a Dutchman, that's all! Well, Ned Franks," cried the jovial carpenter aloud, "how many brass farthings has Bat Bell pulled out of his hoard to prop up the houses in Wild Rose Hollow?"

Franks waved the crisp, fluttering bank-note in reply.

"You don't mean — what — no — not a *bank-note* — a five-pound note!" exclaimed the astonished Stone, scarcely able to credit his eyes. His exclamation was echoed by his wife and two neighbors who joined him at the moment.

"It must be a toy-note," suggested Mrs. Stone.

"No," laughed Ned, "it is a good honest note of the Bank of England, worth five sovereigns of any man's money. Bat Bell was unexpectedly repaid a large loan at the very time when I was with him to ask help for Wild Rose Hollow; the first note which he touched he gave to God, and I trust that God will bless him for it," added Franks, with fervor; "it was more from him than a much larger sum would have been from another man."

"The sum's pretty large from anybody," said the carpenter, with rather a rueful face, for Bat Bell's generosity had taken him by surprise in an inconvenient way. "I hope that I'm not expected to hold to my unlucky offer; where Bell gives once, I give a hundred times; he may plump out a five-pound note and not miss it, but I've not the knack of turning deal shavings into gold."

"No, no, neighbor," cried Franks, "no one would think of holding you to such a bargain.

You have not suddenly come into money like
Bell, or, I've not a doubt, you'd give to the
full as large as he."

"But I'm not the man to flinch from my
word," said Stone; "if I can't give the
money, I'll give the money's worth in work
when I've time to spare; so you may count
that five pounds as fairly doubled, my
friend."

"That will be a lucky bank-note to you,
Mr. Franks," observed the carpenter's wife;
"for now that you've brought in such a sum
to help the collection, I'm sure and certain
that you'll be the man fixed upon to be clerk
at our church, instead of John Sands."

"Instead of Sands! why, he's not going to
resign the place, surely?" cried Franks.

"He'll have to give it up; he could not
for shame stand up just below the reading-
desk, give out the psalms, and lead the singing, as if nothing had happened," observed
Ben Stone, with a shake of his head.

"Why, Sands is the most quiet, steady,
sober—"

"But his wife, she's the mischief, she's the
ruin of him; a man is what a woman makes
him," quoth the jovial carpenter, giving a

self-complacent nod towards his own partner. "Parsons, we're told, must have their own houses in subjection, and I guess the same rule holds with their clerks. All Colme is talking about it. We'll have you, our one-armed sailor, clerk as well as school-master; there's no one so fit for the place!"

VII.

𝔅rightness and 𝔊loom.

"So there's a chance of my being made clerk as well as school-master of Colme," said Ned Franks to himself, as he walked towards his home. "Such a breeze of good fortune is more than I ever could have hoped for. Why, there would be twenty-six pounds a year, besides what I have now, and no trifle in the way of fees! Now that I am a family man, I shall find plenty to do with the money. I shall be able to fulfil my heart's desire, to give my boy, when he's old enough to learn, a first-rate education. Little Ned shall have every advantage, bless him! There's no saying what he may turn out in time, — may be a parson, maybe a bishop, one of these days!" Franks laughed to himself, and walked on with brisker step at the thought. "Then I'll be able to insure my life, so that if anything should happen to me, my Persis shouldn't be cast adrift on the waves, or have to pull the oar herself in a heavy sea! And we'll have something to give to others. I think that I'll devote the fees for the first year, at least, to the repair of the old almshouses in Wild Rose Hollow. Persis will approve of that, I am sure. Grand news I have to carry home to wifie to-day! When I was nothing but a poor Jack-tar, and then lost my arm by an awkward accident, and thought that the storm of misfortune was throwing me back on my native shore like a battered wreck that never would float again, how little I dreamed what a prosperous gale that storm was for me! Here am I, as far from being a wreck as ever I was in my life (barring that instead of my left arm I've timber and a hook, which serve my purpose quite well), scudding along, buoyant as a cork, with the best of wives and the sweetest of babes and the happiest of homes, with teach-ing work, which is just to my liking, and now with the prospect in addition of being appointed Clerk of Colme, in the place of John Sands!"

But the last words, like a touch to a sleeper, broke the charm of Ned Franks's pleasant day-dream.

"Shame on me!" he muttered, half aloud; "here am I rejoicing, like a shameless wrecker, in the ruin of a poor fellow who never did harm to me or mine! The proverb says, 'It's ill standing in dead men's shoes,' but this is something worse. If poor Sands has to resign the snug berth he's held with credit for the last ten years, it will be because he has the misery of having a wife who has taken to drink; her disgrace falls upon him, and because his home is wretched, he may have the very bread taken out of his mouth! Instead of feeling for him, as any man, let alone a Christian, should feel, I, who have had my cup of blessings already filled to overflowing, I am counting on his loss as my gain; because his happiness is shipwrecked, I'm looking to get my share of the spoils! Out upon me for a selfish, covetous fellow!" exclaimed the indignant tar. "That same prosperous gale that I thought so much of seems to be blowing me right on that sand-bank of love of money, from which I've been warning others. I must take care to sheer off myself!"

The road along which the school-master of Colme was passing, led him by the cottage of Sands the clerk, and he glanced, as he went by, at the untidy, weed-grown garden, the window with the broken pane stuffed with rags, which told a sad tale of sorrow and neglect. The cottage was rather a large and good one, and a few years back had worn an appearance of comfort and prosperity, such as befitted the home of the respectable Clerk of Colme. Franks remembered the lines stretched out along the garden, whitened with linen hung out to dry; for Nancy Sands, a strong and active woman, had added many a pound to her husband's gains by her skill in laundry-work. Now one of the poles lay rotting on the ground; a broken, dirty cord, hanging loose from the wall, was all that remained of the lines. Families no longer cared to trust Nancy Sands with their washing, and, if report spoke truth, the poor clerk had sometimes to iron his own shirts himself, to keep up the decent appearance indispensable to one in his station.

Ned Franks had not gone many yards past the dwelling of Sands, when he saw before him the poor man himself, advancing slowly, as if there were little to attract him towards his home. The figure of the Clerk of Colme, by its peculiar stiffness and formality, was easily recognized at a distance. He always dressed in black, and so appropriate did the cloth appear to the wearer, that no one could imagine John Sands appearing in any less grave attire. Even in his best days the Clerk of Colme had seemed as if he could never look happy. The closely cropped hair, black and almost as thick as the fur of a beaver, was seen above a thin, sallow face, always so solemn and serious that it was supposed to be incapable of smiling. There had been some thought, years before the beginning of this story, of appointing John Sands as schoolmaster at Colme; but there was not one of the scholars who would not have regarded such an appointment with exceeding dislike and disgust. The boys were certain that the old raven, as they called the clerk, must have been brought up in an undertaker's shop, and been cradled in a coffin; they believed that he had never laughed when a baby, nor played at cricket or football when a boy; indeed, a doubt was expressed as to whether the clerk had ever been a boy at all, but had not rather grown out of a Liliputian man, clad in a tiny black coat, and miniature white neck-cloth. No one was very intimate with John Sands; no one ever addressed him by his Christian name, or thought of clapping him on the shoulder, or telling him a bit of good news, or asking him to "come and share pot-luck." Yet nothing could be said against the clerk, except that he did not rule his own house well, and was thought to be henpecked by Nancy.

When the sailor (for such Franks still considered himself, and was considered by other to be, though he had not been afloat for years) saw John Sands coming towards him, he had something of a feeling of shame; it seemed to his kindly, honest nature as if he had done his neighbor wrong by even thinking of taking his place. Franks lifted his cap with a courteous "Good-day," as he was about to pass John Sands, but the clerk stood stock-still on the path, and clearly did not wish to be passed.

"Mr. Franks," he said, to the sailor, "if you could spare me a few minutes, I should like to have a quiet talk with you. The church is hard by; will you come with me into the vestry?"

Now Franks was in great haste to get home; he was impatient to tell his wife of his wondrous success with Bat Bell; besides, having given away his breakfast, he was exceedingly hungry; for, having risen at four o'clock that morning, and having eaten nothing since an early breakfast, his sharp appetite reminded him that it was long past his usual dinner-time. Franks had calculated on having just a quarter of an hour in which to satisfy hunger, and tell all his news, before his pupils would gather again for afternoon lessons. Had John Sands not been in trouble, Franks might have asked him to put off his proposed quiet talk; but the sailor was sorry for Nancy's husband, and only reminded the clerk that lessons would begin again at two, and that the school-master must be at his post.

Franks doubted whether Sands had even

noticed this hint. The clerk turned back, and, at a slower pace than was pleasant to his hungry companion, proceeded towards the village church, not uttering a single word as he went. The two passed along the little walk which led to the back door which opened into the vestry. The clerk very slowly, at least so it seemed to Franks, drew the large key out of his pocket, and fitted it into the lock. The creaking door was opened, and the two men entered the little room which looked so neat, solemn, and silent, with the light from the diamond-paned window falling on its green cloth-covered table, with the heavy desk, and the big registry book upon it. It is probable that the clerk felt more at home in this place than in his own cheerless dwelling; here at least there was peace.

There were in the mind of Ned Franks very pleasant recollections connected with that vestry-room. The very chair which he now took had been occupied by his bride, when, for the last time, she had signed herself "Persis Meade;" in that place he had first called her "wife," and there, but two days ago, their first-born babe had been registered as received by baptism into the church. The clerk also seemed to have the latter event in his mind; for, as he seated himself under the window, with his back to the light, he observed, in the slow, measured tone which he always used, "Your child was christened in this church on last Saturday, Mr. Franks."

"If that is all he has to say to me," thought the half-famished sailor, "I need scarcely have lost my dinner for it;" but he waited, with what patience he could command, for the next slow sentence which might drop from the lips of John Sands.

These two men, who had once been rival aspirants for the post of school-master at Colme, formed a singular contrast to each other, — Sands, with that primly-cut hair, which lay like a judge's black cap on his head, and his face as grave as if he were that judge pronouncing sentence; Franks, with light brown locks, which seemed to curl themselves round with very good humor, and bright blue eyes, always ready to sparkle with fun, as well as to beam with kindness. No one could wonder at the preference felt by the boys for the one-armed sailor, though he had not half the learning of Sands. We know that *he that hath a merry heart hath a continual feast;* and where such a heart is possessed by a school-master, his boys enjoy, as it were, the crumbs of that feast. Ned Franks's inspiriting "Now, my hearties, let's to work," would set his scholars to their tasks with a cheerful energy almost as great as that with which they rushed out to play. The sailor felt that these young beings were entrusted to his care, not merely that he might teach them to be wise, but help them to be happy ; and the influence which he thus gained over their affections greatly aided Franks in reaching the very highest mark of education, — that of training young immortals to be wise unto salvation, and happy because serving the Lord.

VIII.

Pleading.

"MR. FRANKS, you have a happy home," said the clerk, after a little pause; and then he added, with a sigh, "so had I once."

7

Ned knew not what to reply; he thought that all England held no two women more unlike each other than Nancy Sands and his own sweet Persis.

"You see, Mr. Franks," continued the clerk, drooping his head, and looking on the carpet, " it was all sorrow that did it.　There was not a better manager in Colme than Mrs. Sands, till — till we buried our only boy; " the poor man's voice faltered as he spoke; " and then she fancied that there was comfort in a drop.　I don't mean to say she was right, but it's too common a mistake; I — I think the world's hard upon her, Mr. Franks, — she has been tempted, grievously tempted; but there's very good metal in her yet."

There was something touching to the sailor in the effort of the poor injured husband to throw a veil of indulgence over the glaring fault of his wife.　Though her intemperance was ruining his comfort, and disgracing his name, and might seriously injure his worldly position, Sands's anxiety was to find some excuse for his wretched partner.　For the affections of the quiet, stiff, formal man still clung to the choice of his youth.

John Sands had loved Nancy almost from

his boyhood; often had he been jested about his fancy for the boisterous black-eyed girl, who cared so little for him. When Nancy had grown into a bold, self-willed woman, ready enough to receive his attentions, but trifling with his feelings, and not returning his love, Sands had seen, time after time, some rival preferred to himself, and had heard, with silent anguish, that the only girl that he had ever cared for was to be married to some one else. Yet, somehow or other, every engagement of Nancy's was broken off; perhaps few men, when it came to the point of decision, would have wished to be linked for life to Bangham's termagant daughter. So, after many long years of patient, sorrowful waiting, John at length had the wish of his heart granted, and found, as too many find, that he had chosen ill for his own peace of mind. Nancy might have made a good, hardworking wife to a man who would have ruled as well as loved her, — one who would have taught her to obey; but where she should have had a master, she found a servant; she despised Sands for his very anxiety to please her, and readiness to yield to her wishes. There was no open rupture between them;

the wife ruled and the husband obeyed and never complained, till at length Nancy's indulgence in the vice of intemperance made John's misery a thing which no longer could be concealed from the world.

The clerk seemed to expect some reply. The sailor was puzzled what to say; he feared to hurt Sands by expressing any pity, and he was too sincere to express any hope. But as the dead silence became very painful, Ned broke it by saying, "I wish with all my heart I could help you."

"That's it, that's just it," said John Sands, raising his drooping head a little; "you're the only man I could have asked. You see," he continued, uneasily, "Mrs. Sands is always right, as she should be, when I'm by; she has the best of hearts; the metal is good, very good; but I can't be always beside her, and I'm called up to London to-morrow on business, which I cannot put off. I thought that perhaps, somehow, you'd look in a little, or — or take a sort of kind of care," — the poor man looked wistfully into the face of Ned Franks; he knew not how to finish his sentence.

"Really, Mr. Sands," said the embarrassed

sailor, "I do not see what I could possibly do. I'm not in high favor with your wife; any interference on my part she would certainly take amiss."

All the village knew that Nancy had done all in her power, by trying to blacken Ned's character, to prevent his being appointed school-master at Colme, and that she cordially disliked him.

"It was your wife's influence I was thinking of," said the clerk. "I know that Mrs. Sands has a high opinion of Mrs. Franks. I have myself heard her say"—He stopped short, for he could hardly have repeated the compliment to the wife in the presence of the husband, as it was that "Persis Meade was fifty times too good for that canting fellow with the wooden arm."

"I am afraid that even my wife would be unable to do anything," replied Ned.

"Oh! don't say that, Mr. Franks," cried the clerk piteously, as if his last hope were being cut away. "It's wonderful what the influence of a woman can do. Do we not all know that Mrs. Franks, and you helping her, were able to convert even a hard-hearted, unbelieving Jew! Is not the baptism of Benjamin

Isaacs, and of Benoni his son, down in the register there, and was it not all from the speaking of you and your wife? If she could do so much for a Jew, don't say she can do nothing for a Christian."

Franks was touched by the earnest appeal, but could not help thinking in his heart that Benjamin Isaacs, with all his Jewish prejudices, had been a more hopeful subject than Nancy Sands. He did not, however, speak; he only shook his head to express a doubt.

"Mrs. Franks could make her way with Mrs. Sands, I feel certain of it," said the clerk, after another painful silence. "Women know how to speak to women. Could she not take the babe with her? Nancy is fond of babies." Sands's voice dropped almost to a whisper, as he added, "She'd have gone through fire and water for our boy; there was never a better mother; it was sorrow that set her wrong."

Ned could hold out no longer. "I'll ask my wife to call upon Mrs. Sands to-morrow, and to take the baby, and maybe she'll get her to return the visit," said the sailor, cheerily. "Keep up a good heart, neighbor; there may be better days in store for you yet."

There was a little sound in the clerk's throat, something between a cough and sob, and he pulled his handkerchief hastily out of his pocket, for his eyes were brimming over with tears. Franks, who hated to see a man cry, made his departure rather abruptly. "It is getting very late," he observed; "I must wish Mr. Sands good-day."

"I could not help it; I could not help striking my flag when he boarded me like that," muttered the sailor to himself, as with long strides he hurried towards his schoolhouse. "But to think of my engaging my poor Persis to tackle a tigress, who's too much for the parson himself! But how could I say him nay? He's nigh broken-hearted, poor fellow! Certainly, if any one in the world is likely to say a word to Nancy that will help her to sheer off from the whirlpool that's drawing her in, that one is my sweet cherub of a wife."

Franks found that he was even later than he had supposed himself to be; the pupils were already thronging to school; and heated, hungry, and tired as he was, the master had almost directly to set to work. He had not even time to snatch a hasty meal. The benches were half filled with their noisy young occupants before Ned Franks took his usual place behind his high desk. He fancied that he heard a little tittering amongst the boys, for at their very last meeting he had given them a lecture upon punctuality.

"So, my lads, you think that you have caught me napping for once," cried Ned Franks, in his cheerful tone; "but I'll not be hard on any one who is a minute and three-quarters beyond time," Franks glanced at the large clock on the wall, "if he brings as good an excuse for delay as I do now. Here," he cried, waving his bank-note triumphantly, "here are five pounds given to the collection for Wild Rose Hollow, by our friend, Bat Bell, the miller."

A deafening shout arose from the boys. The miller had so long been regarded as a money-making, money-saving screw, that they cheered him at the top of their voices in his new character of a money-giving man.

"I can match your piece of good news with another," said Persis Franks, who had come into the school-room on purpose to tell her tidings to her husband. "Mr. Leyton called while you were out, to let us know that his aunt had this morning received a letter from Mrs. Lane, enclosing for the same purpose a check for ten pounds."

There was a cheer for Mrs. Lane, but not quite so uproarious, because the announcement excited less surprise.

"I'll top your story," said the smiling sailor, speaking so that all the boys might hear. "Ben Stone, the carpenter, has kindly promised to give five pounds' worth of his labor to repair the tumble-down almshouses in Wild Rose Hollow."

A very loud hurrah followed this announcement, mingled with clapping of hands. The young curate, who chanced to be passing the school at that time, paused in some surprise on hearing such a shout, and thought that the naval school-master must have a novel and curious way of educating his pupils. But Ned Franks was teaching his boys a lesson quite as important as even the multiplication-table.

"Now you see, my lads," said the sailor, raising his hands to enforce attention, "that he who cannot give much money to a charity, may give his own honest hard work. Now, I've lately read in a capital book* of school-

* Liefde's " Six Months amongst the Charities of Europe."

boys, who, when shown how to go about it, actually built a house for themselves, that the purses of generous friends might be spared as much as possible. Now, I think that there's no one here present, but myself, that has not two hands, and on those hands ten fingers and thumbs. If any one here present wants to help to set the almshouses to rights, and is willing to give an odd hour of labor every week-day till the job is done, let him now hold up his right hand."

Instantly, above the dark cluster of boys, a number of hands — white, red, clean, and soiled — were held up.

"Or," continued Franks, "as the days are now long, if there be any one who could and would give two hours daily to serving God, by thus helping his poor, let that one now hold up both hands."

Up went all the left hands, to the sound of a cheer louder and more joyous than the first; and then all the hands were employed in clapping, as if, instead of an invitation to labor, the boys had received an invitation to a feast.*

---

* I wish that the united energies of the children of every school in Britain, whether for the rich or the poor, could thus be enlisted

"Blessings on the noble-hearted little fellows!" thought the school-master, as he looked down on that mass of bright young faces. And Persis, as she fixed her proud eyes on her husband, thought, "Ned can lead these boys wherever he will; for he never asks them to do a brave, or kind, or generous thing, without first showing them how to do it by his example!"

IX.

The Invitation.

"Was it a shame in me, my darling, to bring you into this engagement about Nancy Sands?" asked Ned at a later hour of the day, when, seated at a comfortable meal, he made up for lost time by attacking the food with a vigor which amused his wife, who did

---

in some good work. Masters and mistresses would find the beneficial effect in the minds of their pupils. Even Ragged Schools might have a collecting box for farthings; or children's sympathies might be enlisted in behalf of some charity near them. Working *together* for God promotes union, and it is a blessed thing for the young to learn to delight in such work.

not know of his having given away his sandwich to the wayfaring man.

"Nay, I think that it would have been a shame had we refused to do what we could for poor Mr. Sands in his trouble. Besides there is nothing very formidable in paying a morning visit to Nancy," added Persis, with a smile; "she has always been rather civil to me. I remember that when I lived in the dell, before my marriage, when my poor old grandfather was ill, Nancy once brought me some broth of her own making, to keep up his strength, as she said."

"Perhaps what her husband told me is true; there may be good metal in her after all, though I own that I don't like the ring of it. He ought to know her best; but I'm not very hopeful about Nancy Sands," said Franks, pushing back his empty plate; "you see, wifie, when once a *woman* takes to the glass, they say that there's not a chance of her ever getting rid of the habit."

"I never like to hear that said," observed Persis. "Why should a woman, any more than a man, be beyond reach of God's mercy and grace? A woman has often strong, deep affections, and especially shrinks from dragging down her family to misery and ruin."

"But when she is once right in the middle of the whirlpool, can she help being sucked in?" said the sailor, gravely. "Intemperance is like a whirlpool, wifie. Round about it, at some distance from the centre, it looks not much more than a ripple of the sea; the careless pilot might venture upon it, and, unless he keep a sharp lookout at his bearings, scarcely guesses what a strong current is drawing him in, closer and closer, to the down-whirl of waters. Let him sheer off at once, and he is safe; if he slacken sail, and let the vessel drift, why, he's lost, — he comes to a point where he *can't* get her off, let him strain every muscle as he may. And it's just so with the drinking. A man feels sick, or a woman feels sad; a drop of something will warm and cheer them, they think; and I don't say but that it may often do so, and that spirits may be used as medicine, and be found a good gift of God. But when the 'drop' comes to be taken pretty often; when there is less of water and more of spirits mixed together; when the man (or woman) begins to relish the glass, and think

that he can't do without it, — then's the time
to sheer off!   Don't let him wait till the habit
begins to draw him in as with the grasp of
a giant, till he finds that the ship won't answer
the helm, that he's getting into the wild whirl
and will soon be carried whither he would
not; let him fix his quantity, measure it, and
not go one oar's breadth beyond it; or, if he
has not the firmness for that, let him, at any
cost, give up the drink altogether, neither
taste, nor touch, nor look at it, lest he be en-
gulfed in the treacherous Maelstrom, and soul
and body perish together!"

"O Ned," exclaimed Persis, "how fearful
it is to think what multitudes are lost in that
whirlpool!   God grant that poor Nancy be
rescued in time!"

"We'll not forget her in our prayers," said
Ned Franks.

On the following day John Sands started
for London, with a heavy, anxious heart,
only lightened by the thought that the sailor
was certain to keep his word.   Sands lingered at the door of his home, with his car-
pet-bag in his hand, turning half round in a
hesitating manner, as if he fancied that something might have been forgotten.

"I suppose that you've left your papers behind, or maybe your purse," said Nancy, who stood on the threshold to see her husband start on his journey.

"No, it's not that, my dear," half stammered the clerk; "it's that I'm not just easy in mind leaving you here all alone."

"I don't care three farthings for being alone," cried the ungracious wife; "I can find occupation enough, and amusement enough, if I choose."

"That's it, that's just it; I wanted you to promise, dear, — while I'm away, just while I'm away, you understand, — that you — you won't step over to the 'Chequers.'"

"I'll not promise that to you, nor to nobody," said Nancy, with a toss of her head and a snort of disdain; "a pretty pass it's come to, indeed, if I mayn't go and have a gossip with a friend. Mrs. Fuddles of the 'Chequers,' was my school-fellow; you know that as well as I do."

John Sands drew a heavy sigh, and wished from the bottom of his heart that Mrs. Fuddles and the "Chequers" were somewhere at the other side of the world, instead of down in the dell, just beyond the mill. He felt, however, that there was no use in his saying anything more; so Sands set off on his walk to the nearest station; and Nancy stood at the door watching him, as long as the prim figure dressed in black remained within sight. Then she went back into her parlor and sat down, resting her hands on her knees, and gazing with a fixed, dull, joyless stare on the opposite wall. Nancy felt very desolate at that moment, for she had parted with the only being in all the world who really loved her. Mrs. Sands knew that she was already "the talk of the village;" that her neighbors, who had once looked on her as "a thriving, well-to-do woman," now regarded her with contempt; she knew that she was lowered in the eyes of all; and, though she would not have owned that she was so, Nancy was lowered in her own. She scorned, she despised herself for the very vice to which she clung so strongly. She could not bear to be alone with her thoughts; she must drown them in the fiery poison which was already consuming her credit, her happiness, and her peace. Nancy rose, walked up to the cupboard, and took out of it a bottle and a glass. Just as she had pulled out the cork from the former, she heard a soft tap at the door.

"Why, Mrs. Franks, who would have thought of seeing you! and you've brought the baby!" exclaimed Nancy, her face relaxing into an expression of something like pleasure; for she was gratified by the unexpected visit of one whose character stood so high in the village, at a time when her own had so grievously sunk.

Persis took the seat which was offered to her, and listened complacently to the praise of her beautiful boy, and when she marked the shade of sadness in Nancy's tone as she said, "Oh! I know what a mother feels with her first-born babe in her arms," she was glad that she had come on her errand of kindness to the lonely and tempted woman.

"I did not think as you'd have walked as far as this, Mrs. Franks, leastways carrying the child, for you're not over strong," said Mrs. Sands. "You've not been here for a long time; we met oftener when you were Persis Meade."

"Yes, you came to see me in the dell. I remember well your kindness in bringing broth to my poor old grandfather; excellent broth it was; I've no doubt that it did him good."

This little acknowledgment of a single act of past kindness had more effect in thawing the heart of Nancy Sands than Persis could have expected. Nancy's pride would have rebelled at the idea of Franks's wife conferring any favor upon her, but her owning herself to be the obliged party set Mrs. Sands at once at her ease. She liked to talk over past days, happy days as she now thought them, when her own poor boy was living. No one who had only seen Nancy Sands on that morning, sitting chatting with Persis Franks, would have thought of her as the "tigress" whose temper, especially when she was under the influence of drink, made her the terror of her neighbors.

"I'm glad of your visit," she observed after a while; "I was feeling a bit dull all alone."

"I hope that you will return my visit," said Persis; "could you not come over this evening at seven to tea?"

"I suppose your man's out?" said Nancy, shortly. "I warrant you he'd not care to see me."

"Oh, no, my dear husband will be at home; he knew that I was going to invite you. I never do anything without his consent."

"Humph!" grunted Nancy; "that's what I call slavery. I take it a wife's not like a red Indian, tied to a stake."

"No," replied Persis, smiling; "rather like a vine fastened to a supporting, sheltering wall."

"I'm none of your creepers!" cried Nancy, with a saucy toss of the head. "I'm a standard for the matter of that, and don't want to lean upon nobody;" and certainly she did not look like anything that needs a prop, with those stout, strong arms, bared to the elbows, and a red face which might once have been handsome, but which now looked only coarse. "I suppose," continued Mrs. Sands, "that you're one of them meek ones as have old-fashioned notions about wedlock and its duties."

"Very old ones," replied Persis, gently swaying herself to and fro, to rock to slumber the soft little burden so tenderly folded in her arms; "as old, or more so, as the days of Abraham and Sarah."

"I'm one as sticks up for woman's rights," said Nancy, and she drew herself up proudly.

"So am I," observed Persis, looking down on her babe; "but I see them in a different light, perhaps, from what you do. I fancy that it is the husband's right to support, the wife's to lean; the husband's to guide, the wife's to obey; *both* to honor, to cherish, and to love; at least, it's so with my Ned and me."

Nancy glanced at the happy wife and mother before her, and though she might not choose to imitate, she could neither pity nor despise. She only said, however, "There's no doubt but that wedlock's a yoke to most. If I'd been fastened to one who chose to pull hard one way, why I'd just have dragged the harder the t'other way, and — "

"And I am afraid that then no great progress would have been made either way," said Persis, timidly yet playfully.

Mrs. Sands gave a short, harsh laugh. "I for one could never abide to be dragged down by such clogs as what folks call duty and obedience. Why do you smile, Mrs. Franks?"

"I smiled because your words reminded me of a little fable of a clock."

"What's that? I never heard the fable," said Nancy.

Persis bent down and kissed her baby two or three times, perhaps to give herself time to collect her thoughts, and then began, —

"Once upon a time, all the upper parts of a great kitchen-clock rebelled against the weights. 'Of what use in the world they can be passes my understanding!" cried the wheel. 'Great, heavy, leaden clogs as they are, always dragging down towards earth!'

"'I'm sure that I've nothing to thank them for,' exclaimed the minute-hand, briskly; 'every one looks at me as I go travelling round and round, but who would ever care to stoop to look at the weights below?'

"'They're not fit to be seen!' added the hour-hand; 'if they could be twitched off at once, I dare be bound that I'd go as fast as you do!'

"'I'm tired to death of them!' clicked the pendulum. 'I'm certain that I don't need 'em to keep me swinging steadily backwards and forwards. I'd get on much better without 'em!'

"'They're dumb as fish!' observed the little bell inside. 'I wonder that any clock-maker in his senses ever burdened a clock with weights!'

"One day an idle boy in a fit of mischief pulled both the weights off the clock. It was not long, as you may believe, ere the different parts of the machine found out the effect of the loss.

"The wheel could not turn itself round; the pendulum grew feeble and would not swing.

"'I've come to a dead lock!' cried the minute-hand.

"'I can't get on!' groaned the hour-hand.

"And though both were pointing to twelve, the little hammer could not strike on the bell.

"'Ah,' said the key, that was hanging close by, 'I guess that the clock-maker knew what he was about when he hung on those weights.'"

When Persis Franks stopped, Mrs. Sands laughed.

"I suppose," she said, "that the moral of your fable is that wives get on better with the clogs of duty and obedience than they would do without them! But I find that *my* hands will move fast enough, and my clapper strike readily enough without my bothering myself to please my man, much less to obey him! But you're not going away yet, Mrs. Franks?" Persis had risen as if to depart.

"I hope to see you so soon again; you are coming, — at least will you not come and take tea with us this evening? You will not wish to stay all alone."

"Oh! I'll not be alone anyhow," said Nancy, also rising from her seat; "I thought I'd look in on Mrs. Fuddles."

This made Persis press her invitation. "You've never passed an evening with me since my marriage," she said; "I'd take it so kind if you'd come."

"Humph!" said Nancy, doubtfully. An evening at the public-house was more suited to her degraded taste than one at the school-house; but she felt the advantage of being able to say to her neighbors that she had taken tea at Mrs. Franks's.

"I want you to see more of my husband," pleaded Persis.

A suspicion flashed across Nancy that there might be some design to convert her. Suddenly and almost fiercely she asked,

"Franks won't be after preaching goodness and that sort of thing?"

"No, he'll not preach," answered Persis, quietly, "but he will *practise*," the added to herself. "My husband has many amusing sea-stories," said Persis aloud. "Did you ever hear of his crocodile adventure in Madagascar?"

"Well, I'll come; seven is your hour, I think, that you told me."

"Yes, we take our meal later now, as Ned goes after lessons, with his boys, to work in Wild Rose Hollow."

The invitation being accepted, Persis was about to leave the place, when her eye fell on the bottle which Nancy had taken out of the cupboard. The scent which pervaded the room told that its contents must be gin.

"What avails it to keep her from the public-house," thought Persis, "if she has the poison with her at home?" Mrs. Franks's foot was on the threshold, but she suddenly turned and came back; her heart fluttered and her cheek flushed, but her resolution was taken.

"Mrs. Sands," she said rather nervously, "I see that you have a bottle of spirits in the house. Poor Walter Baynes, who is almost sinking, has been ordered strong stimulant by the doctor; it is almost necessary to keep him alive. As you happen to have gin at hand, will you, to do me a favor, let me carry that bottle to him?"

Persis was astonished at the boldness of her own request, and Nancy was scarcely less so.

"He can get it elsewhere," she said sharply.

"I should like so much, so very much, to take it to him now from you. I pass his cottage on my way."

Mrs. Sands put her stout arms a-kimbo, and Persis was alarmed at the savage expression which came over her features as she said, "Don't you think I don't guess what you're after. Some one has been slandering me to you. You think that that bottle is safer in your hands than mine."

Franks's wife, trembling, pressed her baby closer to her heart, but she did not utter any denial of the truth.

" You'd be a-wanting to get me to give up the drink, not just for to-day, but always."

" And if I could do so," said Persis, speaking with agitation, for she was nervous and frightened, "if I could persuade you to give it up for your own sake, your husband's, the father of your poor boy, should I be acting the part of an enemy or of a friend?"

Nancy Sands was silent for some moments, painful moments to Persis. She could not read that woman's heart; she did not venture to glance into her face, or she might have seen in the heart the pang of remorse, in the face the sullenness of shame. Mrs. Sands knew, felt, that she was being drawn into misery and degradation, and that Persis, the gentle, pure-minded wife, was only acting as a guardian angel might act, seeking to save a perishing soul. Anything like stern rebuke Nancy's proud spirit would not have borne; but Persis, trembling while she pleaded, with moisture glistening on her downcast lashes, did not stir up all the fierce wrath and resentment that would in a moment have silenced conscience. Suddenly, half fiercely, Nancy cried, "Take the bottle; I don't care; I can get more; the poor fellow is welcome to the gin."

Persis did not let the opportunity slip. In a minute she had possessed herself of the dangerous bottle, and after stammering thanks, to which Nancy would not listen, Mrs. Franks hurried away from the place.

"Oh, I'm so thankful that visit is over!" she exclaimed half aloud as she passed through the garden-gate; "and I shall be thankful when the evening also is over. I hope, oh, I do hope, that she'll come to us sober!"

X.

A Happy Home.

Nancy did come perfectly sober, and Ned Franks kept his engagement made for him by his wife. Not a word was uttered which even the irritable Mrs. Sands, conscious of her own evil habit, could possibly twist into a reproach. On the contrary, Persis took care to thank her guest for her kindness in sending what had been valuable medicine to Baynes, and let her know how the poor sinking sufferer had seemed to revive under its effect.

Everything was done by the Frankses to make the evening pass pleasantly to their

guest.   Their parlor with its jars of fresh flowers, the snow-white cloth spread on the table
covered with the pretty tea-service, which
had been a wedding-gift to Persis, tempting
bread and butter and the home-made cake for
which the school-master's wife was famous, —
all formed a picture of neatness and comfort.
Mrs. Sands could not help contrasting Franks's
cottage with her own.   How different the
home where holiness and love went hand in
hand, from the untidy, comfortless dwelling
of the drunkard !

Ned made himself exceedingly amusing;
he told some of his very best stories, and
Nancy, under the genial influence of pleasant
society, brought out some of her own, which
she related with a good deal of spirit.   Persis
was surprised to find that her guest could be
really agreeable, and Franks, for the first
time, was able to guess what could possibly
have made poor John Sands take a fancy to
Nancy.   There was nothing to ruffle Mrs.
Sands's temper, much to amuse and please
her, and the buoyant cheerfulness of the one-
armed sailor was infectious to every one near
him.

So passed the evening till a quarter before

nine, when Persis glanced at her husband. It was the time when they always had prayer and Bible-reading together.

"Mrs. Sands," said the sailor, "I don't think you'll mind our going on in our own old way; we have a little reading and prayer at this hour, and perhaps you'll like to join us."

The clerk's wife expressed no objection, though Persis fancied that her face clouded over a little. "He'll be reading at me, or praying at me," was the unspoken thought of the conscious guest.

But Nancy Sands was mistaken. The short portion of Scripture, impressively read by Franks, was about the joys of the blessed, the exquisite description of the white-robed ones rejoicing before the throne. And when the Frankses and their guest knelt down to pray, there was nothing in the words of the sailor that might not have been uttered had Nancy Sands been as lowly and pure-hearted and meek a Christian as Persis herself.

The proud sinner felt humbled and subdued. She felt as if she had been nearer to heaven on that evening than she had ever been before in her life, and yet that there was some terrible, impassable barrier shutting her out from closer approach.

"Now I must go home," she remarked in a tone of regret.

"But you will come again and take tea with us to-morrow," said Persis, after asking Ned's consent with a glance, and receiving it in a smile. "Mr. Sands will not be back till Thursday."

"Yes, I'll come; you're very kind," replied Nancy, wondering what could make her company desired by one like Franks, to whom she had shown so much rudeness, or by his wife, who was herself such a pattern of sobriety and quiet behavior.

"I'll convoy you home," said Ned Franks, taking down his cap from its peg.

"Oh, dear, no. I could find my way blindfold, and there's clear moonlight to-night."

"I'll see you safe in port," said the sailor, with quiet firmness. He remembered that the "Blue Boar" must be passed on the road.

It was a night of exquisite beauty. The softness of the breeze, the silvery light of the moon, seemed in perfect harmony with the holier feelings which had been wakened in

Nancy's breast by the sight of a Christian home.

"You are very happy," she abruptly observed, as she walked by the sailor's side.

"We *are* happy," was the brief but fervent reply.

"Perhaps clocks do go better with weights after all," muttered Nancy; a remark which to Ned sounded so odd, and so utterly foreign to their subject, that, had he not known that Nancy had had nothing stronger than his wife's good tea, he would have suspected that she had taken "a drop too much."

As Franks and his companion passed the church, the soft moonlight lay like a silvery robe on the graveyard, throwing deep shadows from the tombstones over the mossy mounds. Nancy heaved a low sigh;—in that quiet spot lay the remains of her only son.

"Life is a bitter thing," she murmured.

"It would be if this life were our all," said Franks.

The sentence was short but suggestive; Nancy knew that the world had been *her* all; that she had thought little of, and cared less for, anything beyond the cares and pleasures of this life. She knew that what shed radiance on the home of Persis was not merely the domestic love and peace within it, but the hope of a better home beyond earth, and that such hope, like the moon, could beautify and brighten, not only the cheerful cottage, but even the silent grave.

Franks was more pleased with the quiet, subdued manner in which Nancy bade him good-night at the door of her dwelling, than he had been with her lively conversation in his own. Never had Mrs. Sands felt more disgusted with the untidy aspect of her parlor than when she entered it on that night. How unlike it was to that which she had quitted! What a different wife she had been from Persis! Nancy thought of what she heard at church about a broad way and a narrow way. She had a terrible consciousness that the broad was that which she herself was pursuing; she knew that it must — not only according to Scripture, but the natural course of events — end in destruction, and she felt more keenly than ever that *the way of transgressors is hard.*

Nancy Sands was very low in spirits,—a reaction after excitement, — and she also, no doubt, missed the stimulant to which she had been accustomed. But for Persis having carried away the gin, which had not been replaced, the clerk's unhappy wife would certainly have all at once drowned uneasy thoughts by indulging in her fatal habit. Happily, however, on this night no supply of spirits was at hand, and perfectly sober, but deeply sad, Nancy Sands retired to rest.

But the enemy, who *goeth about as a lion seeking whom he may devour*, will not lightly leave hold of a victim on whom his deadly gripe has once been laid. While the Frankses were thankful for success of their first attempt to win Nancy from her course of misery and sin, they felt how utterly unable they were in themselves to work any effectual change. Fervent were their prayers to Him who willeth not that any should perish, that he, by the might of his Spirit, would rescue the tempted one from Satan and from herself.

XI.

Temptation.

"WELL, Franks, you're an odd chap," exclaimed Ben Stone, the jovial carpenter, as Ned, on the following afternoon, was passing his shop, going with a party of young volunteers to work in Wild Rose Hollow.

"Why, what's in the wind?" asked Ned.

"To think of your having the tigress to tea with your wife! I wonder she hasn't left marks of her teeth and claws!" The carpenter gave his merry chuckle. "But, joking apart, I don't think that Nancy is fit company for Mrs. Franks. I can't think why you should ask her; it's really encouraging vice."

Ned Franks attempted no explanation. The easy-going, self-satisfied Ben would not have understood the motives of one who, like his Master, could show kindness to sinners whilst abhorring their sin.

"If you've any idea of *converting* Nancy," the carpenter continued, laughing at the idea as utterly absurd, "you might as well try to turn my old lathe into a lady's piano-forte!

Why the woman's just passed this on her way to the 'Chequers,'"—he pointed with his thumb towards the dell,—"and if she come back sober, why, I'm a Dutchman, that's all!"

Franks was more vexed than surprised at the news. He quickened his steps, and overtook Nancy when she had almost reached the door of the "Chequers." "On with you, my lads," cried Ned to his boys, "I'll be after you in a twinkling; see if you can be sharp enough as to finish that bit of clearing before I join you." He then walked up to Nancy, and laid his hand on her arm.

"Mrs. Sands, just you come on with us, and see me and my crew at work." There was nothing in the words, but much in the manner, that conveyed an earnest warning.

"I will, presently; I must just step in here first," said Nancy, looking restless and annoyed.

"Mrs. Sands, you joined us last night in the prayer, *lead us not into temptation;* are you not steering right into the middle of it now?"

Nancy's face flushed very red; there was anger, but also some irresolution. She stood for a moment as if she could not make up her mind, when a shrill voice was heard from the open window of the tap-room, "I say, Nancy Sands, I've been wondering what has become of you. I thought as how you must have jogged up to Lunnon on a spree!"

That call from Mrs. Fuddles decided the hesitating woman. Nancy roughly pulled away her arm from Franks, and hurried up the path to the "Chequers."

"Can't save her against her will," said the sailor, sadly, as he went on his way. "I've no more power to keep her back from the whirl-pool, than I have to stop that great mill-wheel with a touch of my wooden arm." Even the scene of cheerful activity into which the sailor soon entered did not entirely remove the pain-ful impression left by the conduct of Nancy. Ned was, however, too busy to attend much to anything but what lay directly before him. The almshouses in Wild Rose Hollow were, one by one, to be put into perfect repair, gardens, buildings, and all. The funds sub-scribed had not been nearly sufficient to cover the expense; so but few skilled work-men could be employed; but under them, with energy and great zeal, labored the vil-lage boys, whom their one-armed teacher

"To these young volunteers fell the simpler part of the business—fetching and carrying, leveling ground, clearing off rubbish, and digging drains. Sheer off.

p. 105.

had enlisted to help in the work. To these young volunteers fell the simpler part of the business, — fetching and carrying, levelling ground, clearing off rubbish, and digging drains. But they needed an overseer, or, with all their good will, the merry crew might rather have marred than helped on the work. Ned's energies were therefore fully employed, and it was not till working time was over, and the little laborers had begun to scatter on their way to their various homes, that he had much time to think about Nancy.

Ned was sauntering slowly and wearily along the road, and had nearly reached the water-mill, where the clack, clack of the revolving wheel showed that the miller's day of labor did not close at sunset, when he was startled by a loud and piercing cry. It was succeeded by another and another! The first idea of the sailor was, that one of his boys, in careless play, had fallen into the mill-stream. He darted forwards, and in half a minute was in the centre of a group of lads, who, with alarm and horror, were gazing into the water, and shouting out frantically, " Stop the wheel ! stop the wheel ! She'll be under it ; she'll be torn into pieces ! "

Franks saw a form struggling under the water, and one red hand raised above it. He had no time to distinguish more, not even an instant to pull off his coat, before plunging into the stream, lest the poor wretch, dragged on by the force of the current, should be crushed by the ponderous wheel. Ned was a bold and skilful swimmer, but he was a maimed man, and encumbered with his clothes; and, though he had not paused to reckon chances before dashing in to the aid of a drowning woman, he felt, when he was once in the water, that he was quite as likely to share an awful fate as to succeed in saving her from it. The rush of the stream was terrible. Never had the struggling swimmer found himself in greater danger. The cries and shouts of the boys on the bank, who were far more anxious for the safety of their beloved teacher than for that of the intoxicated Nancy, the terrible clack of that merciless wheel, for weeks afterwards haunted the memory of Ned Franks.

He reached the woman, he entangled his iron hook in her clothes, — for his right hand, his only hand, could not be spared from swimming, — and wrenched her back by main force from her awful position close under the wheel. By desperate efforts Franks succeeded in struggling back near enough to the bank to be caught by a dozen eager young hands, and, gasping, choking, almost exhausted, he and his still shrieking burden were drawn up to a place of safety. Ned could scarcely distinguish, through the dull, booming sound in his ears, the exclamations of horror around him, "Her arm! oh, it's smashed, smashed to bits!"

A fearful appearance was indeed presented by Nancy; her dripping, clotted, tangled black hair hung over a face now pale as that of a corpse, and the sight of her arm, mangled and crushed, shocked and sickened the bystanders. "What shall we do, — where shall we take her?" was the question passed around, for her hurts were evidently too fearful for village treatment. Nancy herself answered the question, for, though she had fallen intoxicated into the stream, the sudden plunge, the terrible shock, had effectually sobered the miserable woman.

"The hospital, — the hospital!" she gasped.

Every one knew that there was one in the town but a few miles distant. There was a cry of "Bring a shutter from the 'Chequers,'" when the sound of wheels was heard, and Mr. Leyton, the curate, in a small open carriage, drove rapidly down the dell. The clergyman knew from the cries and shouts of the crowd, that something terrible must have occurred.

"Lift her in here, gently, — gently. I'll take her to the hospital at once," exclaimed the kind-hearted curate. A blanket brought from the "Chequers" was hastily wrapped round the dripping woman, and the carriage was driven off at speed, that its fainting occupant might be placed as quickly as possible under a surgeon's skilful hands.

It was not till the chaise had disappeared from his view, that Ned Franks had leisure to think of himself. He felt sick and faint, and thankfully took the glass of hot brandy and water that was brought to him by one of his boys, but he declined the offer of the miller to come in and warm and dry himself at his fire, and change his dripping clothes.

"Thanks to you all the same, Bat Bell, but a quick walk home will heat my blood, and Persis will soon set all to rights with me," said the sailor, as he shook the drops from his curly brown hair. "I've got no real hurt, thank God! I wish we could say as much for poor Nancy. Sands will have a sad coming home to-morrow when he hears of this dreadful accident."

"No man can say but that it serves her right," was the observation of Ben Stone, when he heard of what had happened to Nancy. "She was walking into something worse than a mill-stream with her eyes wide open; Providence stopped her, when man could not stop her. There are worse evils than a plunge into a mill-stream, or even a broken arm."

Franks rose the next morning before sunrise, that he might have time to go to the town for news of Nancy before his scholars met. All during the night the frightful scene of the preceding evening had disturbed him in his sleep, and he had repeatedly awoke with a start, fancying that he was dragging the shrieking Nancy from under the wheel.

Persis anxiously awaited her husband's return from the hospital. "Have you seen Nancy?" she eagerly asked, as, tired and heated with his long walk, Ned re-entered the school-house.

Franks shook his head sadly. "The poor

arm has been taken off," he replied; "they could not save it. She has passed a very bad night, but there are good hopes that she may recover. Poor Sands, — poor fellow! 'twill be a terrible blow to him!"

"And yet, dear Ned, who knows but that a blessing may come even out of this grievous trial? In the hospital poor Nancy may be broken of her sad habit; she will have time for thought, for prayer. Oh, how can we be thankful enough that she was not suddenly summoned, when in a state of intoxication, to appear in the presence of her God!"

XII.

Ice Below.

SINCERE and strong as was the pity felt by the Frankses for the sufferings of Nancy, a letter, which came by the post a few minutes after Ned's return from his visit to the hospital, diverted their attention to a subject of still closer interest to themselves.

"Why, Ned, here's a letter to you from our Norah!" cried Persis to her husband, who, wearied with his long, early walk, was snatching a hasty breakfast.

"That will be something pleasant; Norah's letters are always pleasant," said Ned Franks, as he broke open the envelope with the help of his hook. "It's come to cheer us a bit, for I don't feel up to much this morning."

"You're not looking well, Ned," said the wife, glancing anxiously at his pale and haggard face. "That plunge into the mill-stream yesterday to save poor drowning Nancy has, I fear, given you a chill, and all your extra work to repair the almshouses after school-hours are over is too much for your strength."

"Yes, if one is to be kept awake half the night with a squalling baby," added Franks. "Our little man seemed determined that we should have enough of his music. I suppose that one will get used to it some time, just as one gets used at sea to the noise of the winds and the waves. Why, there he's at it again!"

The baby, which Persis held in her arms, began crying loudly, as he had been doing at intervals all the night through.

"I'm afraid that the darling has something the matter with him," said Persis, rocking the child gently to and fro to hush his cries.

"Nothing the matter with his lungs, any-how," observed the sailor, who, though fondly loving his boy, had become somewhat weary of his roaring, and who had awoke with a headache, — a bad preparation for playing school-master to a swarm of noisy young rus-tics. "But let's see what Norah has to say for herself; dear girl, her letters are always like sunshine ! " and the sailor began reading to himself the note from his young orphan niece.

"I fear there is not much sunshine in that letter," thought Persis, as she saw a cloud gathering on her husband's brow, usually so open and clear.

"I don't know what to make of this ! " ex-claimed Ned, in a tone of irritation, starting up from the table on which lay his unfinished breakfast. "Just listen to this, Persis. Oh, can't you stop the child's crying for a minute? It's enough to drive a fellow distracted ! " and the sailor read aloud the letter from Norah, with the accompaniment of little Ned's squalling.

"DEAR UNCLE, — I am so grieved, but mis-tress has given me warning, and I'm to go to-morrow. I hope you won't be very angry, after all you've taught me, and all my resolutions. I can't stop in London just now, as I would not know where to go to; so I'm coming down to you by the train that arrives at half-past three. I hope that you won't mind; that it won't put auntie out much. My love to her and the baby. Your sorrowful niece,

"NORAH PEELE."

"When we thought her so comfortably settled in a good situation, doing so well," muttered Franks. "What can Mrs. Lowndes mean by cutting the poor lass adrift at a day's notice!"

"Norah must have got into some scrape," observed Persis.

"Ay, that's plain as a flag-staff. She might have given us a notion of what the scrape is, instead of writing about my teaching and her own resolutions, which we knew all about before. But poor Bessy's motherless girl must always find a home under our roof."

"Oh, yes," said Persis, cheerfully. "While you are busy with the boys, I'll see to clearing out the little room, and having all right and tight for our Norah. I think that she is as dear to me as to you, and that is saying a good deal."

"I loved the lass from the first day I saw her, and I thought there was the making of a very good girl in her, too, only she and her brother had been brought up so badly, scarce knowing a lie from the truth. But poor Bessy, — she's gone, and it's not for her brother to be diving down to bring up her failings to the light. She loved her children, anyhow, and couldn't teach them what she didn't know clearly herself. But who's to meet Norah at the station?" added Ned Franks, abruptly. "You can't go because of baby, and I can't go because of the boys."

"I am afraid that Norah must find her way home by herself," observed Persis, "unless the miller is going to the town. I'll walk over to the dell and ask him. But Norah knows the road so well that her coming alone matters less."

"It matters a great deal," cried Franks, with impatience. "Here the lass is returning with a wet sail and a heavy heart, I warrant ye, and she finds no one to take her by the hand and welcome her to port, or to carry her bundle for her. I'd not have minded it if she'd been coming with colors flying to pay us a visit. Why on earth should she choose an hour when she knows I'm always in the school-room?"

Persis did not know how to answer the question, and had no time to do so had she known, for the sound of young voices, and the trampling of heavy boots in the adjoining room, told that the boys were beginning to assemble. Never had Franks been less inclined to begin his daily labor; never had he met his scholars with less of kindly good-humor.

For Ned was no model of perfection. He was naturally of a hot and hasty spirit; and though, from Christian principle, he usually held his temper under such command that he had the reputation of possessing a good one, it had cost him many a struggle to make it obey the rein. On this particular morning, with an aching head, weary frame, and worried mind, he felt irritable and impatient. He was angry with the dull lad who could not remember that *seven times eight* is not *seventy-eight;* and when Bill Doyle, repeating his natural-history lesson, said that horses ran wild on the *staircase* in Russia, instead of the *steppes*, Ned, who at another time might have smiled at the blunder, which was probably made half in fun, muttered something about "blockhead," and sent the boy to the bottom of the class.

Bill, the son of Sir Lacy Barton's groom, being a sharp, pert little fellow, was not disposed to take his punishment quietly, or to be called blockhead on any subject connected with horses. He whispered to the boy who sat next him, "He don't know nothing about horses hisself."

"What's that?" exclaimed Ned Franks, whose sharp ear had caught the whisper.

"Father says sailors have never no notion of riding," said the saucy little urchin, "and when they mounts a horse, are as likely to get up with their face to the tail as the head." At which observation a little titter ran round the school.

It has been remarked that few things nettle a man so much as to doubt his skill in riding; and Ned, who was always jealous for the honor of his old profession, was in no humor to take as a jest the slight thus cast on the whole of the navy.

"Then you may tell your father, when you

go home," he said, angrily, "that there are no better horsemen than some of our blue-jackets; and as for riding,—when we were lying off Alexandria, every day that we could get leave ashore, I and my messmates mounted and galloped at a pace that would have made your jockeys stare."

As the word of the one-armed school-master was always implicitly believed, Ned could see that he had raised himself not a little in the eyes of his pupils, especially those of Bill Doyle, by the accomplishment of horseman-ship to which he had thus laid claim. But Ned had hardly spoken the hasty sentence, when he was angry with himself for having been betrayed by foolish pride into uttering it. He felt that for once he had been guilty both of exaggeration, and of (without actually speaking untruth) misleading the boys as to his meaning.

Any one of a soul less transparently candid than that of Ned Franks might have thought it weak scrupulosity to let the mind dwell for a moment on such a seeming trifle as this. There is a marvellous difference between the consciences of men. Some have become hard as the horny hoof of an ass; little short of a bullet (by which figure I would represent some open act of wickedness) can make them feel pain at all. Other consciences are tender and sensitive as the apple of the human eye, and what to many would seem an almost invisible speck of sin greatly disturbs and troubles them. This is one of the reasons why holiness and humility are so often found together; while the hardened offender, whose conscience is seared, seems almost past feeling remorse. Franks knew that he had spoken very idle words, and though he was inclined, as most people are, to make excuses for himself, his honest soul could not rest at ease until he had openly repaired his error as well as he could.

When lessons were over, and the boys were about to disperse, Ned stopped their going out of the school-room by a gesture of his hand. He stood up with his honest face a good deal more flushed than usual, for the acknowledgment which he was forcing himself to make was humiliating and painful.

"Boys," said he, in that clear voice which always commanded attention, "there's something which I want to say to you before you go home. There's nothing that I have more

warned you against than the iceberg of falsehood. A man who habitually lies will, we
know from the Word of God, be shut out
from heaven. Now, an iceberg is a thing
clear enough to be seen, and, unless he come
across it at night, one might say that a pilot
had no excuse for running a vessel upon one ;
but there's a part of the mass which one can't
see, — that's the part hidden beneath the
green waves, and as that may stretch out
much wider than the white peak glistening
above, it is clear that a ship might strike on
the sunken ice while seeming to give a wide
berth to the berg. Now, it's just the same
with falsehood. There's an upper part, easily
seen, and I hope that we all try to steer clear
of it ; that no boy here is so mean and base as
to tell a downright lie. Every boy here
knows that *lying lips are an abomination to
the Lord*. But not all are on their guard
against the *sunken ice* stretching below. We
strike on it when we exaggerate, or when in
any way we deceive, though not a word may
be spoken, or what is spoken may be literal
truth. My own keel grated against the
sunken ice to-day." Ned felt a good deal
embarrassed as he went on, all the more so

from the profound silence of the listening boys. " I said that there were no better riders than some of our own blue-jackets. Now, that may be true, or it may not, but I certainly did not speak from my knowledge, and I'm afraid that I ran foul of exaggeration. And I said that when our ship was lying off Alexandria, we tars rode about on shore as often as we'd a chance, — and that was true enough, though the chance came but seldom; but I suppose that you fancied, from what I said, that we galloped about upon horses?" There was a general murmur of assent. "Now, I never mounted a horse in my life; the beasts which we rode were *donkeys*." There was a laugh from some of the boys, almost instantly suppressed, however, for Ned Franks looked unusually grave. " Now, my lads, I've thought it best to say all this to you openly, both for my own sake and for yours. I want you to feel how hard it is to keep off altogether from that same smooth, slippery ice of deceit, — to know how treacherously it lies under the surface; and I want you to resolve, if ever you find yourselves touching it, be it ever so slightly, to sheer off at once, like honest Christians, and let no temptation draw you from the straight course of perfect truth."

The school-master's effort was over; painful as it had been, Ned Franks was glad that he had made it. His frank confession of so small a deviation from that straight course, had made a deeper impression on the minds of his boys than hours of lecturing on the perils of falsehood would have done.

"If our master said one thing, and half the village said another, I'd take Ned Franks's word against all the rest," was the observation of one of the lads as he left the school-house.

"I never knew any one so partic'lar about truth," said Bill Doyle. "Franks has such a sharp eye for the least bit of deceit, that I guess he'd catch sight of that there slippery ice that he talked of, if it be'd fifty feet down under the waves!"

11*

XIII.

The Return Home.

A SWEET, pleasing-looking girl, of between seventeen and eighteen years of age, occupied a place that day in a third-class carriage of the down train from London. Norah Peele — for it was she — was on her way to her native village of Colme; but she had none of the joyousness which she would have felt, under other circumstances, in making a journey home. All the brightness was gone from that young face, the drooping eyelids were red with the traces of tears, and she looked rather embarrassed than glad at finding that the Clerk of Colme chanced to be one of her travelling companions.

Certainly, John Sands was not one to enliven any society, though he served as a very good protector to the young maiden whom he had known from her childhood. He made a few attempts at conversation, and gave Norah the latest news of the village, casting — as was natural with him — a melancholy hue over all. Mr. Curtis continued ill; the clerk was sure that he would not recover, and that his wife would break down with the nursing; the almshouses were rotting to pieces where they stood, and the collection made for them at church had been smaller than he had ever known one to be before. After these not very cheerful communications, John Sands relapsed into silence, keeping his eyes gravely fixed on the knob of his gingham umbrella, while a melancholy train of thought was evidently flowing through his mind.

"Here we are," he said at last, slowly raising his head, as the shrill whistle announced their approach to B——; "if you're going to the village on foot, Norah Peele, we may as well walk there together."

John Sands, with stiff politeness, helped Norah out of the train. She had hardly stepped on the platform, when they were met by Bat Bell, the miller, whose hard, dry features wore a graver expression than usual.

"Mr. Sands," he said, addressing himself to the clerk, with merely a nod of recognition to Norah, "as Ned Franks could not come here to-day, and I had business in town, Persis asked me to wait here and tell you"—the miller dropped his voice as he added the words—"about your wife."

Painful anxiety agitated the sallow face of John Sands; no news of her was likely to be good news. The clerk nervously clutched his umbrella; his pale lips moved, but they framed no question.

"She'd an accident last evening; fell into my pond,—no, no, not drowned; Ned Franks got her out; but her arm is badly hurt, and she's in the hospital here."

The clerk waited to hear no more; turning round, without uttering a word, he went off with long strides in the direction of the place where his wretched wife lay on her bed of pain.

"Her arm is smashed, has been taken off," said the miller to Norah; "but for your brave uncle, the poor, intoxicated wretch would have been torn limb from limb by my wheel."

"And he—oh, is he hurt?" cried the shuddering girl.

"He'd a narrow shave for his life," said the miller, "but he got off without even a scratch. He's a gallant fellow, is your uncle; but I say it was folly in him, a husband and father, to risk his life for a ranting vixen, who'll drink herself to death one of these days. But you'll come with me now, Norah Peele; my cart's waiting near here, and will carry you and your bundle; like a sensible girl, you don't sport much luggage, I see."

As the miller's cart rattled on its way, Bell went on with his talking, at every second sentence giving a cut with his whip to his horse; for the miller liked rapid motion, to "get on" being a ceaseless impulse with him.

"You'll find changes in Colme, Norah Peele. Misfortunes never come single; there was Nancy Sands struggling in the mill-pond yesterday, and to-day, Ben Stone the carpenter, as strong and hale a man as one could find in the county, is struck down, just as he had finished breakfast, with a kind of a fit. They say that something has given way within him, and that though he may live weeks or months, he'll not last to the end of the year. Now, there's a man who looked likely to see ninety; only a little too full-blooded perhaps," added the miller, who had not an ounce of superfluous flesh on his bones.

Tears came into the eyes of Norah. The

carpenter was a popular man in Colne; every one knew so well the portly form, the good-humored, self-complacent smile, the loud voice, the jovial chuckle of Ben, it was difficult to associate with him any idea of sickness or of death. But Bell saw that his news had saddened his young companion, and as his light cart rapidly wheeled round a corner of the road, he as rapidly turned the current of conversation.

"You've chosen a pleasant time of the year for your visit to the country, Norah. How long are you likely to stay with your uncle?"

"I don't know; I can't say,—I suppose till I get another place," answered the girl.

"Ah, you've tired of London, after a village life; I always thought that you would. Noise, bustle, and bother! Talk of the clack of my mill-wheel,—why, in London there are thousands of wheels perpetually going, and streams of people perpetually flowing; there's something always on the grind. I like you the better for getting away as fast as you possibly can from London."

"I'd have stopped there if I could," said the young servant in a scarcely audible voice.

"Then why did you give warning?" asked the miller.

"I did not give warning," replied poor Norah, blushing and hanging down her head; "my mistress gave warning to me."

"There's simple truth, anyways," said the miller, a grim smile rising to his lips. "You are just like your sailor uncle: Franks is his name, and frank's his nature. I don't believe he ever told an untruth in his life."

Norah turned her head, and gazed sadly on the meadows and groves, clad in spring's fresh green, by which she was rapidly passing; but her thoughts did not follow her eyes. The miller's remark had awakened a train of painful reflections.

"Oh, that it had indeed been so with me!" thought poor Norah; "that I had always kept my lips pure from falsehood; I would not then be returning to be a burden upon my kind and generous uncle. I, whose character stood so high, sent away in disgrace! I, whose word was at once believed! I feel as if I could not bear to tell uncle all, — to let him know of the direct falsehood, and the deceit carried on for months, my mistress's trust so abused by his niece! Uncle will think that all his care and kindness have been thrown away upon Norah; that I am still the foolish, deceitful, bad girl that I was when he first came to Colme, and tried to teach me to be honest and truthful, and straightforward, as a Christian should be.   It seems as if I could endure anything rather than the loss of his good opinion, and that of dear Aunt Persis! And yet,"—thus Norah pursued her reflections, to which the miller now left her, his mind being occupied in reckoning up the amount of his savings deposited in the county bank of B——, — "and yet, the safest, the best course for me now, must be to be perfectly frank and open. Alas! I cannot recall the past, but I can draw from bitter experience a lesson for the future. I will confess everything to my uncle, conceal nothing, make no excuses; and oh, may the God of truth help me from this time forward indeed to *take heed to my ways, that I offend not with my tongue!*"

I will not dwell on the kindly welcome given to Norah Peele by Persis and Ned Franks.   She was received as a daughter, no questions asked, no painful inquiries made as to the cause of her leaving her place. "Leave the lass to tell her own story when and how she likes," the one-armed sailor had said to his wife. So the baby now happily sleeping, was shown and admired; topics of general interest were alone spoken of at the evening meal which followed Franks's day of toil; the state of the almshouses in Wild Rose Hollow, the progress made in their repair, the accident to the clerk's wife, the sudden and serious illness of Stone the carpenter, the good report of improvement in the health of the vicar,—all these were made subjects of conversation, everything being avoided which might possibly embarrass the guest. All was done to make her feel at her ease. Norah, it was said, would be so useful in helping to nurse the baby; Norah would look after the flowers, now that her uncle was too busy all day to have time to work in his garden. How delighted old Sarah Mason would be to have Norah to read the Bible to her again!

The poor girl felt grateful for the kindness and consideration thus shown her, and thankful that such a home was left to her still; but a burden was weighing on her mind, and even while conversation was going on, in which she appeared to join, a smothered sigh, or a

sudden moistening of her eyes, showed that
her thoughts were wandering to something
painful. When the tea-things had been
cleared away by the active Persis, assisted
by Norah, when cups and saucers had been
washed and replaced on the shelf, and the
outer door closed for the night (it never was
bolted or barred), Norah sat down on a little wooden stool at the feet of her aunt, and
recounted, with simple truthfulness, all the
circumstances that had led to her hasty dismissal from the service of Mrs. Lowndes. I
shall give you the story, not in Norah's words,
but my own, beginning it by a short account
of her early days in Colme.

XIV.

Norah's Story.

Norah and her brother were the only children of the half-sister of Ned Franks, Bessy
Peele, a woman who, in every important
respect, had been an utter contrast to her
brother. While Ned's maxim was to do
everything in clear daylight, Bessy was one

who, if possible, always took an underground way. He considered the straight road always the shortest; she wound and doubled like a fox. He was convinced that honesty is the best policy; she looked upon cunning as wisdom. One of the earliest lessons learned by Mrs. Peele's unfortunate children was that the great thing in life is to pick up money by any *safe* means; by "safe" being meant whatever would not lead to the prison or the gallows. There was no harm, she said, in telling a lie, — at least a *white* lie, that hurt no one, and helped one's self on in the world. What need was there to be so very particular about a little slip of the tongue? She was sure, for her part, that God would not notice such tri fles as these.

It is said that some Chinese parents are actually so inhuman as to blind their children, that the poor, wretched creatures may earn more money by begging. Mrs. Peele, a fond though a foolish parent, would have been horrified at the idea of inflicting such an injury upon her children, while actually doing them a wrong yet more cruel. For was it not such to *blind their consciences*, to make them unable to distinguish the wrong from the right, at the risk of their walking, through the darkness of their souls, into everlasting destruction? And this all for the sake of paltry gain, miserable profits of sin, more dearly bought than the alms given to the poor blinded Chinese beggars!

The mischief done to the characters of Bessy Peele's children was very serious as regarded her son, and had Norah long remained under the roof of her mother, the principles of the young girl might, like his, have been utterly ruined. Happily Norah went early into service, and became the attendant of an aged Christian lady, who gave her every opportunity of hearing the gospel faithfully preached, and made her read to her the Bible and other religious books. Under her roof Norah received religious impressions; her young and tender heart turned towards Him of whose love and compassion she heard so much. But, alas! the poison-seeds sown in childhood had left their evil roots in the soil. Norah would one hour be listening in church with tearful eyes to the account of Peter's sin and repentance, and the next hour be falling, *without repentance*, into a similar sin of untruth! She was fearfully inconsistent,—not

because she was insincere, but because she
had actually no clear line drawn in her mind
as to where innocence ended and guilt began.
Norah had been led to fancy that little sins
were no sins, — "white lies" no falsehood, —
picking *not* to be classed with stealing. She
wished to please a merciful God and go to
heaven, but she felt not that the God of Love
is the God of Holiness also; that *all* sin, if
unforgiven, must end in death; that the *least*
can be washed out in nothing less precious
than the blood of the Saviour, and that for
every idle, untruthful *word* the sinner must
give account at the judgment.

The return to England of her maimed uncle, the sailor, at this time proved a great
blessing to Norah. She met with one whose
standard of right was the Bible standard, —
one who spake the truth as a man who serves
the God of Truth should speak, and who tram-
pled on deceit as he would have set his heel
on a venomous serpent. Norah's eyes were
opened to see that religious profession is but
a mask if it do not influence the conduct;
that to have prayer on the lips at one moment
and untruth at another is fearful mockery before God! Norah Peele asked the help of the

Holy Spirit to enable her to walk in the path of holiness, which she now found to be so much more narrow than she had before believed it to be. She became watchful over herself, — she set a guard over her tongue; the little bark, with heaven's wind swelling its sails, did "sheer off" from the treacherous iceberg of falsehood.

Mrs. Peele died rather suddenly after a few days' illness, and closed her worse than useless life with little consciousness of sin, and no sincere repentance. She had been a good mother, she said; God was merciful; she was going to a better world. The habit of a life continued to the end; and, having constantly tried to deceive others, poor Bessy deceived herself at the last. She had built her house on the sand; there was no solid foundation for her hope; she had heard the word, and done it not; what could she plead, where would she stand, in the last awful day?

Very different was it with Norah's aged mistress, when, about a year afterwards, she gently sank to rest, in humble trust that He whom she had loved and served would receive her unto himself. By that holy, happy death-bed Norah learned a lesson which she never could forget. She nursed her lady night and day, and, when her gentle spirit was released from earthly suffering, the young servant mourned for her loss with grief most sincere.

Norah would then have gone home to her uncle, Ned Franks, had not Mr. Lowndes, the younger brother of her late mistress, at once offered to take her into the service of his wife. He knew well, he said, the value of such a servant as Norah, a really high-principled girl, who would be found honest in word as well as in deed.

In entering the service of Mrs. Lowndes, Norah had made a great rise in life. Instead of being the general servant of a clergyman's widow, whose narrow life-income barely supplied her need, Norah became the trusted attendant of the only child of wealthy parents, and earned wages which nearly doubled what she had received before. The place was one which offered many other advantages. Mrs. Lowdnes was strict, indeed, almost to severity, but never intentionally unjust. She was extremely anxious that her Selina should be kept from all knowledge of evil. The little girl was seldom allowed to mix with other children, lest she should learn any harm from example.   Mrs. Lowndes often boasted to her friends, that her Selina was brought up in such a habit of speaking the truth, that to her to utter a lie would be an *impossible* thing. The lady would not suffer any one to be near her darling in whose scrupulous truthfulness she could not place perfect trust.   Truth, she would say, is the very foundation on which a character must rest.   She would never over-look or forgive in a servant the smallest attempt to deceive.

Norah had passed several pleasant months in London, in the service of Mrs. Lowndes, with the consciousness that she was faithfully performing her duty and giving satisfaction to her mistress, when an incident occurred, which showed her more clearly than ever the importance of having a character for truthful-ness and honesty.

" Why, there's your bell and my bell a-ring-ing together, and rung so loud, too!   What can missus want us both for at once?" ex-claimed Martha, the housemaid, to Norah, who was helping her, as usual, to make the bed in the little girl's room.   Martha's manner was flurried and frightened.

" We'd better go and answer the bells directly," said Norah. "I hope and trust that nothing's the matter with dear little missy!"

The two maids entered the dining-room together. Mr. Lowndes was seated in his large red arm-chair, with his feet on the fender, and his spectacles on his nose, apparently engaged in studying the *Times*. Mrs. Lowndes, a large, tall, and rather formidable-looking lady, dressed in a very stiff silk, sat, even more erect than usual, at the breakfast-table, on which she was resting her folded hands. She had a peculiarly deep-toned voice, and the voice sounded deeper, her manners seemed sterner than Norah had ever thought them before, as she addressed the young maid with the question, "Did you enter my room this morning?"

"Yes, ma'am, to put by your comb and brush."

"And when?"

"Just the minute after you had left it."

"Did you see a sovereign on the dressing-table?" asked the lady, with the air of a magistrate questioning a witness.

"No, indeed, ma'am, I did not," said Norah.

"Did *you* see one when you tidied my

room?"   Mrs. Lowndes turned her keen gray eyes upon Martha, to whom this last question was addressed.

"No, I never saw a sovereign, nor nothing like it, ma'am; I could take my oath that I did not.   I did not so much as enter the room till Norah had been there, and gone out again."

Mrs. Lowndes looked very grave, and somewhat perplexed.   "I certainly left a sovereign on that table when I came down to breakfast, and an hour afterwards it as certainly was gone.   There are only two individuals who could have entered, and did enter, that room during my absence, and both deny having seen the money.   I cannot doubt that one of them is uttering a falsehood, and that she who utters it is also the thief."

The idea of being suspected of such a crime as theft covered the face of Norah with crimson; she attempted to speak, but could not bring out a word.

"O ma'am! ' exclaimed Martha, in alarm; "Norah went in first; you heard her own that she went in the first."

"I never saw the sovereign," gasped Norah.

Mr. Lowndes, who had every now and then

" I'll be bound that Norah never touched the gold," said the gentleman.
Sheer off.   p. 143.

been glancing up over the *Times*, which he held in his hand, now laid it down on his knee, and wheeled round on his arm-chair a little, so as to face the two maids.

"I'll be bound that Norah never touched the gold," said the gentleman, who had once been a magistrate. "When I was at B——, about three years ago, my poor sister placed in my hands a bag of money, which had been picked up by Norah, her maid, in the street, and given over into her charge. *A bag of sovereigns,*" repeated Mr. Lowndes, emphatically. "Now, no one in his senses would believe that a girl, who would not take eight sovereigns dropped in the street by a stranger, would rob her mistress, betray her trust, and forfeit her own good character, by stealing *one,* which was certain to be missed and sought after." And, having thus given his decided opinion, Mr. Lowndes again took up his *Times,* and wheeled his chair round to the fire.

"And O mamma!" exclaimed little Selina, running forward from a corner of the room in which she had been standing, a deeply interested spectator of all that had passed, "Norah *could not* have taken the money, because she says that she never saw it. Norah always tells the truth," pleaded the eager little witness, whose presence in the room had been until now forgotten by her mother. "When I broke the tumbler, Martha said, 'Never mind, miss, you need say nothing about it;' but Norah told me never to hide anything from you, for it was always best to speak out the truth boldly; and I did what Norah said, and you were not very angry, mamma."

"I am never very angry except where there is deceit and dishonesty," said the lady, fondly stroking back the light ringlets from the brow of her darling.

"And you are sure that Norah did not take the money, mamma, for she *said* that she did not even see it."

"I am sure," answered the lady decidedly, "as sure of her innocence as I am of your own." Bending her keen eyes on Martha, she continued, sternly, "You had better do what you can to repair your fault by a frank confession."

"Indeed, indeed, ma'am, but I never saw, or touched, or thought of the sovereign; it's

very hard that it should be put upon me,"
cried Martha, bursting into passionate tears.
"I was not the first to enter into that room;
I don't see why *I* am suspected."

"And yet I cannot but feel suspicions so
strong," said the lady, "that I cannot retain
in my household one in whom my confidence
is lost."

"I hope, I hope, ma'am, you are not going
to send me away without a character!"
sobbed Martha, while Selina's heart was so
much touched by her sorrow, that the child
could scarcely forbear from crying herself.

"I shall tell the exact truth to any lady
who may inquire for your character. I shall
mention why I send you away, but I shall add
that you were not the first to enter the room,
and that I have no proof that you touched the
money."

"But, mamma, mamma, if she's sorry, if
she will promise never to do it again, won't
you try her a little longer?" cried the tender-
hearted Selina.

"No, my child," replied Mrs. Lowndes;
"had I no other cause for displeasure against
her, I would never have any one near you on

whose word I could not depend. A girl who would teach my daughter to hide anything from her parent is not likely to be very open when the fault committed is her own."

The maids were then dismissed from the dining-room. How different were the feelings of the two as they quitted it ! Norah hurried upstairs to her own little chamber, and, falling on her knees, fervently thanked her heavenly Father for having preserved that character which was to her more precious than life. She remembered the struggle in her own mind about that very same bag of sovereigns to which Mr. Lowndes had referred. She had found it just at the time when her uncle's influence was beginning to tell powerfully upon her, when she was seeking with earnest prayer to give herself wholly to the Lord, and live as a child of God and heir of heaven should live. That had been a turning-point in the life of Norah. She had then by faith resisted the devil, and he had fled. Had she yielded to that temptation, and a very strong one it had been, the whole course of her life would have been altered. Now, against suspicious appearances, her word was trusted at once ; her character was spotless in the eyes of her master and mistress, a great danger had safely been passed, and the heart of the young servant-maid overflowed with thanksgiving to God.

––––

XV.

Norah's Story Continued.

Let him who thinketh he standeth take heed lest he fall. Norah was soon to experience how much needed is this warning from the Scriptures.

A few days before the dishonest Martha left Mrs. Lowndes's service, as Norah was returning home after making some little purchases for her mistress, on turning a corner she came suddenly upon an old friend, and gave an exclamation of pleasure at a meeting so unexpected and so pleasant.

"Milly — Oh, I'm so delighted to see you!" cried Norah, shaking her friend by both hands. Had they not been in a street, she would have warmly embraced her. For had not Milly, when housemaid to Mrs. Lane, shown her kindness in many ways; had she not helped her to nurse Norah's dying mother, and sat up all night with Mrs. Peele when the girl's strength had given way? There were very few indeed whom Norah regarded with so much affection as she did the kind-hearted Milly.

"Who would have thought of seeing you here in London!" continued Norah, whose face was beaming with pleasure. "I have not met you since your marriage. What has brought you and your husband up to town?"

"My husband, — don't talk of him!" cried Milly, in a tone of anguish which startled Norah. Then looking closer into the face of her friend, Norah could see a sad change there. The features of Milly Bligh had grown sharper and thinner; there were furrows on her brow which Norah had never seen there before. She observed now, also, what in the excitement of first meeting her friend she had not noticed, that the dress of Milly looked shabby: though it was winter-time, she wore a thin shawl, which was quite insufficient to protect her from the cold.

"Why — what — has he" — a feeling of delicacy prevented Norah from finishing the sentence.

"*Deserted me!*" moaned Milly, as if to utter these two words was to wring blood from her heart. "O Norah, if you knew what I've had to bear! But it's all over now, — I don't know where he is, — I'm never like to see him again!"

The street chanced to be very quiet; Milly turned, and, as she walked by the side of her friend, in low earnest tones they went on with their conversation.

"Then what will you do, my poor dear Milly?" asked Norah, with heartfelt sympathy and pity.

"I must go into service again. I've come up to London to look out for a situation. My difficulty is that Mrs. Lane, with whom I lived all my years of service, is somewhere abroad, I don't know where, and, as I left her to be married, I did not so much as secure a written character from her."

"Oh, I'm so glad!" exclaimed Norah, suddenly.

"What, — glad that I've not a corner to turn to?" asked Milly.

"Oh, no, not glad of that, but glad that I may be able to help you. Mrs. Lowndes — she's my mistress — asked me only this morning if I knew of any nice housemaid who could take Martha's place. My lady had nearly fixed on one yesterday, but the character did not suit, so she's in a hurry to find another."

"Mrs. Lowndes is not likely to take a servant on your recommendation, I should fear."

"You don't know what confidence she has in me, what trust she puts in my word," said Norah, with a little natural pride. "If I tell her that you have been five years in one place, and that I have known you all the time, and that I'm certain that if your mistress were not abroad, she would give you a first-rate character, I'm sure — at least I'm almost sure that she'll take you."

"O Norah, you're like a comforting angel!" cried poor Milly; "if you only knew what a service you're going to do me! I've been almost in despair; half of my clothes are in pawn; I thought that I'd never succeed in getting a respectable place!"

"And this is such a good one!" cried Norah, quite excited with pleasure; "and how delightful it will be for us both to be always together! A companion whom I could love as a friend was the only thing wanting to make me perfectly happy, and there is no one on earth whom I should so gladly have as my Milly."   Norah could hardly refrain from skipping for joy as she walked.

A thought, however, occurred to her mind, which somewhat damped her pleasure.   "The only thing that makes me afraid that you may not get the place," she said, "is that I know that Mrs. Lowndes objects to married servants.   I have heard her say myself that she will never engage one, the husbands give so much trouble."

"I do not even know where mine is," sighed Milly; "but I don't see why anything at all need be said about my being married."

Norah became very grave.   "Would it be right to hide such a fact?" she said; " would it not be like deceiving my mistress?"

"Well, if you're going to let out a poor friend's secrets, and deprive her of her best chance of earning her bread in an honest way, you're not the girl that I took you for," said Milly, with bitterness.

There is no need to relate all the conversation that passed, nor to tell how Milly tried to persuade Norah, and how Norah tried to persuade herself, that to suppress the truth was no falsehood; that it was not in the least necessary that Mrs. Lowndes should ever know that her housemaid was married. Norah promised to do all that she could to procure the situation for Milly, and on reaching home at once went to her lady, and pleaded the cause of her friend.

"Five years in one place, — that looks well," observed Mrs. Lowndes; "there would at any rate be no harm in my seeing the girl. You have known her, you say, all your life. You may tell her to call this evening, and I will judge for myself. It's hard for good servants when they lose their places by a mistress going abroad."

Norah knew that Milly had not lost her place on account of Mrs. Lane's going abroad, but she was only too glad that her lady should think so. We may always suspect that we are in danger of striking against the iceberg of deceit, when we allow ourselves to *wish* something to be believed which we *know* to be quite untrue.

"Stay," said Mrs. Lowndes, as the eager Norah was about to retire from the room; "of course your friend is not married?"

Norah was taken by surprise; in an unguarded moment the false "no" slipped from her tongue, and she passed through the doorway biting her lip, and wishing — fervently wishing that she had not been betrayed, even by friendship, into uttering a lie. "But I cannot go back now. Oh, no!" thought the conscience-stricken girl.

Mrs. Lowndes saw Milly that evening, liked her appearance and manner, and engaged her as housemaid at once. Norah could not feel as happy as she would have done had her mind been at rest, but dared not confess her fault, as she deemed that to do so would be cruelly wronging Milly. She resolved to be more careful in future; she hoped that this would be the very last time on which she would be guilty of speaking untruth. Alas! lies link themselves on one to another like the rings of a chain; and who that harbors one unconfessed, unforgiven sin dare hope that it will be *the last?*

Months passed quietly over. Norah now seldom thought of her falsehood. If she was colder in prayer, if she was less able to lift up her heart to God, if she took less pleasure in recalling the counsels of her uncle, she hardly

traced these effects to their real cause, —
peace of conscience forfeited by sin.

One morning Norah found Milly in her
room weeping violently, and trembling with
agitation. An open letter lay on her knee.

"What has happened?" cried Norah,
anxiously.

"He's found, — my poor, poor lost one is
found!" sobbed Milly; "but he's in the hospital dying; he wants to see me at once. O
Norah, I must go to him this day! Ask mistress to give me leave for an hour; she's kind,
she'll not have the heart to refuse it!"

"Do you wish me to ask her to let you go
to the hospital to see your *husband*, when she
does not know that you have one?" asked
Norah, feeling extremely uneasy at the idea
of her falsehood being found out at last.

"No, no; that would never do, that would
get us both into trouble, and, oh, I've
trouble enough already! Go and ask her to
let me go to the hospital to visit a dying
mother."

> Oh! what a tangled web we weave,
> When once we practise to deceive!

Norah found herself now in a position of
greater temptation than ever. Milly was in

such a state of misery and excitement that Norah dreaded that any opposition might throw her into a nervous fever. The poor, anxious wife would listen to no objection, had patience for no scruple, and was almost wild when Norah showed hesitation about doing her bidding. Miserable, and hating herself for the deceit into which she was drawn, Norah went to her mistress and told the falsehood put into her mouth by Milly.

Mrs. Lowndes was all kindness. Day after day the housemaid was permitted to go and see her sick mother, carrying sometimes little delicacies sent from her mistress's table. When Milly, from the effect of distress and excitement, herself fell ill, Mrs. Lowndes sent Norah instead of her to the hospital two or three times to see " the poor old lady," and questioned her on her return as to the sufferer's state. Thus Norah was led deeper and deeper into deceit. She had to speak of *her* illness, *her* danger, *her* thanks, when coming from the death-bed of a young man, and she felt that her whole character was becoming gradually lowered and degraded. Never since she had first sought the Lord had Norah been in so low a spiritual state; even to

speak of religion to little Selina appeared to
her to be an act of hypocrisy now. Norah
had sometimes a terrible doubt as to whether
she had ever been a Christian at all!

Happily for Norah she was suddenly to be
stopped in this downward path. It was a
mercy to be arrested even by a blow.

One afternoon in April the bell summoned
Norah to the presence of her mistress. She
went down the stairs with a sinking at the
heart, a feeling of misgiving from which she
now very frequently suffered. What was her
alarm, on opening the drawing-room door, to
see, seated near her mistress, the chaplain of
the hospital, whom she had met before on one
of her visits to Doyle! Norah dared not even
glance at her lady, but the sound of that terrible, deep-toned voice, so expressive of subdued indignation, made the wretched Norah
guess but too well what was coming.

"Mr. Chancie has called to ask me to break
to my housemaid the news of the death of her
husband." There was a marked emphasis on
the last word. "Am I to understand that
this is the person whom she, and whom you
have visited again and again, and spoken of

repeatedly to me under the name of her *mother?*"

Norah pressed the nails of her right hand so tightly into the flesh of the left that traces were left for days!

"Am I to understand," continued the lady, speaking in the same low, terrible tone, "that you and Milly have deliberately conspired together for months to deceive the mistress who trusted you?"

Norah wished that she could sink down anywhere out of sight, into the cellar, or into the grave.

"You leave this house to-morrow," said the lady, who could not but read confession in the silence of her maid, and her aspect of misery and shame. "If your family were in London, you should not stay here for another hour. To think that I should have entrusted my child to the care of such a" — Norah could not catch the concluding word, perhaps none was uttered, but her own conscience supplied the blank with "viper." "Of course you can expect no character from me; your vile deceit has done much to shake my faith in all my kind; I shall never trust a servant again as you were trusted by me. I could no more answer for your honesty now, wretched girl, than I could for your truth. She who could deliberately carry on such a course of deceit would be capable of taking my money."

Norah was utterly unable to speak a word in her own defence; she was miserable, crushed, almost in despair. Milly was, of course, involved in the same disgrace as herself, though not so hastily sent out of the house. Mrs. Lowndes found it more easy to show some indulgence to her, because she had never placed in her the same absolute trust; she had never given to Milly the charge of an only, a much-loved child.

Norah wrote off a hasty note to her uncle at Colme, and made her preparations for leaving her place with an almost bursting heart. One of her keenest pangs was that caused by the distress of little Selina, who could not at first be persuaded to believe her dear Norah to be capable of speaking an untruth.

"You never did tell a story. Oh, I'm sure that you *could not!* Say, only say that it's all a dreadful mistake!" cried the child, bursting into tears.

Norah was too wretched to weep; she did

not close her eyes all that night; the house in which she had once been so happy had become to her now like a stifling prison. Yet she dreaded returning to her native village; she shrank from meeting the clear blue eye of her uncle; she felt herself unworthy of any kindness, —she who had sinned against light, she who had stained her soul with falsehood! Norah's only comfort was in the thought that at least her course of deception was over; she need play the hypocrite no longer; prayer was not now a mockery as it had seemed lately to be. Sin is in itself a thing more dreadful than the sharpest punishment for sin.

XVI.

Passing Events.

Norah had finished her sad story in tears. Neither Ned Franks nor his wife had interrupted the thread of it by a single question; they had sat grave and silent listeners. When all had been confessed, the sailor gently laid his hand on the shoulder of his sobbing niece. His manner was subdued and kind.

"Norah, my girl," he said, "let's be thankful that all was brought to daylight at last. I'd rather have you coming here, even in trouble and disgrace, than seeming to prosper in a course so dangerous to your soul. I only wish that your lady had known all through your own confession, instead of — but let that pass; I trust and believe that henceforth you will always be true as steel, and avoid the slightest approach to deceit all the more carefully because of your sufferings now. I need not say that we will never mention the subject to you again; you are heartily welcome to stay here as long as you will; you'll live, please God, to be a comfort and credit to us yet."

Of course there was much gossip in the village as to the cause of Norah's sudden return. There was a succession of visitors to the school-house on the following day. Many questions were put to Ned Franks and Persis, by those who were more curious than kind, as to the cause of Norah's so unexpectedly leaving her place. Both husband and wife maintained a resolute silence; they made no evasions, threw out no hints to mislead.

"People need not trouble themselves about

my niece's concerns," was Ned's rather impatient remark when hard pressed for an answer to some impertinent question. "She has come to us for quiet and peace, and no one shall annoy her whilst she is under my roof."

Of course curiosity was not satisfied nor gossip silenced in Colme. Some of the neighbors guessed that Norah had done something very foolish or wrong; some that she had had a disappointment in love; but as no one had the means of proving the truth of his guesses, it might be hoped that curiosity would at last die out like a fire unsupplied with fuel. To be exposed to painful remarks, to be viewed with some suspicion, was the heavy but just penalty which Norah must make up her mind to pay for her sin.

There were other subjects of interest at that time to divide the attention of the gossips of Colme, — the illness of the carpenter Stone, and the accident to Sands's wife, being constant topics of conversation. Day after day the cottagers saw the poor clerk plodding on his weary way to the town to visit his suffering Nancy. He looked neither to the right nor the left, nor even stopped to speak to a neighbor, and there was always the same unvarying expression of dull care on his sallow face. On Sundays alone his duties as clerk made it impossible for the anxious husband to go to the hospital at B——; and then, as the miller observed, Sands always looked at church like a condemned man, hearing the sermon preached before his own execution.

John Sands was not the only person to visit poor Nancy in the hospital at B——. Several times, at considerable inconvenience, Persis, with her babe in her arms, found her way to the ward, cheering it by her presence, like one of the rays of sunshine which streamed through the window to brighten the couch of pain. And more often yet, Mr. Leyton came to visit the poor afflicted member of his flock, who no longer scorned to listen to his words. The shyness of the young curate wore off in the presence of suffering and sin; he forgot himself in his work. Nancy, at first a silent, gloomy listener, began at last to look forward to the minister's visits. Mr. Leyton was wont to bring fruit to the sufferer during her tedious illness, and flowers from the vicar's gardens; but it was not this alone that made his visits welcome.

Nancy, during the long, sleepless days and wearisome nights, had much time for thinking; her mind also was clear, for she had no longer the power to procure the fatal stimulants which had so nearly been her ruin. There was no sudden change in the violent, high-tempered woman; but influences were at work upon her, which, like the morning shower and the evening dew, were gradually softening the hardened soil so that it might receive the word of truth.

And so passed the month of April, that month of mingled sunshine and shower, when the fruit-trees burst into blossom, and the groves into music. To Persis and Ned it was a very happy and very busy time. They watched their own little blossom opening under the sunshine of their love, and felt that for them life had a new interest and delight. Poor Norah, who was in very low spirits, tried to hide her sadness, that she might throw no shadow over the cheerful home of the Frankses.

And in the mean time work proceeded briskly in Wild Rose Hollow. Never did nobleman, building a proud mansion for himself, watch the progress of its erection with more pleasure than did Ned Franks the repairing — with some almost rebuilding — of the old thatched dwellings. He threw his heart and soul into the work, and infected even the money-making miller with some of his own enthusiasm. We usually take an interest in that which has cost us a sacrifice, and the more men do for any cause the more they are apt to be ready to do. Pleasant to the ears of Bat Bell were the sounds of labor from the direction of the almshouses which his money was helping to restore. He sometimes would take his little Bessy to the spot to see the one-armed sailor and his boys hard at work, — and a goodly quantity of straw for thatching found its way from the mill. Bat Bell had begun to taste the luxury of doing good; he was realizing the truth of that divine declaration, *It is more blessed to give than to receive.*

Ned Franks, on his way to Wild Rose Hollow, had daily to pass the cottage of Sands and the workshop of Stone the carpenter. The door of the first was always closed, and the place wore an air of desolation and neglect, which often drew a sigh from the kind-hearted sailor. It was equally sad to him to pass the empty shop, to hear no more from it the sound of the hammer or saw, or the whizzing hum of the lathe, mingled perhaps with snatches of jovial song. Ben Stone was so well known in the village where he had spent all his days that his illness could not but cause a blank there. The portly form, so familiar to all, was missed from the accustomed place in church; the voice, rather loud than tuneful, from the music of the hymns in which it had so constantly joined. The responses of Ben Stone had been almost as clearly heard as those of the clerk. Even the children of Colme missed the sight of the carpenter in his Sunday clothes, with his wife, rather showily dressed, resting on his strong arm, as with his big prayer-book in hand he used to walk through the porch into the church-yard with a smile or a nod, or a cheerful greeting to every one whom he met, all being his neighbors, and many his friends. Ben Stone was a man who had known very little of trouble, and even when trouble had come, it had no more rested on his soul than rain on a sloping roof. He had hitherto been prosperous, healthy, and strong; and though a kind husband to a wife who often was sickly, Stone never let his easy serenity of soul be disturbed by the pains and aches of his partner. Now, illness, serious and sudden, had come upon himself, and the question was, how would he bear it? The trial would not be sharpened by poverty, for Stone had, as he was wont to say, laid by for a rainy day, and his wife had money of her own. He was in no distress for the necessaries, nor even for the comforts of life; but how would the carpenter bear to have his working-days brought to so unexpected a close? Above all, how would he look forward to the great change which was slowly and painlessly, but not the less surely, approaching? Would not the current of a life, lately so smooth and shallow, become both rougher and more deep when near the point where the great final leap must be made, and the small concerns, the petty interests of this life, be swept away into eternity's ocean?

XVII.

Perilous Peace.

In a quiet and peaceful nook stands the vicarage of Colme, almost in the village, yet entirely screened from it by extensive shrubberies. High, green walls of luxuriant laurel, and rhododendra, with their thick buds swelling into blossoms, border the winding drive, and girdle the lawn, on whose smooth slope lies the shadow of a lofty cedar, the pride of the place. The vicarage itself is not large, but exceedingly pretty, with its rural porch and picturesque gables, and mullioned windows overhung with honeysuckle and clematis. If we were to pass over that velvet lawn, and glance in through the window at the right of the porch, we should see the vicar himself resting in his arm-chair, very pale and very thin from recent dangerous illness, but looking calm and serene. Though this is Saturday, there is no sign of preparation for the morrow's service; there is no desk open, no book on the table save the well-worn Bible. The vicar has been called into the "wilderness" of sickness to "rest for a while," and he may not yet venture to enter the church even as a worshipper, far less as a preacher. It is only to-day that his wife has been able to leave his side for a long round of visits amongst his parishioners. Mr. Curtis is anxious to hear of each and all of those amongst whom the good pastor has lived for twenty years as a father among his children; so his wife has set out this afternoon with a large basket on her arm, to visit half the cottages in Colme.

Mr. Curtis is not sitting alone; his wife's nephew, the young curate, Mr. Leyton, is beside him, giving him an account of his own work on that day. Claudius Leyton is, as has been before mentioned, of extremely youthful appearance; the smooth cheek, small features, and slight, delicate frame of the curate might induce a stranger to guess his age as scarcely beyond eighteen years. Summoned immediately after his ordination to take entire charge of the parish of Mr. Curtis, then alarmingly ill, the curate, whose life had been spent in London, Eton, and Cambridge, and who had scarcely ever so much as entered a cottage, had found himself at

first almost overwhelmed by the sense of re-
sponsibility. Mr. Leyton had felt somewhat
as a landsman might feel should he be called
to take the command of a vessel on the very
first occasion on which he ever entered one.
The curate lacked neither talent nor devotion,
but he had no experience in the peculiar
work of a village pastor, and with a tender
sensitive disposition and natural shyness, it
seemed as if he had undertaken a task beyond
his strength. The change was great from
the easy luxury of home and college life to
the position of a hard-working curate, with
long church-services to tax a weak voice, and
the various needs of a parish, in which almost
every one was to him a stranger, to try his
energies and test his discretion. Mr. Leyton had prayerfully resolved to do his very
best to be a faithful minister to his flock, and
overcome the difficulties before him. He
had, some time before his ordination, left off
some of his favorite pursuits, that he might
devote himself to his duties; he had given
away his cigar-case, had parted with his
books of light literature, locked up his flute,
and left his paint-box untouched for months.
Claudius Leyton had resolutely turned his

thoughts to sermons and schools, and other matters connected with parish business. But it had been a great trial to the young clergyman to have, as it were, to find his way almost alone in, to him, a new country. He was unable for weeks to avail himself of the experience of the vicar, and but for the information and help always cheerfully given him by Ned Franks, the curate would often have felt utterly discouraged by the difficulties attending his charge. It was no small relief to the young man to be at last able to consult the vicar, receive his sympathy, and ask his advice; for Claudius had none of the proud self-confidence which too often accompanies inexperience and youth; he was not one of those who need to be taught modesty by a number of failures.

"And where have you been this day, Claudius?" asked the vicar, as the curate, tired with a long, hot walk, seated himself beside him, and wiped his own heated brow, where the pressure of the hat had left a reddened line on the smooth, fair skin.

"I have been to the hospital to see Mrs. Sands."

" And where have you been this day, Claudius?" asked the vicar, as
the curate, tired with a long, hot walk, seated himself beside him.

p. 170

"Ah! the poor creature who nearly lost her life by falling into the mill-stream."

"When in a state of intoxication," gravely added the curate.

"And who has had to endure the loss of her right arm,—a terrible loss to any one, especially to a working woman," said the vicar, in a tone of compassion.

"It is a mercy that she did not lose her life," observed Claudius; "but for the gallant conduct of Ned Franks, who risked his own to save it, the unhappy creature must have perished, a victim to that horrible vice of intemperance. Bad as it is in a man, it is doubly disgusting in a woman."

"It seems almost like a possession by a devil," said the vicar; "but we have the encouragement of knowing that our Master has power even to cast out devils. Does poor Nancy seem conscious of her sin before God? Does she show any sign of repentance?"

"I do not know what to think," replied the curate, undecidedly. "The woman listens in silence to what I have to say; she does not fire up as she would have done a short time since at anything like reproof; her black eyes have lost their fierceness, but I fear that

rather sullen gloom than humble contrition
has taken its place. I cannot tell what to
make of her manner; it is so difficult to read
the human heart."

"Difficult, indeed," said the vicar; and he
added, but not aloud, "especially for those
who have but lately mastered even its al-
phabet."

"I have suggested to her total absti-
nence," continued Claudius Leyton. "I have
read and heard that where there is a passion
for strong drink, the only chance of overcoming that passion is by never tasting a
drop."

"You are right; there are cases where
temperance is impracticable without total ab-
stinence from all intoxicating liquors. The
enemy is so determined to gain admission,
that the door must be, as it were, bolted and
barred against him, for, if the smallest opening were left, he would rush in with irresistible force. But how did Nancy take your
suggestions?"

"In sullen silence, as usual," replied Mr.
Leyton. "She stares fixedly at the wall before her, and I scarcely know whether she is
listening or not to what I say. I fear that it

shows a want of charity in myself," continued the young clergyman, "but I own that that woman inspires me with a feeling of repulsion."

"Hers is a case which needs much prayer and patience," observed the vicar.

"I certainly should never go to see her but from a sense of duty," said the young man, who had scarcely yet acquired the grace of patience, and to whom a violent-tempered woman, addicted to intoxication, was rather an object of disgust than of pity. "How different was my next visit to a sick-bed! How refreshing to the spirit it was to sit by that excellent man, Ben Stone, and see how calmly and cheerfully a Christian can bear sickness, and look forward to death!"

"Ah! so you have been with our poor friend, the carpenter? How did you find him?" asked the vicar, with interest.

"Perfectly peaceful, perfectly happy; not a cloud over his soul!" replied Mr. Leyton.

The curate's fair young face brightened as he spoke, but its brightness was not reflected in the countenance of the vicar. It was in a grave, rather anxious tone, that he inquired,

"Is he resting on the Rock? Has he found true peace through Christ?"

"Surely, I should have no hesitation in saying so," answered Claudius Leyton. "His manner, however, was not quite so decided as his words; it seemed rather to convey an idea that an unpleasant doubt had been unexpectedly suggested to his mind. Stone is evidently glad to receive spiritual comfort; he listens, he agrees to everything."

"Agrees! yes, he always listens, always assents. How glad I should often have been to have heard a question from him, — I had almost said a contradiction; that would have served to show, at least, that some interest in spiritual things had been aroused."

"You surprise me, my uncle," said the curate. "I thought that Stone was a very good man; everybody speaks well of him; everybody seems to like him."

"*I* like him," replied the vicar, emphatically; "but it is because I like him so much that I am the more anxious about him. If my only desire for my flock was to have them moral, respectable, regular in church-going, quiet citizens, kind neighbors, honest men, I should be well pleased if all in the village were like the carpenter Stone. And yet, during my twenty years of labor at Colme, there is not one of my parishioners on whom those labors have, I fear, made less impression than on him. Stone has not only heard thousands of sermons in church, but I have repeatedly conversed with him in private on the concerns of his soul, and I have always left him with the discouraging conviction that he is not so much as grounded in the first principles of our religion ; that he has always the same assurance of going to heaven, because such an honest, respectable, sober man as he is must by a kind of necessity go there. Satisfied with this false assurance, he has never been induced to make the slightest effort to examine whether it have any safe ground to rest on. I have felt myself, when conversing with Stone, like one firing cannon at a thick earthwork. There is no strong resistance, such as is made by a stone wall, but the balls sink into the soft mud and are lost, and the fortification, seemingly so easy to be assailed, remains as firm and unmoved as if no efforts at all had been made to shake it. I have found, in the course of my long ministry," continued the vicar, " that it is easier to impress a profligate or to convince an infidel, than to lead to true faith and repentance a self-satisfied, self-sufficient soul like that of poor Stone."

Claudius Leyton gave a sigh of disappointment. "I fear that I have been doing harm, then, where I meant to do good," he observed, "saying, *peace, peace, where there is no peace.* I took it for granted that such a kind-hearted, respectable man as Stone must be a Christian indeed."

"My dear boy," said the silver-haired vicar, kindly, "yours was a most natural mistake, especially for one so young in the ministry. It is extremely difficult to distinguish mere outward good conduct and amiability from that which results from the hidden life of faith in the heart. The sad thing is," continued the pastor, "that the individual who misleads us is usually himself misled; while in danger he believes himself to be perfectly safe, and may approach even the hour of death without the slightest fear or misgiving. With him there is no cry for mercy to the Saviour of sinners, no looking unto him who was lifted up, as the brazen serpent in the wilderness, as the one only means of salvation offered to the perishing sons of men."

The invalid had spoken with animation, and a sensation of exhaustion immediately followed. He leaned wearily back on his pillow, and closed his eyes. Claudius Leyton, aware that the interview had lasted too long for his uncle's strength, quietly arose and quitted the study. The young minister sought his own room, feeling more strongly than ever how difficult it is to be a good physician to souls, and not give an opiate to a conscience already too much inclined to sink into dangerous sleep. Mr. Leyton unclosed his Bible with a sigh, but the promise on which his eye rested came with comfort to his soul: *If any of you lack wisdom, let him ask of God, that giveth to all men liberally and upbraideth not. But let him ask in faith, nothing wavering.*

XVIII.

Self - Reproach.

"Are you going to see poor Stone to-morrow?" said Persis Franks to her husband on the evening of that same Saturday.

"Ay, Sunday is the only day when I can find time now to visit a sick friend."

"I am sure that in this case it is 'the better day the better deed,'" observed Persis, as her fingers briskly plied the needle, while the pile of unmended stockings on her right hand was gradually growing small, as pair after pair, neatly darned and folded, were transferred to the left. "Mrs. Stone was saying to me to-day how much her husband enjoys your calls. You will never regret these visits, Ned."

"Now it's odd enough, wife, that at the moment when you spoke to me I was thinking of these same visits of mine to poor Stone, and thinking of them *with* regret. I might use a stronger word," continued Franks, as his wife glanced up with mild surprise; " I've

been taking myself to task for these same
Sunday visits."

"Surely, dearest, *it is lawful to do good on
the Sabbath day;* that is what our Lord himself has told us."

"Ay, *to do good,*" repeated Franks; "but
I'm not clear that I've not rather done Ben
Stone harm. You and I are alone, wifie, and
I don't mind saying to you what I wouldn't
say to any one else." Franks lowered his
voice as he went on. "Stone's voyage
through life has been a very easy one; it
seems almost as if his vessel had been one
that could guide itself without any pilot at
all; he has never met a storm that I've heard
of, — all has been smooth sailing with him.
And yet, wifie, I fear that Stone has not had
his eye fixed on the Pole-Star, nor his finger
tracing the right course on the Bible-chart.
Self-righteousness is a sunken rock, none the
less dangerous for being sunken, and if a poor
bark go to pieces upon it, we know that it's
just as surely lost as if it had gone down in
the whirlpool of drunkenness, or of any other
open vice."

"But I do not exactly see what *you* have
to reproach yourself with if poor Stone think

himself a better Christian than he actually is," observed Persis.

"Don't you see I've a kind of credit in the village for hanging out my colors boldly, and trying at least to sail by the chart? When I go Sunday after Sunday and sit with a sick, I fear a dying man, and join with him in cheerful talk, as if I'd never an object but to make the time pass pleasantly, I only cause him to think, 'There's Ned Franks, a dreadfully strict and precise old tar; he must be sure that I'm steering all right, for if he saw danger he'd be certain to bid me *sheer off.*' "

"But I have no doubt that your conversation often takes a religious turn," observed Persis.

"A religious turn!" repeated Franks, in a rather sarcastic tone; "ay, a kind of sop to my conscience, and, perhaps, poor fellow, to his. We talk, maybe, of the sermon, and the way in which busy hands are getting on with repairing the almshouses, and what a good minister the vicar is, and how glad we shall be if the Lord lets him fill the pulpit again. There's a text put in here and there, and Stone says something about being thankful for having no pain, and having been given a

good wife and a comfortable home, and such
peace in his mind. But I know that such
conversations as these held with one who, in
a few months, will probably suffer that great
change for which I cannot in charity think
him prepared, is but a kind of idle beating
and tacking about; it is not going to the
heart of the matter; it never makes him ask
himself when I leave him, 'Am I in the right
course? Is this peace of which I talk the
peace of a converted or of a dead soul?
What shall I plead when I stand, as I soon
must, in the immediate presence of a heart-
searching God?'" Franks rose from his
seat, and paced up and down his little room,
as he was wont to do when anything disturbed
or perplexed him.

"Do you intend then," asked Persis, lay-
ing down her work, "to speak faithfully to
our poor friend when you visit him to-morrow?"

Ned passed his hand through his curly
hair; he looked perplexed and undecided.
"I wish I were fit for such speaking," said he.
"If Mr. Curtis were able to get about, he'd
go right to the point with Stone at once; but
I don't think there's anything in life so hard

as to convince a self-righteous man that he's a sinner in need of a Saviour."

"Surely," said Persis, very softly, "it is the Holy Spirit alone that can convince of sin; it is only God himself who can open the eyes of the blind."

"Then to God we must turn for the blessing, wife, but we must not neglect the means. I'll try to drop in a word of warning to-morrow, though it's just such an office as I'd gladly make over to any one else if I could; but I really care for poor Ben, and I can't help thinking of the lines, —

> "'Who speaks not needed truth lest he offend,
> Hath spared himself—but sacrificed his friend.'

I hope that my visit to Stone to-morrow may not be as utterly profitless as I fear that the three last have been."

XIX.

The Test.

WHILE Persis and Ned Franks are conversing together in their little parlor, we will turn for a short time to Norah, whom we shall find in their little garden, with a full glow of the setting sun around her, as she is stooping over a flower-bed busily engaged in weeding.

Even in the bright season of spring, even in the cheerful home of the Frankses, since her return from London, the time had passed wearily and anxiously to Norah. She shrank from notice, she dreaded questions, and, though nothing was said to make her feel that it was so, she knew that her maintenance must be a burden on the slender income of her uncle. The accommodation in the school-house was small. Persis, at some inconvenience, had given up her only store-closet to serve as a sleeping-room for Norah; and if the good housewife cheerily laughed over her own little difficulties in finding a place where she might stow away jams and bacon, and Franks declared that the closer people were packed together, the less danger there was of their chafing one another, Norah felt that the little domestic circle had been complete without her, and that her pale, sad face could not add to the cheerfulness of a married pair. Even the food of which the orphan guest was so kindly pressed to partake freely must make a sensible difference in the household expenses of those who had so little to spare. Norah longed for the means of earning her own bread; but employment in needle-work, even had she been clever at sewing, could scarcely be procured in the retired neighborhood of Colme. The young girl would gladly have gone again into service; but to whom could she apply for a character? How often, with bitter regret for the past, did Norah ask herself that question? Her only resource was prayer. She entreated him whose mercy, as she trusted and believed, had forgiven her sin, to open for her some door of usefulness, to give her some means of honestly earning a livelihood. Norah was ready to take the lowest place, the hardest work, the smallest wages, if she might but struggle back to a position in which she could again maintain herself by her labor.

As Norah rose from her stooping posture, she saw Mrs. Curtis, the vicar's wife, approaching towards her. The lady, who was the general counsellor and friend of the villagers of Colme, had always shown kindness to Norah, and to be spoken to by her would, in former times, have called up a beaming smile in the face of the girl; but Norah now

met the vicar's wife with a feeling of shame
and fear.

"Good-evening to you, Norah Peele; I am
glad to find you alone, for I wish a little
quiet talk with you," said Mrs. Curtis." Let
us go to yon arbor at the end of the garden,
where we shall be undisturbed."

Norah followed the lady along the narrow
gravel path which Franks had bordered with
box. The poor girl dreaded the interview
before her, but silently prayed, as she walked
along, that she might be enabled to answer
truthfully whatever painful questions might
be asked her.

When the arbor was reached, Mrs. Curtis
seated herself on the rustic bench, which was
the handiwork of the one-armed sailor. No
one could approach the spot unseen; the
lady had chosen it in order that the conversation between herself and Norah might not
be interrupted or overheard.

"Norah," said Mrs. Curtis, "my housemaid is about to leave me to be married to
Rob Gates, the nephew of the miller. I am
therefore looking out for a trustworthy girl
to take her place. Knowing both you and
your family for so long as I have done, it is

natural that my thoughts should turn towards you."

The girl's heart throbbed fast with a newly awakened hope which she yet scarcely dared to indulge.

"But," continued the lady, (what a terrible word was that *but!*) "I cannot offer you a situation without a clear knowledge of the cause of your leaving your last one. The information which has reached me may or may not be correct. Many innocent persons are hardly judged; some are the victims of a slander. A mistress may be injudicious, or she may be unjust to her servants."

"Oh, no, Mrs. Lowndes was not unjust, at least not in sending me away," said Norah, the large tears gathering in her downcast eyes. "She was kind and generous, and good to me, till — till"— a smothered sob closed the sentence.

"Norah, you must feel that no idle curiosity leads me to question you thus. I would give no needless pain. But will you tell me, as a friend who has your best interests much at heart, the simple truth regarding the circumstances which led to your leaving London? I cannot know how to serve you, I cannot know how to advise, without that full information which can only really satisfy me when given by yourself."

"Have I not suffered enough yet?" was the silent thought of poor Norah. "Must I tell to her, whose good opinion I prize so much, that which will make me lose that good opinion forever, and prevent her from thinking of taking such a deceitful girl into her service?" And then came the strong temptation to soften and gloss over her own fault, to lay the chief blame upon Milly, or to avoid telling of any direct falsehood, or long-carried-on scheme of deceit. Again the bark was in danger of striking against the iceberg. Again rose the silent prayer, followed by the brave resolve to be honest and truthful now, at however painful a cost.

The happy bees were humming amongst the blossoming limes, but Norah did not hear them; she did not notice how richly perfumed came the breeze from the hawthorn full in flower; there was that on her mind which shut out surrounding objects. Briefly, but as clearly and truthfully as she had told her tale to Ned Franks, she now confessed all to Mrs. Curtis, without attempting to make the slightest excuse for her fault. Norah closed her account with a deep sigh, and stood as if awaiting with humble submission the rebuke which she knew must follow.

But Mrs. Curtis uttered no word of reproach; her voice when she spoke was more kindly and cheering than it had been when she had first addressed Norah Peele on that bright evening in May.

"I am very thankful, my child, that you have made a statement so frank and truthful, one which so perfectly accords with what your last mistress has written." Mrs. Curtis drew a note from her pocket, and Norah at once recognized the familiar handwriting of Mrs. Lowndes. "Before speaking to you of the situation in my household, I thought it well to write to London, to ascertain facts from the lady whom you had served. Her reply, I own, startled me a little; I thought at first that I must give up all idea of engaging you in my service. But I consulted the vicar, and he took a different view of the question. 'The young girl,' he said, 'has no doubt committed a serious fault, but she may at this moment be sincerely repenting it; if so, let us give her an opportunity of retrieving her character here.'"

"Kind, merciful!" murmured Norah.

"'But how,' I asked, 'can we know whether she sincerely regrets her fault?' 'The surest sign of true repentance,' replied my husband, 'is *amendment*. Go and question Norah Peele; see if she now makes any fresh attempt to deceive. If she be candid and open with you, we may take it as a proof that no habits of falsehood are formed, and that, warned by the past, she is likely to become as truthful and trustworthy as her sailor uncle himself.' I have done as the vicar advised; I have tried you, Norah Peele, and you have well stood the trial. I am quite willing, if you wish to come to me, to engage you from this day week."

Then, indeed, Norah could hear how merrily the bees were humming, and feel how delicious was the scented breath of May on her cheek, and admire the glorious glow of the sinking sun! All nature seemed to brighten around her, and she thought that life might be to her again a peaceful and happy thing. Eagerly she closed with the offer of Mrs. Curtis. With a heart and a step how much lighter than what they had been an hour before, Norah retraced that gravel walk along which she had passed so sadly, and, after showing her new mistress to the gate, ran into the house to carry to her uncle and aunt her good tidings, sure of their ready sympathy in her joy as well as in her sorrow!

XX.

The Momentous Question.

"Ah! glad to see ye, Ned Franks, always glad to see ye!" cried Ben Stone, holding out both his hands to the school-master of Colme. "I sent my Bell off to afternoon church, for I said, says I, there will be Ned Franks sure to drop in and give me a bit of the news. There, take a chair, my good fellow, you're always heartily welcome."

Stone himself was reclining on a bed, and well propped up with soft cushions; a flannel dressing-gown wrapped round his large form, and a scarlet shawl over that, with a red nightcap on his head. There was an air of comfort and of neatness visible in the partly darkened room. Stone liked, as he said, "to have things look respectable-like" about him. The appearance of the sick man would have conveyed to none but a practised eye the idea of serious illness. There was no wasted cheek, no hollow eye, to tell the insidious fatal disease within. Even the voice of Ben Stone, though not perhaps as strong, sounded as jovial as ever. Franks could hardly realize, as he drew his chair near to the bed, that he who rested upon it was actually dying by inches. Ned made inquiries how the patient was feeling that afternoon.

"Not just up to felling an oak-tree, or splitting it up into planks," said the carpenter, gayly; "the doctor says I can't last till winter; but who knows? 'the greatest clerks are not always the wisest men,' as good Queen Bess once said."

"No one can indeed know whether you or I will be taken first," observed Ned; "but it's well to be prepared for the end, whether it comes sooner or later than we have been led to expect."

"Yes, yes, I'm not one of those as is afraid of hearing the worst," said Stone, still in the same easy manner. "Death must come one day or another to all, and it's no such great odds when we go."

"The question is certainly not *when*, but *whither* we go," remarked Franks.

"There's the comfort of religion," said the carpenter, complacently folding his hands. "Don't we all hope to go to heaven when we die?"

"Yes, heaven's the port we all hope to land in," replied Ned Franks; "but I should just like, neighbor, for us to talk the matter over a little together; to see if you and I have embarked in the same boat, since we wish our cruise to end in the same harbor. Would you mind now telling an old friend what reason you have for thinking that you're bound for heaven?"

Ben Stone looked half perplexed, half amused, at the question. "It's not for a man to speak up for himself," he said good-humoredly; "but you and all the village know that I've not wandered far astray. I don't pretend to be such an out-and-out saint as you are," he added with a smile; "but I'm

not worse than my neighbors, and I don't
doubt but that we'll both land in heaven at
last."

"And do you suppose that *I* dare start in
the voyage to eternity in such a cockle-shell
as my own merits, all leaky and worthless!"
exclaimed Ned Franks. "No, no, neighbor;
I know too well that if I did so, I must go to
the bottom. As when the flood was coming
upon the world, there was but *one* safe vessel, and that was the ark, so there is now
but *one* means of salvation, which God himself has provided, — *faith in the Lord Jesus
Christ.* Can we fancy that in those old days
of the flood there were no boats and no
sailors, — that none could row, and none
could swim? It's likely that there were men
who had vessels, and trusted in them, and
were proud of them, too, — who believed that
these vessels could ride through the fiercest
storm that ever blew; and that may have
been the very reason why, despite of warning, these men would not fly to the ark; and
so, when the flood came, they perished. *My*
only hope of heaven is in the merits and
death of my Lord. I don't fear death, because I know that I've already taken refuge

in the ark of salvation, which is faith in Christ, the Saviour of sinners."

"These things are too deep for me," said the carpenter. "I'm a simple, plain man, and don't puzzle my head with matters of doctrine. I never can make out what you thorough-going people consider yourselves to be. There are saints and sinners in the world, that's clear. Nancy Sands is a sinner, and you are a saint, —nay, don't stop me, I must have out my say. Now, I don't count myself much either of a saint or a sinner; I'm a plain, honest man, who don't like extremes, and I dare say that I shall do just as well as others in the end. But what puzzles me," continued the carpenter, "is that the saints will insist upon it that they are the sinners; they flare up, as you did now, at the very notion of being taken to heaven because they are good, and seem to think that they can't be safe unless they declare that they are sinful!" The invalid would have laughed aloud, had there not been a grave earnestness in the face of Franks, which checked any such unseemly mirth.

"And is not the prayer in the Litany, Have mercy upon us miserable sinners, put into every mouth?" observed Franks, who had a clear recollection of the very audible tone in which Ben had joined in that prayer when attending church service.

"Yes, to be sure. I could say half the Litany by heart."

"What a wide difference there is," thought Ned Franks, "between saying it *by* heart, or *from* the heart! Do you think," he asked aloud, "that that prayer is suited for *every one* who repeats it?"

Ben Stone hummed a little before he replied. "Well, I should say, suited better for some than for others; but there's no harm in any one saying it."

"There would be harm in any one calling himself a sinner before God if he did not *believe* himself to be one," observed Franks. "But I've no doubt, neighbor, that if St. Paul and St. Peter had lived in these days, they'd have been able to cry from the bottom of the heart, 'Have mercy upon us, miserable sinners.'"

Ben Stone gave a look which seemed to say that he neither understood nor cared to understand how that could be. Ned Franks's feelings were much like what Mr. Curtis had described as his own. It seemed a hopeless matter to try to make any real impression upon that mass of quiet, self-complacent, good-humored insensibility. Ned had to repeat to himself, "He's a dying man, and dying without looking to the Saviour," in order to overcome his own strong inclination to give up in despair all attempt to convince or to move.

"I suppose that you'll agree," said the school-master aloud, "that Job was a saint if there ever lived one in this world; God himself declared that there was none upon earth like him; and yet, what were the words of Job? *I abhor myself, and repent in dust and ashes.*"

"I never can make out why Job should feel that," observed Stone; " there was nothing in what the Almighty had said to him to bring him to such a confession."

"I believe that it was not so much what God had *said*, as what he had found God to *be*, that so humbled Job as to make him confess himself to be a miserable sinner. The truth is, neighbor, we think so little of our own sinfulness, because we think so little of God's holiness. The clear light of his purity does not stream into our souls, and therefore we don't mark the spots and the stains in those souls. We think sins small and trifling which in the Lord's eyes are hateful and deadly. Eve plucks a forbidden fruit, Moses loses his temper, a man of God lets himself be drawn into what we might deem a small excusable act of disobedience : it is clear enough from the punishments which followed, that a holy God did not regard these things as *trifles*, though man in his blindness might do so."

"Ah ! all these examples are from the Old Testament," said Ben Stone ; "as for me, I hold by the New. There's none of that terrible strictness now."

"The God of the New Testament is the God of the Old," observed Franks ; "the same just and holy Being who hath declared, *The soul that sinneth, it shall die*."

"You talk like a Jew," said Stone ; "yet you know as well, and better than I do, that we've the gospel to look to now, and that's all mercy and love."

"The New Testament rests on the Old ; it has grown out of it ; it forms with it a complete whole. We cannot really accept the one without the other," replied Franks, with an animation of manner which strongly contrasted with the carpenter's stolid composure.

Ben Stone shook his tasselled cap, and half smiling observed, "The New is enough for me."

Ned Franks glanced around for something that might serve to illustrate the important truth which his companion could not, or would not, understand. He took up a cut flower which had been placed in a glass of water on the table.

"The Old Testament is the bud of the New; or rather as the green sheath enclosed the bud, so in the Old-Testament Scriptures is the precious gospel held and enclosed," he said, looking down on the flower.

"Granted, if you wish it," said the carpenter; "but now we've done with the sheath, and only the flower is left."

"Not so," cried the school-master eagerly; "look here, this is the green sheath of the bud, the green cup or calyx, as they call it, still holding and supporting the flower; less noticed, certainly, under the bright petals, but keeping them all together. What would happen, Ben Stone, were we to tear that green part away?"

"Why, the flower would of course fall to pieces."

"And if it were possible to separate New-Testament truth entirely from that contained in the Old Testament, — but it is *not* possible," exclaimed Franks, interrupting himself in the midst of his sentence. "*The word of the Lord endureth forever!* The Old Testament is the very support and foundation of the gospel. If we would know *who* the Lord Jesus is, we learn, from the Old Testament, that he is *the mighty God,* whose goings forth have been from everlasting;† the man that is my fellow, saith the Lord God of Hosts.‡* If we should know *why* he died, again we find the gospel enclosed in the ancient Scriptures, like the bud in the sheath : *He was wounded for our transgressions; the Lord hath laid on him the iniquity of us all.§*

"Still, there's ever so much in the Old Testament that does not concern us Christians at all," said the carpenter; "and though I don't pretend to have the Bible at my finger-ends,

* Isaiah ix. 6.   † Micah v. 2.   ‡ Zechariah xiii. 7.
§ Isaiah liii. 5, 6.

as you have, I can show you that in a moment. We have no concern whatever with all those endless sacrifices of bullocks and lambs, which the Jews were perpetually making; you might cut out of the Bible every chapter about them, and we should never miss them at all."

Franks's expressive face showed surprise at the utter ignorance betrayed by such a remark. "Why, the very *keystone* of Gospel truth rests on the doctrine taught by those very sacrifices!" he exclaimed, bending forward in his eager earnestness. "There were two mighty lessons taught by those sacrifices, which were ordained by God himself; these lessons were, that *without shedding of blood there is no remission,** and that justice would accept of one life as given *instead* of another. No Israelite, no, not even the holy Moses, could be forgiven and accepted without a *sacrifice* for sin, the sprinkled blood of atonement; no Christian, not even a St. Paul, can be forgiven and accepted, without a sacrifice for sin; and ours, in One of which all the burnt-offerings made by the Jews was but a type, the sacrifice, once and forever, made

* Hebrews ix. 22.

on the cross by Him who is *the Lamb of God that taketh away the sins of the world!* O Ben Stone, my friend," continued the sailor, with emotion, "I believe, from my soul I believe, that *there is none other name under heaven given among men whereby we must be saved,** but the name of Him who died for sinners; that there is nothing that can make the soul pure, but *the blood of Christ which cleanseth from all sin.*† Faith in that name is the ark in which alone I dare hope for salvation, and through that blood shed for me, I have the blessed assurance of being received after death into that heaven which the Lord hath prepared for them that love him!"

Ned Franks rose hastily from his seat as he concluded the last sentence; for, after what had been uttered on a subject so solemn, he could enter on no common theme. He pressed the hand of the sick man, and, with no other form of taking leave, quitted the carpenter's cottage. The sailor sighed heavily as he passed from the darkened sick-room into the glowing sunshine without.

"How weakly I have spoken, how little have I said of what I wished to say!" he mur-

* Acts iv. 12.   † 1 John ii. 7.

mured to himself. "The words of my Persis are true indeed: it is only the Holy Spirit that can convince of sin. Then I know that my manner is too impetuous. I am always running the chance of offending, rather than persuading; and I don't know how to put into words the thoughts that are swelling within me like a stream that is bursting its bounds. I cannot restrain myself, when any one would put aside (as if they could be worn out by time) those Old-Testament Scriptures which our Lord himself bade us search, as testifying of him; when any look upon the faith of Abraham, Isaac, and Jacob, as quite a distinct thing from that required of us; when, like poor Stone, they seem to conclude that justice and holiness are confined to the Old Testament, mercy and love to the New! Ah! the truth is"—Franks quickened his steps, as if to keep pace with the current of his thoughts—"the truth is, that Satan knows that he has a terrible advantage over us, if he can but persuade us to try any way but God's way to reach the kingdom of heaven. Satan is willing that we should look on the Lord as a great example, or a great teacher, or even as a great king, if he can only keep us from acknowledging Christ as also a great sacrifice for sins, for *our* sins ; and so prevent us from throwing ourselves entirely upon his mercy and merits. To draw us back from the ark, that is Satan's chief aim ; to make us believe that we do not require a Saviour. As if the Son of God would have died, had there been any less costly means of purchasing heaven for his people ; as if we did not see most clearly, in his sufferings on the .cross, the *holiness* of God that abhors sin, the *justice* of God in punishing it, joined with the boundless *mercy* and *love*, which made God not spare even his Son, but give him freely for our salvation ! "

XXI.

An Old Letter.

" WELL, Bell, my dear," said the carpenter, as his wife returned from afternoon service, " tell me what you've heard to-day, and I'll tell you what I've heard."

" Mr. Leyton preached as usual," replied Mrs. Stone, as she unloosed the red strings of her bonnet. "I think he's getting less shy, and more earnest. His text was, '*If we say that we have no sin, we deceive ourselves, and the truth is not in us.*' "

"Why, that would ha' done for the text of the sermon I've had all to myself," said Ben Stone.

"Sermon, — what do you mean?" asked his wife, pausing in the act of taking off her shawl.

"There's Ned Franks been here, and — talk of earnestness — he's earnest with a vengeance! There was nothing would content him but that I should own myself to be a downright, miserable sinner; and he threw out something more than a hint, that I'm like to come to the same end as those who wouldn't go into the ark, and so were drowned in the flood."

"I wish that Ned Franks would mind his own business," exclaimed Mrs. Stone, indignantly. "I'm sure that he, and every one knows that there's not a better man in the parish than you are; it would be well if, with all his fine talking, Mr. Franks were but half so good!"

"Softly, softly, my dear," said Ben Stone,

amused and pleased at her warm defence. "Ned Franks is a capital fellow; a brave, noble-hearted man."

"Let him be what he likes," exclaimed Mrs. Stone, angrily pulling off her boots. "If he comes here a worritting and lecturing you, I shall shut the door upon him!"

"His visit was certainly very unlike that which the young curate paid me. Mr. Leyton, with his gentle way and soft voice, spoke of my trials and my hope; and said that a true Christian is not afraid even of death. Then says I, 'Sir, I'm never afraid of death;' so, of course, he takes it for granted that I'm a true Christian, and all right, and goes away quite pleased and happy. But as for Ned Franks," — Ben Stone gave his little chuckling laugh, though it sounded less merry than usual, — "he'll take nothing for granted, except that I *must* be a sinner. He leans forward and looks right into your eyes, as if he meant to read you through and through, and let you see right into his soul also. I can just fancy," continued the sick carpenter, laughing again, " what sort of a sailor he was when he served the queen, — how he'd stick by his colors, and go slap-bang at an enemy!"

"But you're no enemy," cried Mrs. Stone, "neither his nor any one else's, and I'll not let him go slap-bang at you! Let him preach away as much as he likes to that wretched Nancy Sands whom he pulled out of the mill-stream!"

"There's not much chance of *her* deceiving herself, and saying that she has no sin," observed Stone.

"It was small kindness to her husband to save her," continued the carpenter's wife; "Sands has little cause to thank Ned. The poor clerk is growing thinner every day, and looked at church this afternoon as if he was going to be hanged. He knows that when Nancy comes out of hospital she'll be at her old tricks again, drinking him out of house and home; far better for *him* if all had been over at once! I couldn't help giving her a bit o' my mind about that, when I went to see her yesterday!"

"You did!" exclaimed Stone, in amused surprise; "how did she take it? If Nancy returned you a bit o' *her* mind," he continued, with a laugh, "I guess you'd the worst of the exchange. You never were a match for Nancy, my dear."

"She said nothing, but looked as if she could have eaten me," replied Mrs. Stone.

"Her accident must have pulled her down a bit, if she'd not something sharper than a look to fling at you," observed Ben. "You and she used to go at it like poker and tongs, but Nancy could hit hardest and longest; she'd a tongue like a mill-wheel if once you set it a-going. But put the kettle on the fire, my dear, and lets have a drop of good tea. In the evening I'll do what I've been intending to do for these many years past, — look over that box of old things belonging to my poor mother, whom I lost when I was a little chap but nine years of age. I want to sort 'em, — put by what I mean to keep, and burn what's of use to no one. Ned Franks himself would say it was right for a sick man to put his house in order."

The task of looking over the contents of that old box, which had been stowed away in a cupboard for a great length of time, was one which the carpenter had put off from day to day, and year to year, perhaps because — till illness came — he had led a busy, active life, or more probably because his cheerful, easy nature disliked any occupation that might

awaken melancholy thoughts. And who but
is saddened by turning over memorials of one
loved and lost, even though, as in the case of
Stone, forty or fifty years may have elapsed
since the friend departed. This Sunday
evening, as twilight came on, Ben Stone fulfilled the long-deferred task. His wife brought
the old box, — a deal one covered with faded
paper, — and placed it on a chair close to his
bed, that he might examine its contents with
ease. She lighted a candle and put it on the
table beside her husband, and then sat down
with some little curiosity to see her mother-
in-law's hoarded treasures, but a secret conviction that the box would hold nothing but
" old-fashioned rubbish."

The late Mrs. Stone had not been an orderly
woman, or perhaps death had taken her by
surprise, so that she had left her things in confusion, — such was the silent reflection of her
son's wife, as Ben went slowly over the contents of the box. They were a strange medley. There were two gilt lockets, a nutmeg-
grater, an old tooth-brush and silver thimble,
a collar, an unfinished bit of embroidery, a
sampler, several skeins of silk and cotton of
various colors in a tangled mass together,

fragments of gimp and tape, a red leather
pocket-book much the worse for wear, a
prayer-book without a cover, and a padlock
without a key. There were also heaps of
papers, recipes for cures, and recipes for
dishes, old patterns, old letters, old bills, a
jumble of all sorts of things which it was
scarcely matter of wonder that no one had
cared to reduce into order.

"You may use all these receipted bills to
light the fire with, my dear," said Ben Stone;
"they at least can be useful to nobody. But
I'll keep this old bit of an Almanac, — 1815!
Well, well; how time passes! It seems
strange to look back to the days when this
Almanac was a new one!"

"I think that this may go into the fire too,"
said Mrs. Stone, who had been vainly trying
to unravel a silken tangle.

"Ah! here's something curious," observed
Ben, as he drew out an old letter, written on
very coarse paper, in a very round, childish
hand, a letter which had been fastened with
a big red wafer pressed down with a button,
and which was soiled with many a blot.

"Here is, I suppose, the very first letter as
ever I wrote. I didn't remember that I had

18*

ever written to my mother. She died — poor, dear soul! — the week after I first went to school."

Mrs. Stone was of course interested, as any good wife would have been, in the first specimen of her husband's handwriting. She pushed the candle nearer to him, and read over his shoulder, as she might have done at the distance of half the length of the room, the school-boy's big, blotted scrawl.

"Dear Mother, I hope your well. I am ill my head is so bad pleas get me home *quick* QUICK your dutiful son B. S."

Mrs. Stone smiled, but her husband looked grave. Strange old recollections, and those by no means of a pleasing nature, were brought back to his mind by the sight of that — till now — forgotten letter to his mother. Ben put up his hand to his forehead, and pushed up the nightcap from his temples.

"Yes, yes," he muttered to himself," I remember writing that letter as if it were but yesterday; I remember the very button which I used to press down the wafer. I was very wretched on first going to school, — the boys bullied me, and I could not bear regular work; so to get my poor mother to take me home, I wrote that letter with a big falsehood in it. It was the first, — the only note as ever I sent her, and it was full of lies! Strange that that should turn up now!"

"There's nothing to take to heart in such an old matter as that," observed Mrs. Stone, struck by the unusual gravity of her husband, who generally turned everything into a jest. "Nobody thinks of raking up what they've done wrong forty or fifty years back."

"Tut, I should not care a toss of a straw about it," replied Stone, "had I told the falsehood to any one but my mother, and that just a few days before I lost her. I'd never an opportunity of telling her that I'd deceived her, or of asking her to forgive me, for I did not go home till she lay in her coffin. To think of that vile bit of paper turning up against me now!" Ben doubled the note, and, tearing it into pieces, threw the fragments on the floor.

It may be a matter of surprise that a sin of childhood should have in the slightest degree ruffled the easy conscience of such a man as Ben Stone. He had thought very little indeed of sinning against God, but his natural affections made him feel pain at having sinned against a sick mother. Perhaps the words of Franks had not been so utterly unheeded as they had seemed at first to be, and had served to rouse a suspicion, confirmed by the school-boy's letter, that there might be many a forgotten fault of the highly respectable man that would "turn up against him" some day; faults for which forgiveness had never been granted or asked. Be that as it may, Stone suddenly found out that he was tired and sleepy, and bade his wife shut up the box and take it away. The evening was getting on; it was time for him to take his night-draught, and go quietly to rest.

Though the night-draught was taken and the pillows carefully beaten up and sleep soon closed the invalid's eyes, it was not quiet rest. A confused medley of thoughts shaped themselves into dreams, which took their color from what had occurred during the day. Ben Stone in his sleep was still looking over and examining things of the past; his whole room appeared to be filled up with boxes, one piled on another, and there seemed to be a necessity for him to open and put them all into order. This was in itself an oppressive feeling to the dreamer; but the oppression became much greater when he found that each box was filled to overflowing with bills,—old, forgotten bills,—and that not one of them was receipted; not one had ever been paid. Stone had a dim idea that all these debts were connected with unforgiven sin, from that falsehood contained in his first letter to the last "idle word" which had fallen from his lips. As box after box was emptied, and every unpaid bill thrown down in despair, the white paper seemed to turn into foam, a sea was rising around him, and it appeared to Stone as if his numberless debts would drown him at last. Ned Franks was by the side of the dreamer, helping him to look over his boxes, and saying, every now and then, in an earnest, anxious tone, "Ben Stone, if you don't pay, you are a ruined man!—if you don't pay, you are ruined forever!" So strong was the impression left on the dreamer's mind, that he awoke with the words on his lips, "If you don't pay, you are ruined forever!"

Very still was the room when Stone opened his eyes with a start, relieved to find that he had, after all, been but dreaming. One feeble night-light was making "darkness visible" in the chamber, where no other object could distinctly be seen. · Even so faint a light had Stone's conscience hitherto thrown upon spiritual things, as different from the clear radiance of Truth as the night-light from the sun. The sinner had not known his sinfulness because his light had been too dim to enable him to see it.

As Ben Stone lay silent and still on his pillow, the breeze bore to him, more distinctly than he ever before had heard it in his cottage, the sound of the church clock striking ONE. For once Stone felt something solemn in the sound; he felt that time was being meted out to him, that his remaining hours might be few, and that he *was not prepared* for eternity.

Then Stone thought of Ned Franks. The sailor was not afraid of death, but his reason for not fearing it was something utterly different from the easy reliance on his own goodness which the carpenter knew to have been his own. Ned Franks had shrunk from the idea of his safety depending on his merits. On what then *did* it depend? The invalid, with a dawning perception that he himself might not be quite as secure as he had lately thought himself to be, felt desirous to know more clearly what was Franks's hope of salvation; and when, in the morning, Mrs. Stone was preparing her husband's breakfast, he asked her to stop the sailor when next he should pass their door, and ask him to step in and see him.

XXII.

Peace from Above.

"You went off in such haste yesterday that we'd not time to have out half our say," said Ben Stone to Ned Franks, as, called in by the carpenter's wife, he walked up to the patient's bedside.

Franks smiled, agreeably surprised to find that Stone wished to renew such a conversation.

"Take a chair, my good friend, and sit down. Bell, you needn't stop in for me. I know Franks won't grudge me a half-hour for once, even on a week day."

Mrs. Stone soon quitted the cottage, but not till she had warned her visitor with raised finger and shake of the head, "Don't you bother my husband about anything to make his mind uneasy."

When she had closed the door behind her, Ben Stone turned to Franks, and said, "I was looking over old papers, yesterday, which reminded me of my boyhood, and I suppose it's that which has brought back to me a bit of rhyme which I learned from my mother, and which has been running in my brain all this day, though it had gone clean out of my memory for years, —

> "'There's not a sin that I commit,
>   Or wicked word I say,
> But in Thy dreadful book 'tis writ
>   Against the judgment-day.'

"Now, do you suppose," said Stone, with an effort to speak in his usual careless tone, "that God keeps an account like that, as a creditor with his debtors, and that when folks die there are all the old bills, as it were, brought up, even debts that they'd clean forgotten?"

"Yes, assuredly, *unless all those debts have been paid*."

"That's the very nail that I want you to hit," cried the carpenter. "How are we to make sure that the debts *are* all paid, — I mean, that God has forgiven us outright? Are you sure that *your* debts are all paid?"

"Yes, thank God!" cried the sailor; "my debts were paid, every one of them, when my Saviour died on Calvary. Does not St. Paul say that Christ blotted out *the handwriting of ordinances that was against us, which was contrary to us, and took it out of the way, nailing it to his cross?*"

"Were every one's sins blotted out then?" asked Stone.

"The sins of all who have living *faith* in the Lord."

"Ah! *faith;* that's what you're always talking about, and I can never quite make out what it means."

"It simply means that we believe from the heart that the Son of God *died for us*," said Ned Franks.

"Is that all?" exclaimed Stone, in surprise. "Why, a poor wretch like Nancy Sands might believe that as well as yourself!"

"And if poor Nancy does believe that *from the heart*, her sins, be they few or many, *are* forgiven her for the sake of Him who bore the punishment for them all."

"That's a dangerous doctrine, a very dangerous doctrine," said the carpenter, shaking his head; "you wouldn't put Nancy, I hope, on the same footing as yourself or as me?"

"The ark of Salvation is as open to Nancy as to us," replied Franks; "and if any of us reach God's heaven, it can only be in that ark."

"I don't understand what you mean," said Ben Stone. "Would you put bad and good all together?"

"Perhaps I can explain myself best by referring to Noah's ark," replied Franks. "God made known that a deluge was coming on the earth, and that the only way of escaping it was by going into an ark which Noah was commanded to prepare. It is clear that those who were *saved* were those who *believed*. It was *faith* in God's word that made Noah and his family enter the ark; they were saved because they were *in it*, and not, as I tried to explain yesterday, because of their merits as sailors or swimmers. It is clear, also, that they could not be *half* saved by the ark, and *half* by their own boats or rafts. So, if we trust our souls to Christ, we must do so *entirely;* we must give up all notion of saving ourselves, and own that our hopes of forgiveness and heaven rest on *nothing but his mercy and merits.* We own ourselves, indeed, to be miserable sinners, but we are able to take our firm stand on the Gospel doctrine that *Christ died for sinners,* — for that is our ark."

"I'm afraid that people who make sure of being saved by faith will lead very careless lives," said the carpenter, who could not get over his repugnance to being classed with Nancy Sands.

"They can only be saved by living, true faith," replied Franks. "Merely to say that we believe is nothing; nay, a cold conviction that the Bible is true, is nothing, — *the devils also believe and tremble.*"

"How are you to know true faith from false faith?" asked Ben, with rather a sarcastic smile, as if he thought he had driven Ned Franks into a corner.

"How do you know a real fire from a painted one?" asked Ned.

"Well, it does not need much wit to tell the one from the other, if the painting were ever so clear," replied Stone; "the real fire warms us, of course; it aint a thing only to be looked at."

"And so real faith warms the heart, fills it with a glow of grateful love towards Him who gave himself for us. And that love makes us loathe and detest sin, because it is displeasing to our Lord, — the one thing which he hates. True faith and sin are just as much opposed to each other as fire and water. You said just now that you were afraid that people would live very careless lives if they hoped to be saved by faith. Do you find it to be so in your experience of men, Ben Stone? Those who are the most active in good works, the most steady in conduct, the best husbands, parents, neighbors, are they not the very people who have no hope of heaven but in the great Sacrifice for sin?"

"I can't deny that," answered Ben Stone, who knew that Ned Franks himself had a standard of duty that made his own appear but a low one. "But I can't see how that should be."

"Because every man *that hath that hope* in Christ, *purifieth himself even as he is pure;* * because true faith is a gift of God's Holy

* 1 John iii. 3.

Spirit, and it must be followed by two others, — the love of Christ and that *holiness without which no man shall see the Lord.* * As a good man once said, 'We come to Christ just as we are, but not to remain as we have been.' When we are once in the ark, Stone, it will lift us above the waters of wilful sin, as well as the waves of destruction ; none serve God like those who have received the assurance, — 'Go in peace ; thy sins are forgiven thee.'"

The conversation was here interrupted by the entrance of Mr. Leyton. Franks respectfully rose, and gave up his chair to the young clergyman, and, at his request, brought the large Bible, which always occupied a conspicuous place in Ben's home. Very few words were exchanged, but Franks felt that the portion of Scripture selected by the curate was peculiarly well suited to deepen any impression which the late conversation might have left. It was the fifty-first psalm which Mr. Leyton read, almost without comment, by the sick-bed of one just beginning to have his eyes opened to the truth that he, too, had need to cry, *Have mercy upon me, O Lord!*

* Hebrews xii. 10.

19*

Create in me a clean heart, and renew a right spirit within me!

The eyes of Ben Stone were never again to be utterly closed to that truth; as life's day waned, a better light dawned on the invalid's soul.

XXIII.

The Wife's Resolve.

ON, on flowed the stream, round and round went the mill-wheel; and even so flows the current of time, and the circle of daily occupation goes round and round. Little Bessy, the miller's child, used every afternoon to watch Ned and his little band of workers going cheerfully to their toil; for the short cut to Wild Rose Hollow was through the wooded glen. Whistling and singing, laughing and shouting, the boys came along, and often a nosegay from a cottage garden, or a garland of flowers from the hedge, was left on the way for Bessy. The almshouses she always called *her* cottages, and the boys who labored to repair them *her* workmen; and the child's day-dream, as she sported by the stream, was to build a whole village of cottages, the prettiest that ever were seen, so that every poor old woman in England might have one with a garden all brilliant with flowers.

Before Ned and his "jovial crew," as he called the school-boys, had left off working in Wild Rose Hollow, just at the hour of six they always saw John Sands return from visiting the hospital of B——. The Hollow, though a little apart from the high road, yet commanded a view of it, and, punctual as the clock, with his black coat, white neckcloth, and a narrow-brimmed hat surmounting his close-cropped black hair, the lean, stiff figure of the clerk was seen passing a certain thorn-tree which grew by the dusty highway. The boys were so much accustomed to this sight of the poor husband pursuing his silent, joyless way back to his solitary home, that he would certainly have been missed by them, had he on any day failed to appear. It was as natural to catch that glimpse of him passing the thorn-tree, as it was on Sundays to see him in his place under the reading-desk in church; whatever John Sands did, there seemed to be a kind of necessity that he should go on doing it forever.

It caused no small surprise, then, amongst the boys, when, on one evening in the latter part of May, as the clerk appeared at his usual hour, instead of passing the thorn-tree as usual, he turned off to the left from the high-road, and, at the same pace, descended the narrow path which led down into Wild Rose Hollow. Any deviation from John Sands's daily course appeared as strange as if the mill-stream had suddenly taken to flowing in some new channel. The attention of the boys was even distracted from old Matthews, the cake and biscuit-man, who, with his well-known basket, had come that evening down into the Hollow to tempt the "jovial crew" to spend some of their half-pence and farthings in buying its sweet contents. Persis, who had brought her baby on that bright, warm afternoon to the Hollow, partly that she might visit old Sarah Mason, and partly that she might watch her husband and his crew at their work, looked up with an inquiring glance from the low wall on which she was seated, as John Sands came, with his long strides, towards the party.

"Why, here comes the old raven himself! What can be a-bringing him here?" cried one of the boys; "sure he's not a-going to work!" The idea of John Sands shouldering a pick-axe seemed so funny, that it set the auditors laughing.

"He's a bit red in the face, — I never seed him look like that afore, — as if he was going to smile; I fear he's been drinking like his wife!" exclaimed another boy; for anything resembling either a color or a smile on the sallow face of John Sands had never been seen in the memory of the oldest of Franks's "jovial crew."

"He's a-walking right up to old Matthews. Oh, if he ben't a-going to buy lollypops!" almost screamed a little urchin, in the excitement of surprise.

Every young eye was watching with curiosity the movements of the clerk, who went up straight to the cake and biscuit seller.

"Will you take half a crown for all these?" asked John Sands, pointing to the contents of the basket.

The wondering boys gathered around, while old Matthews, after a short mental calculation of the value of his sweeties and cakes, signified assent by a nod of the head.

John Sands pulled out an old black leather purse, opened it with fingers that seemed to tremble as he did so, and drew forth a half crown. He gave it into the old man's hand, and then, turning with a kind of nervous little giggle to the boys, he said, —

"There, you may have a scatter if you like it!"

So much amazement was excited by such an unaccountable act of generosity on the part of the stiff and usually melancholy man, that the boys stood staring and gaping at him for one or two seconds before they gave the donor of the sweets the loud, joyous cheer, which was instantly succeeded by a scatter and a scramble.

Meantime, John Sands strode up to Franks, who was standing by the wall with a measuring-line; the clerk took hold of Ned's one hand with both his own, and wrung it hard without uttering a word; then, to complete the astonishment of the beholders, went up to Persis, stooped down, and actually kissed the baby, — a thing which he had never been known before to do to any neighbor's child, and which he could only have done, all were persuaded, under the pressure of most unusual excitement. John Sands then turned on his heel and departed as he had come, anxious to escape from the noisy gratitude of the boys, whom he had treated for the first and last time in his life.

Had one of the jackdaws that haunted the old church-tower taken to soaring and singing like a lark, or had the ancient yew-tree been found on some morning bursting out into rose-colored blossom, it would hardly have excited more amazement than this strange conduct of John Sands, the clerk. Franks looked anxiously at his wife, and unconsciously touched his own forehead with his finger. The same thought was passing through the mind of each : " Grief has turned the poor fellow crazy." But grief had nothing to do with the matter ; Sands was as sane and as sober as he had ever been in the course of his life. If his conduct appeared odd to those who had never known him but gloomy, solemn, and stiff, it was because such a (to him) strange guest had come to the poor man's heart in the shape of *joy,* that it had overturned everything before it ; and Sands, in the excitement of receiving such a guest, scarcely knew what he was doing.

To explain the cause of this strange new sensation of joy to one dried up, as it were, by care and sorrow, we must relate what had occurred not an hour before, when John Sands had stood in the hospital-ward by the bedside of his suffering wife.

Interviews between them had taken place regularly on every week-day. It had seemed as if poor Sands could find little comfort in his visits to Nancy. After his long walk from Colme he would sit, silent and sad, listening to his wife's complainings and moans, or enduring her gloomy silence, which was almost harder to bear. Sands was not a man of many words, at least, words of his own, — well as his voice was known in the responses in church. He never attempted to comfort, but he felt for his suffering Nancy; and — little as he guessed that such was the case — very dear was his sympathy to her who was proving, week after week, the strength of his patient, much-enduring affection. On this particular afternoon Nancy had been more silent than usual, and Sands was thinking of rising and taking his leave at his accustomed time of departure, when his wife broke out suddenly with the exclamation, —

"I'll do it! I've made up my mind she shan't never throw that at me again!"

"Throw what, my dear?" mildly inquired the clerk.

"Bell Stone was here last Saturday," said Nancy, speaking with strong but restrained emotion. "She threw out a hint, — she did, — that it is no great thing for you that I'm getting over my accident, for that a *dead* wife is a deal better for a man to have than a *drunken* one!"

"My dear!" exclaimed Sands, much shocked.

"She did say it!" repeated Nancy, vehemently, "and she thought it, and all the world thinks it, and *I* think it, too, for it's the fact, though I could have torn out her eyes when she said it!" The woman of fiery passions, weakened by illness and pain, lost all her self-command, and burst into a torrent of tears.

John Sands knew not how to soothe her passion of grief, and could only repeat, "My dear, my dear!" in a deprecating tone of distress.

"I'm not angry with her now!" cried Nancy, suddenly stopping in her weeping and drying her eyes. "The young curate came just after Stone's wife had left. I did not think much of the lad at first, but he, too, spoke what was truth, though in a different way from Bell. What he was a-saying I've been turning over in my mind ever since. 'Twill be hard work, but I'll do it. Then I've been thinking, oh, many and many's the time, of that evening I spent with the Frankses just afore I fell into the stream! I've been saying to myself, 'What a different home Persis gives her husband from what I've given to mine! She has a good husband, — I'll not deny it, — but he don't deserve better of her than you do of me, John Sands, let any one deny that as can!'"

"My dear!" repeated the poor clerk, in a softened tone. It was a new thing to him to have a kind word from his wife.

"Now," continued Nancy, who did not care to be interrupted, "I've lost an arm, and my right one, and it's not much as I can do now. But I'll do what I can, John Sands, and I'll *not do* what I've done," she went on, more vehemently. "I'll *not* go a-disgracing you, spending your money, and breaking your heart. I'll take the pledge to-morrow, and, God helping me, I'll keep it; never a drop of the poison shall pass my lips again!"

And this was the piece of good news which had sent the poor clerk on his homeward way almost dizzy with joy, so glad that he could not rest until he had got others to share it, though only by the very simple means of a scatter of sugar-plums and cakes!

But Nancy's conversation with her husband had not closed with her promise to take the pledge. There was something else on the woman's mind.

"We've done nothing yet, John Sands, to show that we're not ungrateful to that sailor whom I've been a worritting and abusing ever since he came to the village; and who yet jumped into the water and saved me, just as I was drawn under that fearful wheel. I'll never forget the horror; — I thought all was over with me then!"

"I'd do anything," began the clerk, but Nancy, as usual, cut him short.

"You go home, and get my pretty cuckoo-clock, the clock as was given me on my marriage, and send it over to the Frankses with a letter, a handsome letter; you're a scholar, and can write one as good as a parson. And, mind you,"— a grim, strange smile came over Nancy's features as she added, — "and mind you, don't forget to send the weights, John Sands. Persis told the truth, and I'll never forget it, — a clock can't get on without the weights."

John Sands did not forget to take down the clock that evening, and to send it to the school-house, with a letter written so neatly that it looked like copperplate. It was a fine specimen of composition also, for the clerk could write well, though he could not speak well; and if ever there was a man inspired by grateful joy, that man was the husband of Nancy. He did not, however, in his letter make the slightest allusion to his wife's late bad habits, nor to her intention of taking the pledge; there was a feeling of delicacy on the part of the husband that made him shrink from unnecessarily touching on so tender a subject. But often and often did the clerk mutter to himself on that evening, before he went to his rest, "Didn't I always say it; she was tempted, poor dear, and went wrong, but the metal was always good, — very good!"

XXIV.

The Blind Maiden.

WE are now going to change the scene of our story, and, leaving for a while the quiet village of Colne, with its rushing stream and blossoming hedges, turn towards busy, bustling London.

My reader may chance to remember a slight mention made by Sands, in an earlier chapter, of a Jew and his son, of whose conversion Persis and Franks had been the happy instruments more than three years previously. It is to the humble abode of the converted Jew that I will now direct my reader's attention.

In a gloomy kitchen in a lodging-house situated in a low street of London, a poor girl sat, not on a chair, but on a box, for scanty indeed was the furniture in that dark, close room. The carpetless floor was uneven, the paper on the walls half peeled away, the plaster in the ceiling smoke-stained, cracked, and broken in several places. But it was not the aspect of the place that distressed Sophy Claymore ; had it been adorned by rich tapestry, and pictures in gilded frames, it would have been all the same to her as far as regarded its appearance, for she was totally blind. Though years had passed since the heavy affliction had come upon her, the poor young woman had never yet become reconciled to the loss of her sight. She longed, she pined to look on the sunbeams once more, to see the flowers, and behold again the faces of men.

And then to Sophy Claymore poverty was a terrible trial. She had not been accustomed to it in her childhood. Sophy, the daughter of a worthless sharper, who had spent lavishly what he had gained wickedly, had known more of pleasure and folly during the first fifteen years of her life than usually falls to the lot of girls in her station. Now she was an orphan, poor, penniless, having hardly the necessaries of life, and owing even those necessaries to the generous kindness of a friend. Isaacs, the converted Jew, though no relative of Sophy, had adopted her as his own child at a time when he was better able to support her, and would not now throw her off, though he had scarcely a crust to share with the poor blind girl.

Then Sophy had sharp pain added to poverty and blindness. Ever since the terrible illness which had deprived her of sight, she had been subject to attacks of rheumatism, sometimes in her limbs, sometimes in her head. As she sat on the box in that low-ceiled room, dreadful shootings of pain from eye and ear and cheek made her ever and anon start and draw in her breath, and then utter a low plaintive moan.

But it was not only these trials, sore as they were, that made poor Sophy's blind eyes overflow with tears, and drew from her that impatient wish that she might lie down and die. Sophy had a wounded spirit as well as a suffering body. She had not the calm rest of that loving faith which has so often made God's children *joyful in tribulation.* She felt very impatient under her troubles, even though well aware that she had partly brought them on herself. Sophy had the fear of God in her heart; but she had as yet but little love, and therefore could hardly keep from murmuring, though she tried hard not to rebel.

"Oh, here comes Benoni, at last!" exclaimed Sophy Claymore, hastily drying her eyes, as a light footstep was heard on the dark wooden stair leading down to the kitchen. Sophy had never seen the face of her little brother, as she called the son of Isaacs; she had never met the smile of the child; but she would sometimes say that she could *hear* the smile in his voice; and she loved to fancy him like the picture of a fair white-winged cherub, with a ray streaming down on his bright, uplifted face, which she had admired when she was a child. If Sophy could have seen Benoni as he entered the kitchen, she would have beheld something very unlike the image in her mind; he would have appeared as a pale, sickly boy, of about nine or ten years of age, with a Jewish cast of feature, and very shabbily dressed. But perhaps Sophy was after all not so much mistaken as many might have thought her, and Benoni, seen with the eyes of the soul, might have looked much like a cherub still. There *was* a ray streaming down upon him, though not such as can be seen by mortal eyes.

"Oh! have you sold them, Benoni?" cried

Sophy anxiously, as she heard her adopted brother softly enter the room.

There was not "a smile in the voice," but there was hope in it as the boy made reply, "Not to-day, dear Sophy. People seemed all so busy and bustling, they would not attend to me. But I hope to-morrow to sell some of your beautiful knitted things;" and Benoni put down a card-board box containing small cuffs and kettle-holders, — a box, alas! just as full as when he had taken it out that morning to try to sell something in the streets.

"I wish that the money thrown away on the wool had gone for bread!" said Sophy, desperately. She was dreadfully disappointed at the failure, and ready to burst into tears.

Benoni went and sat upon the box beside her, took her hand in his own, stroked and fondled it, and looked up lovingly into her face. "Poor sister," he said very softly, "I'm afraid you are still in sore pain; I wish I could take it away!"

"You feel for me, Benoni, you pity me," replied Sophy, almost with a sob; "why does not God pity too?"

"God does!" exclaimed Benoni, looking shocked at what sounded so much like the expression of a doubt of the love of his merciful Creator.

"It does not seem like it," muttered Sophy, half aloud, "or why does God leave us in misery like this?"

"God knows why, and we must trust him," said Benoni, simply. "Why, you trust even *me*, dear Sophy, a poor, foolish, little boy like me, when I lead you about in the street; you are sure that I won't bring you into danger, or take you where you would get any harm. You just hold me tight by the hand and walk on, and are never afraid. I think that's how we should feel about greater things. We should let the good Lord take us by the hand, and then not start back and feel frightened. He sees, you know, though we cannot see, what is the best road to take us along."

"I wish that I could feel as you do," sighed Sophy. "How do you get such comfort in religion? I scarcely ever have any."

"My comfort comes by thinking all about the Lord Jesus," said Benoni. "I'm often getting anxious and sad, and then when I think about him, all seems to grow sunny again."

"I also think of the Lord in his glory," observed Sophy; "but it seems as if in the midst of all the happiness of heaven he would not care to think about me.”

“But I like best to think about the Lord when he was on earth,” said Benoni; “most of all when he was a little boy living at Nazareth with his mother. Then I know he can understand all that I feel, and the little things that trouble me so. Joseph was not a rich or a great man you know; he was only a simple carpenter, and had to work for his bread. Don’t you think that Joseph may sometimes have been ill, or out of work like my father, and that Mary may scarcely have known how to get food to give to her husband and son?”

“Perhaps so,” replied Sophy, thoughtfully, “but one can hardly fancy it. All the pictures of the Virgin Mary that I used to see made her look dressed like a queen, and sitting on clouds, and one can’t imagine that either she or the Holy Child could ever really want a meal.”

“Ah! but one can’t trust *pictures*,” said Benoni; “it is very likely, as I once heard dear Persis say, that the Lord Jesus had a hard, struggling kind of life when he was a boy. And then he lived in a very wicked

place; we know that from the Bible. I dare
say that he often heard bad words and saw
things that would grieve him; and I dare say
that bad boys would tempt him, and jeer at
him, and torment him, because he never
would join them in doing anything wrong.
You can't think what a comfort it is to me to
think that the Lord had such common troubles
as these."

"*In all points tempted like as we are,*" repeated Sophy, the apostle's words recurring
to her mind.

"I do love," continued Benoni, "to remember that it was when he was a boy, not many
years older than I am, that the Lord said,
*Wist ye not that I must be about my Father's
business?* It showed that *doing* God's will
was in his mind then, that he was preparing
when he was a child for the great, great
work, — the business of saving the world.
And perhaps the Lord had something to
suffer, too, when he was a boy, preparing him
for the terrible trials that came upon him at
last; perhaps he had little crosses — like
ours — before he had to take up the great
one, and many a thorn to pain him, even in
his quiet home, long before the cruel soldiers

put the platted crown round his head. Now, being hungry and having very little to eat may have just been one of these thorns."

"But I dare say that the Lord could have covered the table with abundance even when he was a boy, if he had chosen to do so," said Sophy.

"But I don't suppose that he ever did choose to do that," replied Benoni, in a very thoughtful tone, for he was a child who reflected much. "The Lord wouldn't make bread for himself when he was a man; it is not at all likely that he would do so when he was a boy. No, I dare say that the Holy One tried to help Joseph, and to cheer his mother, and told them that he was sure that their heavenly Father would never forget them. I dare say that the Lord looked *then* at the sparrows and the lilies, and thought how God clothed and fed them, and then up to the blue, blue sky, where his heavenly Father dwells, and never doubted that Father's love, however hungry and poor he himself might be."

Benoni Isaacs expressed himself like a child, but Sophy felt that the love and joy and peace that breathed in his simple words were not of earth, but from above. The little one beside her was, like Samuel, early called to listen to the word of God, and to answer in trustful obedience, *Speak Lord, for thy servant heareth.* Sophy envied Benoni his power of looking upwards by faith, and seeing God's love in all things, more than she envied him the sight of his bodily eyes. The girl and her adopted brother might be compared to travellers on a wide ocean. With Benoni there were heavings and tossings, a gale of trouble lifting the waves on high; but love to God was like bright sunshine on that stormy sea, turning the foam into crests of pearls, the billows to waves of gold. But Sophy was like one who journeys towards a frozen north, at a time when the sun for long days is absent. All around her was becoming dreary and chill; the ice of mistrust was gradually gathering and thickening around her, till it seemed as if it would hold her fast as in a prison, so that she should make no more progress towards heaven;—never get forward, never get through to open water and a brighter sea! There is something more terrible in this gradual freezing round the soul than in the sudden shock of temptation. It seems more impossible to " sheer off " from a danger like this. If we can thus find *mistrust* beginning to spread around us its deadly chill, if the slightest doubt of God's love arise like a film on the water, let us instantly turn our thoughts towards the Sun of Righteousness though his rays may be hidden from our eyes; let us not be content to rest for an hour where shoals of unbelief are forming around; let the very north wind of trouble only drive us more rapidly towards the clear south, till we feel at last the warmth of that Sun which has healing and life in each beam.

XXV.

Honorable Scars.

" HERE's father ! " suddenly exclaimed Benoni, as he heard a familiar step on the stair, and rose to meet his parent.

" Oh, may he bring us good news ! " sighed Sophy. Instinctively she turned her head in the direction of the door, longing to be able to read in the face of her adopted parent whether he had met with success in his quest for employment or assistance. All was darkness with Sophy; but Benoni saw in a moment, from the heavy cloud on his father's brow, the compressed lips, the haggard cheek, that he had met with severe disappointment. Benjamin Isaacs almost threw to Benoni the single loaf which he brought, as with suppressed bitterness he said, "Take it — I got it by pledging the last of my tools."

"God has forsaken us!" muttered Sophy, putting up her hands to each side of her head. There had been a shooting pain through it at that moment, but a sharper pang still had pierced through the poor girl's heart.

The one chair in the kitchen had been left for Benjamin Isaacs, but he did not take it; he was too restless to sit down. Under a manner usually quiet, he was a man of passions naturally fierce. These had been kept under control, first by a habit of reserve, then by the principles which he had adopted with the Christian religion, but now and then they broke through restraint, and a short but vivid glimpse was given of an impetuous, fiery spirit.

"Man at least has forsaken us!" he ex-

" Then go to the Christians," he said, mockingly, waving me out of the shop.

Sheer off.

p. 244.

claimed, with but half-suppressed passion. "I went first to Elkanah da Costa, him under whom I worked as a journeyman for years. There he was in his shop, surrounded by the silver and the gold and the gems that are dear to him as his soul. I told him of my difficulties; how anxious I am to find work, even if my wages be much reduced. He knows *how* I work, — many of the glittering jewels in his cases had been set by these hands. 'I don't see you, Benjamin Isaacs, in the synagogue now,' he drawled forth; he who cares less for religion, be it in Christian or Hebrew, than for the lightest grain of gold dust that falls from the graver! 'No,' I replied; 'for these three years and more I have attended a Christian church.' 'Then go to the Christians,' he said, mockingly, waving me out of the shop. 'You will at least give me a certificate of character,' I began. He cut me short with, 'Go to the Christians for *that*,' with a sneer on his face which made the blood mount to mine; and I turned my back on that place with its glittering wealth — forever!

"I had not walked many paces from the shop," continued Benjamin Isaacs, "when whom should I come upon suddenly, on turning a corner of the street, but my near blood relation, my cousin Reuben. He and I had played when children together, shared the same meals, read out of the same book, slept in the same room at night. I had written to Reuben after my conversion, but I had received no reply. I did not doubt that he would be angry at my having left our common faith ; but he is under obligation to me, — deep obligation, — and I scarcely thought that even religious differences would entirely break the threefold tie of gratitude, friendship, and blood."

Benjamin Isaacs paused, knit his dark brows, and pressed his lips tightly together. Benoni thought of that which is written, *Brother shall rise up against brother*, and silently thanked God that he and his father, at least, had at the same time given themselves to the Lord. Isaacs continued his narration ; it seemed a relief to him thus to pour out the bitterness of his spirit in words, —

" 'Reuben,' said I, and held out my hand ; he drew back, and looked as if he would as lief have grasped a viper. 'Turncoat, dog of a Christian!' he hissed forth, and passed me with a gesture, which, had I *not* been a

Christian, would have made me strike him to the pavement, and stamp upon him as he lay there!" The dark eyes of Isaacs seemed to flash fire as he said this, and intuitively he clenched his thin hand.

"O father, dear, then you'll have your scars to show!" cried Benoni. The soft, sweet voice of the boy sounded to Sophy like music after a storm.

"Scars! what do you mean?" asked Isaacs.

"Ned Franks said that what we have to suffer for Christ, because we are his faithful soldiers, will be to us at last like the scars left by wounds got in battle."

There was something soothing in the idea to one who was at the moment smarting from persecution borne for righteousness' sake. The furrows on Isaacs' brow smoothed down; he seated himself wearily on the chair, and drew his little boy towards him.

"You seem to have a good memory, Benoni, for everything done or said by your good friend the sailor, though you were so young when we left the village of Colne."

"We had such happy days there," said Benoni; "the happiest days in all my life, when you and I lodged in the pretty cottage with old Mr. Meade and dear Persis, and every evening Ned Franks came to court her for his wife. He used to take me on his knee, and tell me stories, and I think of them now so often, — most of all at night when I can't get to sleep; it seems as if they brought those dear old times back again." Benoni, in that gloomy London kitchen, could not repress a little sigh. As memory may have recalled to Adam the sights and sounds of Eden, so she pictured to Benoni the cottage mantled with creepers, buried in its green wooded dell, with the gurgle of the stream and the clack of the mill and the happy voice of Persis singing hymns at her grandfather's door.

"And what was it that Franks said about wounds and scars?" asked Isaacs.

"You know that Ned Franks had served the queen, and had been in more than one battle; yet he told me that he had never so much as received a scratch in fight, and that he half envied the fellows that carried away some marks that they'd been in the struggle; for that though wounds may be sore at the time, an old soldier or sailor likes afterwards to look at his scars. Franks said, that if the bright angels in heaven, who have nothing but peace, happiness, and love, could envy us poor mortals anything, it must be the opportunity of giving up something and suffering something for the sake of the Lord Jesus, who suffered so much for us. The angels may have the harps of gold and the crowns of life, but they can't have the victor's *scars*, for no one has ever hated or persecuted them for righteousness' sake. Sometimes," continued the boy, nestling closer to his father, and speaking on, because he felt that his simple words were giving comfort, — " sometimes I like to think of all the Lord's faithful soldiers marching in glory before him, when all their trials and battles are over, and when everything which they have borne for him will be remembered. There will be Joseph, — he got his scar when he was thrown into prison; Daniel, his in the den of lions; the three brave Jews, in the burning, fiery furnace. And then there will be the scars of those who have been reviled and spoken against and laughed at because they would serve the Lord; scars of those who have lost money for Christ, who have given up Sunday gains, or wouldn't take bribes, or get gold in any bad way, and so were sometimes hungry

and poor while they lived upon earth.   And
sometimes it has seemed to me," continued
Benoni, "that even if I *could* get so easily
through life as never to have a hard word or
want a comfort because I served the Saviour,
I would *rather* have some little scars to show,
— not because they would make me deserve
anything as a reward from my King, but because they would be like *marks* to prove how
dearly I had loved him."

"Ay, ay," said Isaacs, calmly and even
cheerfully, "*Blessed are they which are persecuted for righteousness' sake.*   It is the Master himself who bade his wounded servants
rejoice and leap for joy.   If we have never
received so much as a scratch in the long
struggle against the world, the flesh, and the
devil, it looks as if our fighting had been but
a sham, — that we had kept out of the fire, and
thought a great deal more of our own comfort
than of the honor of our Leader.   He bore
shame and loss for us ; we should welcome
shame and loss for him."   The thought was
taking from Isaacs all the venom that had
been rankling in his wounded spirit.

"Such sorrows are blessings and honors,"

cried Benoni, and his pale face brightened as he said it.

"But what are sorrows," thought poor Sophy, "that come upon us, not because we have followed the Lord, but because we have wandered from him?" She had listened to the preceding conversation in silence, bitterly conscious' that the wounds which festered in her heart were not those received in Christian warfare, but rather, in part at least, the consequences of her early folly and neglect of religion. Sophy knew too well how entirely her mind had been set on the world. A gay ribbon or dress, a gaudy bead necklace, a Sunday "lark," or a dance, had been more to her silly, sinful heart than all the truths contained in the Bible. She had not given up one folly for the sake of her Lord; she had not through sense of duty ever renounced the smallest gain; her dangerous pleasures had been torn from her,—not yielded up of her own free will; she had clutched them as long as she could; she had been made poor, desolate, and blind; but this had been because her waywardness had rendered chastisements needful, not because her faithfulness to God had led her into persecution or trouble. And yet Sophy was far more disposed to repine than were Isaacs and his son; she was more tempted to distrust God's love, though her very afflictions were a token of it. Sophy had been a wandering sheep, straying upon the mountains of sin and folly, now near to the brink of the precipice, now close to the den of the lion who lurketh in wait for souls to destroy them. She would not then hear the voice of the Shepherd: she chose her own dangerous path. When her friend, Norah Peele, under the influence of her uncle, had begun to try in earnest to lead a new life, Sophy had done all in her power to hinder and keep her back; had first laughed at her good resolutions, and then quarrelled with Norah because she could not be persuaded to break them. It was in mercy indeed that sorrow and sickness had been sent to Sophy, like the rough sheep-dog after the straying lamb to frighten or drag it back to the fold; Sophy, if left to herself, must have been lost forever. It is not always that trials are blessings, but such they had been to her. Sophy had been suddenly checked in her mad career, shut out by blindness from many temptations which she had never been able to resist, — love of dress, of flattery, of folly, — temptations which were drawing her farther and farther away from her God. Sophy in her misery had learned to pray, but she had not yet learned to praise; as a penitent she was sincere, but as a believer she was weak. She reverenced the Lord as her king, had hope in him as her Saviour; but she did not cling to him with rejoicing trust as the Friend, the loving Friend who bids us cast all our care upon him, because he careth for us.

"Shall we never go back to Colme, father?" asked Benoni, after a long interval of silence, during which the boy's thoughts had been wandering back to what he considered the pleasantest spot upon earth.

"There would be no opening in a village like Colme, for a jeweller like me," replied Benjamin Isaacs. "I finished the business that took me there, — that of arranging and getting into order the curiosities and gems at the Hall. My patron, Sir Lacy Barton, is dead, and his heir knows nothing about me. I would never go to Colme to be a burden upon the kindness of Ned Franks and his wife, — better enter a poor-house, or starve!" There was an independence of character in the Jew which he carried almost to a fault; Benoni knew that his father would suffer the extremity of want rather than beg or borrow from a friend.

"It is long, very long, since we have heard either from the Frankses, or from my dear friend Norah," said Sophy.

"They know not where a letter would find us, my daughter; I have twice changed our lodgings since last I wrote, which I did when returning money most kindly offered. Franks has his own family to care for; I accept nothing but from those who are my relations by blood."

"Or by adoption," added Benoni, glancing kindly at Sophy, and then at her basket of knitted goods.

"You and Sophy are alike my children," said Isaacs; "our purse shall always be one; our good or bad fortune we share together. So," he added more cheerfully, "take you loaf, my boy, and divide it between your sister, yourself, and me. 'Better the dinner of herbs where love is, than the stalled ox and hatred therewith.' We'll thank God for the bread which he gives to-day, and trust him to send more on the morrow."

XXVI.

A Scrap of News.

HEAVY and joyless, Sophy on the following morning arose from her bed, which was little better than a heap of rags, in a kind of cupboard off the kitchen. Heavy and joyless she groped her way into the room where Isaacs and his son were waiting for her coming to offer their daily morning sacrifice of prayer and of praise. Sophy joined them in the former, but when she attempted to sing

"Praise God, from whom all blessings flow,"

her voice faltered, and she broke down; tears came instead of music.

The remains of the loaf were shared for breakfast, and taken with some almost colorless tea. Then Isaacs and Benoni quitted the kitchen, the one to seek again for work, the other, — with the basket on his arm, — to try to sell Sophy's knitting. When they had left her, the poor girl seated herself on the box. She had no materials for work, even if she had had the spirit to labor. She gave herself up to sad thought, with her elbow on her knee, and her brow on her hand. "I wonder where Norah is now, and whether she ever thinks of me! When she and I were merry young girls together, singing, and laughing, and building all kinds of castles in the air, how we used to promise each other that our friendship should last as long as our lives! She will have new friends now,—better friends than I ever was, who will not fill her head with follies and her spirit with pride. If she ever thinks of me, it will be with— But I do not believe that she ever *does* think of me," continued Sophy, in bitterness of soul; "she is happy, earning her living honestly and cheerfully; she is not dependent, despised, despairing,—a poor, blind wretch, like me!"

Surely the ice of mistrust was growing very thick around Sophy, making her doubt, not only the care of her heavenly Father, but the love of her earthly friend!

And on that very day, Norah Peele was not only thinking of Sophy, but thinking of scarcely anything else. One of those strange little incidents which sometimes occur, small in themselves, but hinges on which great events may turn, had brought poor Sophy on that morning forcibly before the mind of her friend.

Norah was on her knees, lighting the kitchen fire at the vicarage, with a bit of the advertisement-sheet of the *Times*, which was used as waste paper in her master's house, when her eye chanced to fall on the following notice :—

"NEXT OF KIN. *If the nearest relative of the late Tabitha Turtle apply to Messrs. Grant, Bold, & Co., —— Lincoln's Inn, he will hear of something to his advantage.*"

"Tabitha Turtle! surely I know that name!" exclaimed Norah, pausing with the lighted match in her hand. "Yes, to be sure, that is the name of poor Sophy's aunt, who lived somewhere near Portman Square. I remember how we two silly young things used to laugh and joke at the name, and wonder whether she who had it was like a turtle-dove or a tortoise! *Something to his advantage — nearest of kin!* Why, what if Sophy herself should be nearest of kin, — if there should be money waiting for her, — she who is living now upon the charity of the Jew who has adopted her, and who, I fear, has but little for himself! Oh, that would be delightful, delightful!" and Norah threw down the match, and tore off the little scrap from the paper, as eagerly as if it had contained the greatest piece of good news for herself. She could hardly settle to her work, so impatient was she to go and ask her mistress's leave to run over to the school-house, to consult her uncle Ned Franks as to what could be done for Sophy. However, it was clear that the harder Norah worked, the sooner her business would be over. She therefore plied her fingers so diligently, that, before eleven o'clock had struck, she received leave to go, "just for a quarter of an hour," to speak to her uncle on something of great importance.

There was no time for Norah to change her working-dress, scarcely time to wash her hands. On ordinary days there would have been no use in going to Ned Franks before school-hours were over; but this was hay-making time, and a week's holiday had been given to his pupils. Carrying her precious little scrap of paper in her hand, Norah hurried along the path to the school-house, where she found Ned Franks, with Persis carrying

her baby, just starting to pay a visit to
Nancy Sands, who had, on the previous day,
returned from the hospital to her home.

"Why, here comes Norah!" exclaimed Ned
Franks, gayly, "scudding along like a yacht
in a race!" and as he spoke, his niece came
up breathless alike in eagerness and the pace
at which she had been going, for her walk
had quickened into a run.

"I've not more than five minutes," she
began, and stopped to pant, her eyes sparkling and her cheeks glowing with excitement.

"Come in, then, and take breath, and tell
us what news you have to bring us. What's
this?" as Norah thrust the scrap of soiled
paper into his hand,—"what have we to do
with Tabitha Turtle? She was certainly none
of our kith or kin."

As they returned into the school-house,
Norah hastily informed her uncle of her
reasons for thinking that the notice might be
of importance to her poor blind friend.
Franks and Persis listened wth interest.

"Certainly Sophy should know of this,"
said Ned Franks; "but she's blind, and
Isaacs is scarcely likely to see the *Times*, and
if he did, it's a thousand chances to one that

he should connect his adopted daughter with the name of an aunt whom she appears never to have seen, and may never even have mentioned."

"We must write to Sophy at once!" cried Norah.

"But how can we write," asked Persis, "when we do not know her address? Ned has not heard from Isaacs for months, and then our friend mentioned that he was about to leave his lodgings, without saying where the next one would be."

"Ned Franks passed his hand through his thick curly hair, as if, by so doing, he could draw out some bright idea. "I've half a mind," he said, "as it's holiday time, to be off to London myself, see the lawyers, and find out if it's likely that there's really any money left to Sophy, and then hunt her out, if I can; though looking for any one in London is like searching for a needle in a hay-stack."

"Oh, if you will only go!" exclaimed Norah, eagerly, "I'll pay the expense so gladly, as soon as I get my quarter's wages!"

"No, no, lass," said the school-master, laughing; "I've enough shot in my locker to

manage without your little store. Only "—
Ned glanced at his wife ; he knew that Persis
had been looking forward with the pleasure
of a child to his holiday-time ; for him to go
to London would spoil a pleasant plan which
the Frankses had talked over for months.
They were to have gone on that very after-
ternoon on a short pleasure-trip to the sea-
side ; for Franks longed, as he owned, " to
smell salt water again," which he had not
done since he had left the profession of a
sailor.

"What do you say, sweetheart?" asked
Franks of his wife. "I leave the decision
to you."

Persis stooped down and kissed her baby,
probably to get a moment for thought, and
then raising her head, said, with a smile
which cost her some effort, —

"I think that you'd better be off to London."

Franks glanced at the clock, Nancy Sands's
cuckoo-clock, which hung in his little parlor.
"I might be off by the 12-30 train if I hoisted
all sail," he cried. "I'll get my kit ready in
no time. If I'm early in town I may see the
lawyers to-day. I must stay over Sunday in

London, but if I've a prosperous cruise, I hope to be back upon Monday."

Persis was too busy helping her husband, and putting up his dinner of cold meat, to have time to think of her own disappointment, till Ned Franks, quick and prompt in everything, had started off for the station at almost a running pace, with his little bundle fastened to a stick hanging over his shoulder. Norah had at once returned to the vicarage, full of hope for her friend, having perfect confidence that whatever business her uncle undertook he would do, and do well. Persis gave a little sigh as her husband disappeared in the distance, and with him all her prospect of a holiday trip; yet she was glad that she had made the sacrifice of her own inclination; and, taking up her baby from the cradle in which she had placed him, at a slow pace she proceeded along the dusty road towards the cottage of her neighbor.

XXVII.

Nancy's Return.

WITH very mingled feelings had Nancy Sands returned to her home. It was in the twilight that she entered her native village. "I do not care," she said, "to have the gossips staring at me, or stopping me to talk."

John Sands would have hired a conveyance for his wife, as the walk from the town was a long one for an invalid just discharged from an hospital; but his wife, in her short, determined way, declined his proposal to get one.

"I've two feet if I've only one arm," she said, almost sharply. "If I've walked that road once, I've walked it a hundred times; the fresh air will do me good."

Mrs. Sands set out briskly at her husband's side; but before they had gone a mile she felt that she was no longer what she had once been,—that the sufferings and confinement which she had undergone had greatly told on her strength. Her pace very sensibly slackened.

"My dear, would you take my arm?" suggested the clerk, timidly, for he was still afraid of a rebuff from his hot-tempered wife.

But this time there was no rebuff; Nancy thankfully took the proffered arm, and leaned on it as she had never done since the first week after her marriage. Whether it were that these old days were brought back to her mind, or whether the very necessity for *leaning* made her realize the position of a wife in regard to her husband, who should be, according to Scripture, her "head" and her "lord," we need not decide; but never had Nancy Sands felt her wilful, wayward heart so drawn towards her spouse as on that homeward walk in the twilight. As for John Sands, his spirit was full of tenderness towards the wife of his youth.

Very few words were spoken by either of the two as they slowly proceeded on their way. Nancy was too weary for much conversation, and so perhaps was her husband; but as they passed the carpenter's shop, she observed, —

" So poor Stone is ill and not likely to live? He and I were the two strongest people in the parish."

Very much tired was Nancy when she re-entered her home. She wearily sank on a chair; exhausted nature craved the support of a stimulant. An intense desire arose for a glass of spirits or a tumbler of ale; but she had taken the pledge, and neither she nor her husband liked to mention what was in the minds of both.

John Sands went to the cupboard and brought out of it the supper which he had provided for his wife, and himself arranged it on the table. There were little luxuries, in which the poor clerk had never thought of indulging during her absence. Pickled salmon,—Nancy had a weakness for pickled salmon,—Bath chop, fresh butter, and white rolls. Nancy noticed the consideration shown for her tastes, and drew her chair to the table, well disposed to do justice to the dainties before her. Sands filled her plate, and then shyly — for he was afraid of hurting his wife by showing that he remembered that she had no longer a right hand — he cut up the viands into small pieces, and quietly pushed the plate to its place, avoiding looking at Nancy as he did so. "It must pain her, poor dear, to be so helpless, though I'm sure it's a pleasure to

me to help her," thought the indulgent husband.

Nancy had scarcely begun her meal when
she stopped short, and fixed her eyes upon a
tumbler of water at the right hand of the
clerk, where she never before had missed at
supper the pint of beer. "Where's your beer,
John?" she asked, abruptly.

"Well, my dear, I thought — I did not
want" — stammered forth the clerk, nervously.

"You do want it; it does you good; *you*
have not taken the pledge."

"No, but" — there was a look of perplexity
on John Sands's sallow face; he did not know
how to finish his sentence.

"The truth is, you can't trust me even to
see it," observed Nancy, gloomily.

"I thought that I should not like to be
different from you, my dear," said Sands, in
a deprecatory tone. He would have made
any other sacrifice of his own comfort, as he
made this, for the sake of rescuing his wife
from her fearful vice.

"Different, — you can't help being different," murmured Nancy, "you who never in
all your born days took one drop too much.

It's hard for you to be kept from your beer. But perhaps you're right, John," she added, looking her husband full in the face; "at least just at the first. I suspect that if I saw any strong drink it would not end with the *seeing;* I'd give the world at this moment for a draught of good double stout."

Nancy rose on the following morning much the better for a calm night's rest, and the breakfast was decidedly more cheerful than the supper had been. The clerk had afterwards to attend a christening, but his wife was not long left alone, for a succession of visitors came to see her, some from curiosity, some from kindness.

One of the first to appear was Stone's wife, the former motive being that which moved her, though she deceived herself into thinking that she was performing a charitable deed by going to see "that wretched creature Nancy, who must be ashamed to show her face."

"I hope that this will be a warning to you, Mrs. Sands, a solemn warning," said Mrs. Stone, after the first greetings and inquiries had been exchanged. "You've lost an arm, but you might have lost your life; if you'd been taken *then*"—Bell paused, for there was something in Nancy's face which told her that the temper of the old tigress might be lurking in her still, and that it might be dangerous to rouse it. It was hardly to be expected that Mrs. Sands would endure that any officious bungler should, as it were, tear off the bandage and probe the yet unhealed wound in her spirit. Had John Sands plied his wife with reproaches and admonitions after the fashion of Bell Stone, it is probable that Nancy would have returned to his dwelling, not as a penitent, but as a savage-hardened offender.

The entrance of Mrs. Fuddles put a stop to what might have ended in what she would have called a "flare up." Mrs. Stone suddenly recollected that she could not stop long away from her poor dear patient, and hurried away, shrugging her shoulders and saying to herself, as she left the place, that it was clear, from the company kept by Nancy, that in spite of all that had happened, she'd be as bad as ever again.

Mrs. Fuddles's manner was an utter contrast to that of the visitor just before her. She was excited and flurried in her greeting;

she declared that she was delighted to see her dear old friend again, and looking well, wonderfully well, all things considered; only she'd need to take plenty of good nourishing stuff to get up her strength again, after such a terrible illness. "A little drop of something, taken hot, just the first thing in the morning, my dear; I've known it work wonders," said the publican's wife, who doubtless spoke from personal experience.

"You forget I've taken the pledge," replied Nancy, who needed no explanation as to the nature of the "drop" recommended.

"Now, really, I heard something about it, but I could not believe it. A sensible woman like you! But people do get round sick folks, and wheedle, and coax, and frighten them so!"

"No one ever wheedled, or coaxed, or frightened *me*," replied Nancy, sternly; "what I did, I did of my own free will, and I'll hold to it too."

"To be sure, quite right; I'd be the last to try to persuade you against your wishes," cried Mrs. Fuddles, instantly changing her ground; "you don't know how I've been cut up about you,—and to think of its having happened after your leaving my house, though I said, and always will say, *that* had nothing to do with a slip of the foot; any one might have a slip of the foot; the parson himself might have tumbled into the mill-stream! But you won't keep away from the old house, Nancy, my dear," continued the publican's wife in a fawning tone, edging her chair nearer to that on which Mrs. Sands was seated; "you and I won't give up our pleasant chats over a—a cup of tea, if you like it; I won't press you to anything to put your husband out, or to offend the young parson; I'll offer you nothing stronger than tea, unless, of course, it was good for your health?"

Mrs. Fuddles thought that she saw symptoms of yielding in her of whom she dared to call herself a *friend*. The woman, doing the work of the tempter of souls, knew well enough that there was something within poor Nancy which was making her only too willing to be persuaded against her better judgment, and that if she crossed the threshold of the "Chequers," that craving for stimulant, which had been like a disease, would become altogether irresistible. Mrs. Fuddles, eager to press her point, was annoyed by the interruption caused by another visitor.

"Why, if here ben't Mrs. Franks!" she exclaimed, rising from her chair with ill-concealed vexation; a feeling which was increased by the very cordial manner in which Nancy received the wife of her brave preserver.

It almost seemed as if the gentle, pure-minded mother, bearing her innocent babe on her bosom, had come as a guardian angel to the aid of a tempted soul. A purer atmosphere was breathed around Persis; the fragrance of the roses, which she had brought from her garden as a gift to Nancy did not contrast more strongly with the odor of brandy which clung to the publican's wife, than did the meek dignity of the Christian matron contrast with the fawning vulgarity of the mistress of the "Chequers."

"My game's up for this time," thought Mrs. Fuddles, as she soon after took her bustling leave. The cottage seemed a holier as well as a quieter place when rid of her presence.

"I am so glad to see you back here," said Persis, looking with kindly interest at Nancy, as one who had so narrowly escaped a terrible death.

"I know that you are, Persis Franks; you have always been a true friend to me," replied Mrs. Sands; and the ear of Ned's wife caught with pleasure the emphasis on the word *you*.

Then the baby was duly exhibited and admired; the heart of poor Nancy always warmed towards a baby. How he had grown, — how much he was improved, — how like he was to his father, especially when the little one laughed and crowed, and showed the dimple on his cheek! Persis was always a patient, smiling listener to the praises of either her husband or her child.

The conversation, however, took before long an abrupt turn. Nancy had something on her mind which, as was usual with her, soon found its way to her tongue.

"Do you think I shall be *able* to keep the pledge?" she asked suddenly, though Persis had made no allusion to the subject. Mrs. Franks, however, easily connected the abrupt question with the visit of Mrs. Fuddles. Nancy repeated it rather impatiently, as Persis hesitated before giving a reply.

"I think that depends upon two things," she answered, looking down as she spoke, perhaps to avoid meeting the gaze of the keen black eyes fixed upon her.

"What are these two things, Persis Franks? You need not mind speaking out boldly; you are not one to force your advice where it's not asked, nor to set yourself up, like Bell Stone, for being a deal better than your neighbors. I want to keep the pledge if I can, if only for the sake of poor John; but how am I to do it?"

"The first thing, at least so it seems to me," replied Persis, "is to keep out of all way of temptation."

"You don't mean to say I'm to cut an old friend," said Nancy, who was longing to renew her dangerous visits to Mrs. Fuddles.

"If I were you I would never venture near the 'Chequers;' at least, not without my husband," replied Persis.

Nancy flushed, and muttered something that sounded like "with a keeper;" but her good sense approved of that which had offended her pride; and, after a short struggle with herself, she said, "Yes, yes, I'll never more enter the 'Chequers' without John, and

that's next thing to saying that I'll never go
there again. What's the second thing that
you meant, Persis Franks?"

Persis lifted up her heart for a moment in
supplication for wisdom before she ventured
to reply. "I think that your next, — your
best safeguard, Mrs. Sands, must be earnest,
daily prayer to Him who alone can keep you,
— or any of us, from falling. While we
shun temptation, we must also *watch and
pray*."

Nancy made no reply, and Persis, after a
pause, went on. "I feel myself, Mrs. Sands,
that I am no more able to stand firm without
the help of God's Holy Spirit, than my babe
is able to support himself without a parent's
embracing arms. I come to God, just as a little child, for the daily grace which I need. I
have no strength to hold him fast, but he will
hold *me* fast, if — with all my weakness and
sinfulness — I give myself up entirely to him."

Tears rose to Persis's eyes as she spoke, and
tears were also glistening in those of Nancy.
"Shun temptation, — watch and pray," she
repeated, as if to impress the words on her
memory; then, looking fixedly at Mrs.
Franks, and speaking in the measured tone

of one who has made up her mind, Nancy said, "I will never forget your advice. I believe that I shall one day bless you for it in heaven."

And from that time forth Nancy Sands was never seen at the "Chequers," and not a morning or evening passed without the voice of simple, earnest prayer arising from what had been once the home of the drunkard.

XXVIII.

A Search.

WITH all the speed which he had made, Ned Franks was scarcely in time to catch the train for London. The journey was without incident, and the village school-master ere long found himself in the centre of the noise, glare, heat, and bustle of the great city in the dog-days.

"Difficult navigation this," said the former sailor to himself, as he made his way across roads crowded almost to blockade. "I suppose it's because I'm not used to the thing;

but I can't understand how children or old folks can manage this steering behind and before and between omnibuses, carts, cabs, and vans, dodging right under horses' noses, and all in the midst of such confusion and noise! I'd not bide in such a rackety place as this to be made Lord Mayor of London!"

Ned's first care was to visit the office of Messrs. Grant, Bold, & Co. He there obtained more precise information regarding the object of the advertisement in the *Times*. Mrs. Tabitha Turtle having died intestate, her little savings, amounting to something above two hundred pounds, would of course revert to her next of kin. She had had no brother, and but one sister, who, as the lawyer informed Ned Franks, had been married more than twenty years before to a man of the name of Peter Claymore; but whether Mrs. Claymore were living, or whether she had had any children, had not as yet been ascertained. No answer had been made from any quarter to repeated advertisements in the *Times*.

"I can pilot you a little lower down, sir," said Ned Franks to his informant. "Mrs. Claymore died long ago, her husband about a year back, — in a penal settlement; he had changed his name more than once, I believe. They have left but one daughter, whose name is Sophy. She is now blind, and, having been adopted by Benjamin Isaacs, a Christian Jew, is probably called by his name, which may make it harder to find her. But it is worth any trouble to do the poor orphan right, for she has not a farthing in the world, and I fear that the generous Jew is scarcely able to support her and his son."

"Can you give me any clue to her present place of abode?" asked Mr. Grant, with a languid air of indifference.

"I'll give you what was Isaacs' address when he last wrote to me, sir," replied Franks; "but that was some months back, and he was about to change his lodging. I've not had a line from him since, but I'll be off to Islington at once, and try if I can't hunt him out. Poor Sophy shall not miss such a chance for want of a friend who will take a little trouble to find her."

Ned Franks took more than a little trouble; not feeling rich enough to afford hiring a cab, he, a perfect stranger to London, was puzzled beyond measure how to find his way through its endless labyrinth of streets. "I'm like a blind man steering amongst shoals," muttered the one-armed sailor. Twenty times had he to ask his way, "veering about and tacking to half the points in the compass," as he afterwards laughingly told his wife, and it was not till after the lapse of several hours that Ned found himself, much heated, tired, and with a racking headache, at the door of Isaacs' old lodging at last.

Here little comfort was to be obtained. The shrewish-looking landlady who had unwittingly quitted her supper to answer the sailor's impatient and repeated summons, seemed half-inclined to shut the door in his face, and told him that she knowed nothing, not she, of Benjamin Isaacs. A working jeweller with a boy and a blind girl had lived there once, she owned, when more closely questioned by Ned; but they had gone long since, she could not tell whither; if they were alive or if they were dead, she didn't know and she didn't care! Slamming the door, the woman went back to her supper, grumbling at being "bothered by impudent fellows like that coming to hunt up old lodgers."

"Where am I to turn up now?" thought

poor Franks, almost knocked up, and a little discouraged by the result of his search. The street lamps were lighted, the public houses flaring, night was coming on; but it seemed as if to London and its suburbs night would bring no interval of quiet or repose. The village school-master longed for food, sleep, and rest.

"But I won't give up my chase yet," Ned said to himself. " Knowing Sophy and Isaacs by sight, I'm much more likely to find them out than a stranger would be; besides, I put more heart into the business than that grand, sleepy-looking gentleman in black, who seemed not to care the turning of a straw whether the money found its way into Sophy's pocket or into the sea."

A thought occurred to Ned Franks as he stood in perplexity leaning against a lamp-post. "I'll step into one of the post-offices, and ask for a sight of one of the big red books that hold all kinds of addresses. Though Isaacs' will not be put down there, I may light upon some relation of his; and if I can but get hold of one end of the line, I may manage to follow out the clue."

After a little more of inquiring his way

along those noisy streets, where no one seemed at leisure to answer a question, Franks found a post-office, which he entered. The shopman was putting up the shutters, and at first desired the sailor to wait till Monday; but, perhaps struck by the worn, weary looks of the inquirer, he good-naturedly let him have a sight of the directory, which he took down from a shelf, bidding the sailor, however, make haste.

Franks hurriedly turned over the leaves by gas-light, and came to the name of "Isaacs." It was perplexing to him to see how many persons in London bore it; how should he choose between them? Ned ran his finger down the closely printed column till he came to the name of "Reuben," and uttered an exclamation of satisfaction as his eye fell upon the word.

"Ah! that's a Jew's name, anyhow; and now I remember Isaacs telling me that he had in London a cousin called Reuben, who was to him as a brother. I'm on the right tack at last! but 'Lisson Grove;' where's Lisson Grove?" asked the weary stranger of the good-natured shopman. "I hope that it's hard by, though I have not seen anything hereabouts like a grove."

The Londoner smiled at the observation. "You must not look for trees there," he said, " but a lot of low, dirty, narrow streets ; and, as for the distance from here, I should say at a guess, four miles."

"Four miles !" repeated poor Ned to himself, as, after thanking his informant, he quitted the shop. "Tired as I am, I'd rather walk forty miles on a country road than four miles through this labyrinth of London. I could scarcely steer my course while I'd daylight; at night I'd not have a chance. I must hail a cab, and to pay for it I'll do without supper to-night, and maybe without dinner to-morrow, for I must keep enough of the ready rhino to pay for my journey back."

A cab was hailed, and in due course of time Ned Franks, at the cost of a half crown, found himself standing in front of a pawnbroker's shop, where the blaze of gas-light fell on a crowd of the poor, thronging around the door, some to pledge and some to redeem articles of clothing, blankets, or plate.

"I'm glad he's not shut up yet, though the hour's so late," thought Franks, as, with a little difficulty, he made his way through the throng. The moment that he caught sight of the pawnbroker, the strong likeness borne to his cousin by Reuben made Franks feel certain that he had "hit upon the right Isaacs." He had to wait, however, which he did with no small impatience, till the pawnbroker had leisure to attend to his business, and then Franks knew that he must put it into as few words as might be, as the night was now far advanced.

"Pray, sir, haven't you a cousin of the name of Benjamin Isaacs, who has adopted a blind girl as his daughter?" asked Ned, in a rapid tone.

"Ay, more fool he!" muttered Reuben.

"That mayn't prove the case in the long run, my friend," said the warm-hearted sailor. "No one's the worse in the end for helping widow or orphan. The girl's just come in for some money. Can you tell me where to find her, or your cousin?"

Little did Franks, himself the soul of candor and truth, suspect the perfidy and malice that prompted the pawnbroker's reply.

"If you're seeking them out to tell them of such a bit of good luck, you're a day too late for the fair. Benjamin, his boy, and the girl, the whole lot of them, sailed last week for Australia!"

"Are you certain of that?" inquired Ned, anxiously.

"As sure as I am that my name's Reuben Isaacs. I saw them to the docks myself;" and the man turned suddenly round to a customer, perhaps to hide the smile of gratified malice which rose to his lips.

"Then my work is done!" exclaimed Franks, leaving the place with a sense of bitter disappointment. "Nothing remains for me now but to find some berth for the night."

And it was close upon midnight before the weary man found one.

XXIX.

Pleasure or Principle?

NED FRANKS had wished to combine cheapness and comfort in his lodging, but this appearing to be an impossible arrangement, he gave up the second for the sake of the first, and passed in a dirty boarding-house one of the most uncomfortable nights that he had ever known. Accustomed as he had been when a sailor to "roughing it," Ned Franks could have slept soundly in an open boat or under a hedge; but the suffocating atmosphere of an almost air-tight room, shared with a dirty Portuguese, made him, weary as he was, unable to snatch more than a few minutes of broken, feverish slumber, to which the name of repose could not be given. Franks was glad when morning broke, and he was able to rise and go forth into the air from what he considered to be "as bad as any black-hole."

"I wish that I were back again amongst our own green fields, or that I'd never had the folly to come on such a wild cruise as this," muttered Franks to himself, he being in a somewhat irritable mood. "Persis and I might have been now,—but there is no use regretting what's done. I believe that the search, useless as it has turned out, was the right thing to be attempted. It's our part in life to try and do our duty; and then, if it seems that we've worked in vain, we must remember that all is in God's hands, and that he has always some wise, good, kind reason for sending us disappointment or trouble." If there was one sin more than another, from which Franks was resolved always to "sheer off" at once, it was *mistrust*, — that gathering shoal-ice. He had been working hard; exerting all his energies, and giving up his pleasures, not so much for the sake of a girl in whom he had no particular interest (for Sophy had never been a favorite of Franks), but from obedience to Him who commends to us the cause of the fatherless and poor. What is done unto the Lord can never be done altogether in vain. When he bids us work for him, he bids us do so in a cheerful, trustful spirit, looking to him for a blessing, thanking him for success when success is granted; and, if it seem to be denied, never daring to doubt for a moment that *he hath done all things well.*

"Now, if this were any day but Sunday," thought Franks, as he walked through the street where, even at an early hour, the cries of the water-cress seller and the hawker unpleasantly broke on the comparative stillness, "if this were any day but Sunday, I'd be off by the first train, and not spend another hour in this hot, close city. And why should I *not* go to-day, although it is Sunday? Would there be any harm? I should be in plenty of time for afternoon service at least, and should pass a much holier, as well as happier, Sabbath in Colme than in London. I should be with my Persis and my boy, and those who love and serve God, and not tossing about here like a stray bit of sea-weed on the waves. Why, in the midst of crowds here, I've not a single being to speak to; and I feel as lonely in a city as Crusoe did in his island! I think that I'd better go back at once to my home!"

Franks quickened his steps as he heard the shrill whistle from a railway station near, which reminded him that there are plenty of travellers from London, every Sunday, bound on errands of business or pleasure. The temptation to Franks was strong; so many excuses offered themselves to his mind for breaking the fourth commandment only *this once.* Health, convenience, economy, the pleasure of giving a joyful surprise to his wife, from whom he had never before been separated for a single day since their marriage, — all combined to draw Franks to the conclusion, that a journey on Sunday was excusable in his case, if not perfectly lawful.

As the struggle was going on in the mind of the one-armed school-master of Colme, a woman, with a basket filled with pottles of strawberries, stopped him with the question, "Buy any nice strawberries, sir, this morning?"

"I never buy or sell on the Lord's day, and I am sorry to see you doing either," replied Franks, gravely but kindly.

"Sir, I can't help it," said the woman, with a sigh. "If I don't sell, my children can't eat."

"Obey God's command, and trust his promise, my friend. His command is, *Remember the Sabbath day to keep it holy*. His promise is, *Trust in the Lord, and verily thou shalt be fed*. God, who has all things in his power, will return unto his servants a hundred-fold in the end, whatever they lose upon earth by faithfully doing his will."

Franks walked on; but the whole current of his thoughts had been changed by the little incident; he felt that in reproving another he had condemned himself.

"Shame on me," he muttered, "that I, who know so well a Christian's duty, should be so slack in performing it! I can see the mote in my brother's eye, indeed; let me pull the beam out of my own! There is no necessity for my travelling to Colme to-day; no one would be really the better for my doing so; nay, my pupils might be injured by seeing the inconsistency of one to whom they look for an example. I must take heed that I *offend not one of these little ones*, by making them think lightly of the sin of breaking the fourth commandment. As for my passing a holier Sunday in Colme than in London, the day or the place is holy to us, whenever the presence of the Saviour is with us. Nothing but sin can divide us from him. I will stay, and take my meals quietly or unquietly, as the case my be, at the boarding-house which I've entered; and if I lack comfort for the body, there's many a church in this great city in which I can get pure and wholesome food for the soul. There are the church-bells ringing for early service, — the sweetest sound I've heard in London! And there goes the railway whistle again! The two calls seem, on this Sunday morn, like God's invitation and the world's. How could I doubt which to accept?"

XXX.

Found at Last.

Saturday had been to Sophy one of the darkest days of her life. Isaacs and his son had been absent during the greater part of it, and the blind girl had been left to her loneliness and pain, the former only broken by a visit from an angry landlord demanding rent which Isaacs had been unable to pay. Isaacs, on his return, had found Sophy in tears, and he was little able to cheer her, for again had the convert been unsuccessful in his anxious attempt to get work. He seated himself wearily, folded his arms, and, drooping his head, sat silent as one who feels that life is full of trials. But who " can suffer and be still," — submissive and uncomplaining?

" If I had but a little capital to start with," he began, speaking rather to himself than to Sophy ; but he cut himself short by the remark, " If God had thought it good for me to have it, he would not have withheld it ; I am content that my portion should not be in this life. *Better the reproach of Christ, than all the riches of Egypt!*"

" Success, success ! see what I've brought !" cried the cheerful voice of Benoni at the door. Benjamin raised his head, — Sophy turned her sightless eyes in the direction of the welcome sound.

" I've sold all; emptied your basket, emptied and filled it again !" cried Benoni. " Here's bread, and delicious bacon, and a nice bit of butcher's meat too ! It's Saturday evening, so I got it for five-pence. Have I not made a good bargain?" The boy turned with an appealing smile to his father.

" How did you contrive to sell everything in the basket?" asked Isaacs.

" And how much did it all bring?" inquired Sophy.

" I'll tell you all about it. I had been wandering about for five or six hours, and had sold but three kettle-holders for a penny a-piece, when I thought I'd try a woman who was standing at the door of a shop where things just like yours are sold. I begged her to buy; she looked doubtful. I told her she might have everything that was left for a shilling, and so she cleared off all that was in the basket at once!"

Isaacs shook his head with a rather sad smile. "You are no great hand at making a bargain in the selling line, whatever you may be in the buying," said he.

"A shilling would not pay for the wool!" murmured Sophy, in a tone of bitter disappointment.

Little Benoni looked mortified and distressed. "You told me to sell the things for what they would bring," he said, sadly. "Yesterday they brought nothing at all. I dare say I've done very foolishly, but I wanted to bring home plenty of nice food for Sunday."

"And you have brought plenty; and we have to thank Sophy for feeding us all by the work of her hands," said Isaacs, kindly. "I wish that I had earned as much to-day as you and she have, my boy."

Benoni looked gratefully at his father, but the cloud did not pass from the brow of Sophy. What hopes she had built on that basket of work! How she had counted on the proceeds of its sale, not only to supply present need, but to buy materials for future labors! She had probably over-estimated the value of her little store as much as Benoni had done the contrary, and now all that it had been sold for would be consumed in two or three meals, and nothing be left with which she might start afresh! Sophy, hungry as she was, scarcely cared to touch the supper, purchased at what seemed to her at so very costly a price.

We know that severe cold is apt to benumb those who are exposed to it, to make them dislike making efforts, even when life may depend on their doing so, and that they are in danger of sinking into a sleep from which they waken no more. The ice of mistrust brings to the soul a peril much like this. A chill of despair often comes over sufferers who doubt the love of their God. They are not inclined to struggle against its benumbing effects, to wrestle in earnest, or to press onwards with resolute faith. Thus it was with Sophy Claymore. When, on the Sunday morning, Isaacs asked her if she were going with him to church, she shook her head, and said that she was not well enough to go. Her sickness was more of the soul than the body, —it came from the tempter's whisper, "Where is thy God? He heareth thee not."

"If Sophy can't go with us, Benoni," said Isaacs, "I'll do as I once promised, — take you to attend service in Westminster Abbey. Now bring me the Bible; we'll have our morning reading, my son."

Isaacs read about the story of the woman of Canaan, — the touching account of persevering pleading, of faith that would take no denial. When the Bible was closed, Benoni, as was his wont, began to talk over the passage to which he had just been listening.

"How happy that woman must have been! — so much happier than if the Lord had granted her prayer directly!"

"I don't see why," said Sophy.

"Do you not?" cried Benoni. "Why, if the Lord had made her child well at once, she would never have heard that delightful word, 'O woman, great is thy faith!' I always fancy that the Lord smiled upon her as he said that, but that he sighed when he said to Peter, 'O thou of little faith, wherefore didst thou doubt?' I suppose," continued the boy, that both the woman and St. Peter really loved and served their Master, but he spoke very differently to them. Sometimes I think —perhaps it is a childish thought—that when

God's people have no more troubles, and they are welcomed up to glory, and see that what looked wrong really was right, those who *trusted* most will be those to *rejoice* the most. To some, then, the Saviour may say, ' Great was thy faith ; ' and oh, the delight to hear him say *that!* But I'm afraid that to most he will rather say, ' Thou of little faith, why didst thou doubt ? ' "

These words from the lips of a child were as a soft warm breeze from the south, melting and stirring the ice round the heart. Sophy felt that her sullen mistrust was dishonoring her Lord, and that, had *she* been in the place of the woman of Canaan, the first discouragement would have driven her away from the Saviour. The blind girl made no reply, but a few minutes afterwards she said, " I'll go to church this morning ; there's really nothing to hinder me."

" Yes, yes, we will all go together ! " cried Benoni, cheerfully giving up at once, and without any apparent regret, the plan of going to Westminster Abbey, a place too distant for Sophy to walk to. It was agreed that the three should, as usual, attend service in their own parish church.

And Sophy, like many other sorrowful ones, found the Saviour in the temple of God. Her burden grew lighter as she listened to the numerous voices around her joining in singing the praise of the Lord. She thought of the multitudes clothed in white robes, come out of *great tribulation*, and felt that those who will share such bliss *then*, may learn *now* to *glory in tribulations also.*

Sophy and the Isaacs were among the last to quit Marylebone church. As the blind girl slowly walked down the steps under the portico, she was almost startled by the joyful exclamation, "Hurrah! I've found them at last!"

"Ned Franks!" cried Isaacs and Benoni in a breath. It would be difficult to decide who was most delighted by a meeting so unexpected, — Franks, or those whom he had so anxiously sought. Isaacs invited his friend to go home with him; then almost repented having done so, for he was ashamed of his miserable abode. Benoni was secretly glad that for once there was something better than a crust to offer to the guest.

Franks was so eager to tell his good news, that he could scarcely wait till they had reached a more quiet place than the Marylebone Road. His eagerness was greatly increased by the poverty betrayed by the appearance of his friends. "Help has not come before it was needed," he thought, as he looked at their thin, sunken features, and their shabby, though still decent, dress. "How thankful I am that I came on this cruise ! and doubly thankful that I did not start for Colme this morning, and so lose the prize which was right ahead of me ! "

Franks kept his great secret tolerably well, only letting the fact that he had some good news ooze out a little, till the party had entered together the gloomy lodging of Isaacs. Then, indeed, he enjoyed to the full that feast to a kindly heart, the power of imparting glad tidings. The very bareness of the kitchen seemed to make his message brighter, like a dark background setting off a pattern of gold. Isaacs' grave features relaxed into a smile ; Benoni clapped his thin hands and could hardly keep from shouting ; Sophy looked at first as if she could hardly believe what she heard, then clasped her hands and raised her sightless eyes towards heaven.

"Father," cried Benoni, "you said that if

you'd but a little capital to start with, you could make your way"—Isaacs hurriedly stopped him short by gesture and glance.

"I shall advise Sophy how to lay out her little property to the best advantage for herself," said the Jew.

"And that is by your taking it, using it, doing what you will with it!" cried Sophy with emotion. "O my father, have you not called me your child; have you not said again and again that our purse should always be one? Have you not shared your little with me, fed and clothed me for years? What is mine is yours and my brother's; let it start you in business, and we will all share together whatever your gains may be. I would rather throw the money into the street, and myself go into the workhouse, than have property and not enjoy it with you and my dear Benoni!"

"The lass says well," observed Franks. "Her money can't be better laid out than in giving you the power to support all three."

"I might take it as a loan, if Sophy would trust me," said Benjamin Isaacs.

"*Trust you!*" exclaimed the blind girl, while joyful tears coursed down her cheeks;

"you to whom I owe so much, you who have been to me as a father, from whom I deserved nothing, and yet have received everything! It would be strange indeed if I could not trust you!"

Did conscience then whisper to Sophy that it had been stranger still that she should mistrust One who *like as a father pitieth his children*, who had loved and watched over her from her cradle, and would love and bless her even to the end?

And so the long struggle with poverty came to a close with Benjamin Isaacs. From that time he was to be as successful in business as he had formerly been unfortunate. The working jeweller was to realize how true is the Word of God, *The blessing of the Lord it maketh rich, and he addeth no sorrow with it.* Sophy laid out her little property to very good interest when she lent it to her father by adoption. The blind girl never recovered her bodily sight, but the darkness had passed from her soul; she had learned to *rejoice in the Lord*, and to wait with trustful hope for the day when all clouds of sorrow and mists of doubts shall be rolled away forever.

XXXI.

The Baronet's Return.

NED FRANKS had an exceedingly pleasant journey home. He arrived at Colme in high spirits, and received a joyful welcome from Persis; to whom he gave a very amusing account of all his adventures in London, and of their happy conclusion.

Persis, on her part, had a good deal to tell, though, like a sensible wife, she let her husband first have out his say. She told of her visit to Nancy Sands. Franks listened to her account with interest and pleasure; and, when he heard that the poor woman had attended church upon Sunday, his honest blue eyes lighted up with an expression of joy.

"It's a real pleasure," he cried, "to see a fellow-creature lifted out of poverty, and given a good start in life, like Benjamin Isaacs; but it's a still greater pleasure to see a poor sinner that was going to ruin raised out of the mire, and turning her face towards Zion. O Persis! I trust that there's many a one that man would have rooted up as worthless tares that will be found in the heavenly garner at last!"

"And poor Ben Stone is, I hear, far more anxious about his soul than he ever was before," said Persis. "I do trust that he is now resting on sure ground; that he is giving up all vain hopes of being saved by anything but living faith in the one great Sacrifice for sin."

"You and I are exchanging good tidings, my Persis," said Franks. "All seems bright sunshine now, within as well as without, in this glorious month of June."

"I cannot quite say that, dear Ned. We had something of a cloud sweeping over Colme yesterday in the shape of a carriage and four, with postilion and post-horn, dashing through the village during church-time, on the way to the Hall."

"You don't mean to tell me that young Sir Lacy Barton has come to take possession of his property!" exclaimed Ned Franks, looking startled at the news. "I had hoped with all my heart and soul that he would have kept away for years. You know that I had but too good an opportunity of judging of the character of that young man when I was a sailor on board the same man-of-war in which he was serving. I don't like to think ill, still less to speak ill, of any one who has served under the dear old Union-jack of England; but I should be sorry to think that the queen has another officer to match that young scape-grace, Barton. I wish that the old baronet had lived till he was a hundred years old; it might have saved our village from the mischief which must be brought by the influence and example of such a man as his son."

Ned Franks, who had been doing all in his power to train the village boys under his charge to be not only good scholars but good Christians, felt like a shepherd who hears that a bear has been let loose in the midst of his flock. The lord of the manor would be like a little king at Colme amongst his tenants, and his influence for good or for evil would be very extensive indeed.

"The new baronet did indeed drive to the Hall yesterday," said Persis, "and he took good care that all the village should know of his arrival; for, as he dashed past the church where we were listening to Mr. Leyton's sermon, the post-boy blew a loud flourish on his horn. The church doors were open on ac-

count of the heat, so you may imagine the
effect of the trampling of horses, and the sudden loud blast upon our little congregation.
Every one turned his head round, half the
people rose from their seats, some of the
children ran out of church to see the great
man drive past! One could hardly blame
them, poor little things. It was strange in
Sir Lacy to return thus to the home of his
poor dead father."

"Just like him, just like him," muttered
Franks.

"You should have seen how our young
curate flushed up to his forehead, and for a
moment or two could hardly go on with his
sermon," said Persis.

"It was a personal insult to Mr. Leyton for
Sir Lacy Barton to have the horn blown at
the very door of his church," cried Franks.
"It is the more strange that the baronet should
behave thus, as our curate is his own cousin,
and, I've heard, the heir to his title and property."

"Sir Lacy might not like him the better
for that," observed the school-master's wife,
with a smile. "Mr. Sands told me yesterday
that he believed that the noise was made on

purpose to spite the young preacher; for Sands, as clerk, had had to carry a message to the curate just before service began, asking him to have the church-bells rung for the next hour in honor of the baronet's arrival in Colme."

"Did you ever hear of such a thing!" exclaimed the indignant Franks. "What answer did our young curate return?"

"Oh, a courteous one, you may be sure! I don't think that Mr. Leyton could be rude to any one if he tried; but I believe that he proposed to Sir Lacy a little delay. Of course bell-ringing during church-service was out of the question, so the baronet gave us horn-blowing instead."

"Mean, sneaking spite!" muttered Franks. "We are likely to have a stormy time of it if Sir Lacy stays long at the Hall."

"You and he are not likely to have anything to do with each other, I trust," said Persis. "Do you think that Sir Lacy will remember having seen you on board of his ship?"

"I don't know, — I was nothing to him, — he was not likely to take much notice of a common sailor, and it is nigh four years now

since we trod the same planks. But if Sir
Lacy *does* chance to remember me, he will not
care to have any one in Colme who knows so
much of his pranks at sea as I do.   I doubt
he'll let me stay here long."

"I don't know what he has to do with your
going or staying," said Persis, speaking, however, with a little nervous hesitation, for she
was aware that the lord of the manor must be
a powerful enemy.

"Do you not know," asked Franks, quickly,
"have you lived here so long without hearing,
that this school was founded and endowed by
a Barton ages ago, and that the family have
a right to appoint the master of it?"

"I thought," replied Persis, turning rather
pale, "that you had been appointed by our
good vicar, Mr. Curtis."

"Oh! the last old baronet let our vicar
appoint whom he would, thinking, I suppose,
that Mr. Curtis knew more about schools
and school-masters than he did himself.   But
the patronage of the place goes along with
the property."

"Then you must walk warily, Ned."

"That's not a thing I can do!" exclaimed
the late sailor.   "When I see an unprincipled

fellow trying to corrupt others, and making use of wealth and position only to do the more mischief, I feel a kind of game-cock spirit stirring within me; it seems as if I must have a dash at him, come what may." Ned Franks's blue eyes sparkled with animation; he looked as one of the soldiers at Waterloo might have looked at the call, "Up, guards, and at them!"

Persis was fondling in her arms her little babe, that smiled up at her, unconscious of the shade of anxious care passing over the mother's face. She gazed wistfully first at Ned, then at their boy, as she said, "Oh, do not forget that you are a husband and father now."

"No," replied Franks, more quietly; "it is wonderful what a difference that makes in a man. It's well that tars are not allowed to take a wife or children to sea, or they'd think twice before they ran a ship within range of the enemy's guns. I could bear a pinch of poverty well enough myself, but I'm a bit of a coward when it comes to seeing you or the baby in want. Bless him!" the father stooped forward and kissed the soft lips of his child. "But I can't answer for my own self-command, if I've much to do with that worthless Barton. I detest him more than any other man in the world."

"Now, Ned, darling, will you let me say a little thing to you?" asked Persis, with a shy, tender glance at her husband, as she laid her hand on his shoulder. "Do you think that our blessed religion allows us to detest any being on earth?"

"It makes us hate sin!" exclaimed Franks.

"But surely *not* sinners, my love."

"The truth is," said the sailor school-master, "that I'm by nature of an impatient, fiery spirit. I'm one of those of whom it is said that they make good lovers and good haters."

"A good lover, if you will," observed the wife with a pleasant smile; "but it always seems to me that the expression, 'a good hater,' can never describe a Christian, who is bound by the Lord's command, not only not to detest but to love his enemies."

"That's a most difficult command to obey."

"I am sure that it is," observed Persis. "But He who gave the command, can also give grace to keep it. It seems to me, as if hatred, revenge, and all the fierce passions so natural to man, are like Satan's fire-ships that he sends against even those who are going on the straightest course towards heaven — ”

“And you would have me ‘sheer off,’” cried Franks, gayly, “as soon as I see one bearing down on me, because I carry a dangerous quantity of gunpowder down in my hold! You're afraid of an explosion, wifie, and you're right. I dare say now that there's something of pride in my very contempt for a fellow like Barton (he really is *not* a gentleman) ; I despise him too much in the spirit of *Stand by, I am holier than thou.*”

“And should we not remember,” said Persis, softly, “that those whom we cannot respect are our fellow-creatures still ; they, like ourselves, have souls, precious souls, that must live forever? If they, through rejecting mercy, will have at last to share the misery of the rich man in the parable, should not our deep, deep pity swallow up every feeling of dislike? And if, on the contrary, they are to be found in the end amongst those whose sins have been forgiven, can we not bear with them a while in patience, even as God has borne so long with them, and with us?”

Ned Franks answered the question by giving his wife a hearty kiss, in return, as he said, for her lecture. He promised to keep on his guard, less against Sir Lacy Barton than against his own fiery temper, and to "sheer off" as fast as he might, whenever he found that Satan's fire-ships of hatred, malice, or revenge, were drifting on the current towards him.

XXXII.

The Bonfire.

THE holidays given on account of the haymaking season were soon over, and with their daily lessons at school, the boys of Colme resumed their cheerful labors in Wild Rose Hollow. Already there was a pleasant change in the aspect of two of the cottages, which, through the combined efforts of workmen and boys, were declared by Franks to be "quite weather-tight and seaworthy." The third was now "to be laid up in dock, and well overhauled." Franks was ambitious to make the almshouses pretty as well as comfortable. He set the boys to gathering a large quantity of tough boughs which, tastefully interlaced, and painted to preserve them from decay, were to form seven rustic porches, round which creepers should be trained to climb.

"They'll be like cool, pretty bowers for the old folks to sit in during the hot summer days," said Franks; and he took especial pleasure in the gradually increasing pile of collected branches stripped of their leaves, which formed one of the most conspicuous objects in what Ned called "the building yard" in Wild Rose Hollow.

Cheerfully, on the day when work was resumed, the one-armed teacher led his jovial crew of noisy young workers along the familiar road which led to the scene of their labors. As Ned passed the cottage of Sands, Nancy came forth to greet him with a good-humored smile on her face, which, if it looked paler and older than when he last had seen it, had certainly gained in pleasantness of expression since her accident in the stream.

" A good-day to you, Ned Franks!" she cried, as she leaned over the little gate of her garden. "I wonder if you and your good wife could just step in and pass a quiet evening with me and John Sands? I can promise you a good cup of *tea*," she added, with an emphasis on the last word which was meant to assure the hearer that she had faithfully kept the pledge.

"I shall be happy to come, if Persis can manage it; but the ladies settle these matters," replied Ned, gayly; "and there's a little troublesome fellow, you know, who will have a voice, though he is not quite up to talking."

"Oh, you must bring the baby of course!" cried Nancy. "The days are so long, and the evenings so warm, that he can't now take any harm."

The invitation frankly given was frankly accepted, and Nancy returned into her cottage saying to herself, "How strangely things do change, and people change as strangely! It's not three months since I used to call Ned Franks that canting Jack with the wooden arm. I hated him,—I hated his ways,—I'd have done him a mischief if I could. And now I've lost an arm as well as himself,—I'm crippled far worse than he, and yet I believe that I'm better off and happier now than I was when I mocked and jeered at him. And, as for these pious ways of his, which made me so mad against him, I only wish I could follow them myself, and have the same look-out for another world as honest Ned Franks and his wife."

"Nancy Sands is a changed woman if ever there was one," mused the school-master, as he hurried along the dusty road after his boys, who had gone on in advance. "There never was a being who tried my patience more sorely than she did, with her waspish temper and her stinging tongue. Why, I remember biting my lip till it bled, to keep in the passionate retort to her very provoking taunts. Yes, the fire-ships were bearing down upon me then; and if I was enabled to 'sheer off' and avoid an explosion, it was because conscience stood at my helm, and my sails had been filled with prayer. Let no one make an excuse for passion by saying, 'It's in my nature;' the office of grace is to conquer nature, and tame the unruly spirit to the meekness and lowliness which become a Christian."

Ten minutes afterwards, Ned and his crew

were busy as bees at their work, sawing and digging, carrying bricks and piling up wood, some of the boys singing cheerily as they labored, while the miller's little girl, seated on a stone, watched the work, and joined in the song with her sweet, childish voice.

Suddenly the singing ceased. Franks, who was working hard with his back towards the path which led up to the high road, did not at first notice the cause of the interruption, till he heard a loud, coarse, and too familiar voice, exclaim, "You boys there, what are you about?"

Ned Franks did not need the murmur of "Sir Lacy — Sir Lacy Barton," which ran through the groups around him, to make him aware who had appeared. He turned round quickly, and saw a young man not more than two-and-twenty years of age, but whose bloated features already showed the effects of the evil habits which must soon have caused his expulsion from the noble service which he disgraced, had not his succession to the baronetcy given him an excuse for quitting the navy of his own accord. As the baronet stood on the path leading down into the Hollow, between his fingers the lighted cigar which he had just removed from his lips, Ned gravely touched his cap out of respect to his position as lord of the manor. The moment that the eyes of the two men met, the school-master felt certain that Sir Lacy had recognized him, though the settled purplish-red on the baronet's cheek would scarcely admit of a deepened flush. He took no notice of Franks's salutation but by a haughty stare, and turned towards one of the boys who was standing with his foot resting on his spade.

"What are you all about?" repeated Sir Lacy.

"Please, sir," answered the boy, "we's be a-building up them old houses," and he pointed over his shoulder with his thumb.

"And what do such young fry as you get for your work?"

"Please, sir, we don't not get nothing," replied the little brown-faced rustic. "Ned Franks, he be our school-master, there; he tells us to work for the pleasure of helping the poor."

Sir Lacy gave a loud, very scornful whistle, and then a still louder laugh. "If you listen to such twaddle," he cried, "I'll tell you what you'll come to, my lad. Your ears will grow longer than your purse, and you'll have to take to browsing on thistles, like a donkey, as you are!" and to give point to his wit, the young man caught hold of the ear of the unfortunate boy, and gave it a pull, apparently to hasten the lengthening process, but which had only the effect of forcing out a sharp cry of pain.

The circle of boys retreated a pace backwards, and Franks had to press his lips very tightly indeed together to keep in the word "brute!"

"And what's that?" asked the baronet, turning to another young worker, who looked by no means anxious to be singled out for conversation with the lord of the manor. Sir Lacy was pointing with his cigar to the great pile collected for making the seven cottage porches.

"Them be branches," stammered out the child.

"I dare say; I did not take them for buttercups, wiseacre! So you've been making preparations for a grand bonfire in honor of my return?"

The poor little boy gave a frightened, appealing glance towards Franks.

"Answer me; I suppose you've a tongue in your head," said Sir Lacy. The boy was trembling for his ears.

"Them be for the porches, sir," faltered the poor little fellow, who had been one of the most active in collecting for the purpose the strongest and most pliable branches.

"Ah! but I say they're for a bonfire, and as a bonfire they shall blaze!" cried Sir Lacy. "Here's a light,—you set fire to the heap!"

Again the frightened child looked to his master, though not daring to refuse to take into his hand the lighted cigar. Franks strode forward, and, with as much calmness as he could command, addressed Sir Lacy Barton.

"I hope, sir, that you will not destroy that which it has cost us some time and trouble to collect, and which is intended to add to the few comforts of the respectable poor."

"Mind your own business, and hold your tongue," was the insolent reply; "and you, little dog, do what I bid you, or I'll toss you on the top of the blaze."

In a few minutes the pile of branches was a crackling heap of smoke and flame, that curled up pale in the yet brilliant light of the declining sun. Sir Lacy laughed, rubbed his hands, and bade the boys give a good British cheer, if they knew how to do it. About half the number obeyed, though the shout sounded different indeed from that which had burst from them freely, at no man's command, —when they had resolved to give two hours daily to working for the poor.

"Now off with ye all to your homes," cried Sir Lacy, as soon as what he called "the fun of the thing" was over; "unless you've a mind to come and look on at a famous match between some game-cocks that I'm going to have up at the Hall."

Several of the boys cheered again at the great man's invitation, and, whether from a regard for their ears, or a mean desire to curry favor, not one of them seemed to be in the least disposed to return to work. In short, as soon as Sir Lacy had lighted another cigar, and turning on his heel began reascending the path, the jovial crew dispersed in one direction or another. They were afraid or ashamed to appear to mind the school-master's "twaddle."

"They've not the spirit of a tom-twit

amongst them!" muttered Franks, almost more indignant at the defection of his boys than at the insolence of Sir Lacy. "They just follow one another like sheep!"

Little Bessy, with her face glowing scarlet, ran up to the sailor, who was standing alone.

"Oh, isn't he a bad, bad man," she cried, "to burn up all in that great big fire, and to make the boys go away? But don't mind him, don't mind him, Ned Franks. I'll work with you, if they won't work. I can carry a brick all by myself!" and she suited the action to the word.

"There's a brave little lass!" said Franks, stooping to pat her curly head. "You won't be daunted by difficulties, nor bullied into baseness by a"—he stopped short; the sight of the still burning pile recalled to him Persis's simile of the fire-ships. He felt the fierce glow rising hotter in his heart than the flame from the branches which scorched his brow. He must not trust himself to say more, even to the child, lest he should utter words which he might in vain desire to recall.

Ned returned to his work, and labored with even greater energy than usual. Perhaps

27*

the strong efforts of the arm relieved the
pressure on the spirits, or perhaps the hard
blows which descended on pillar and post
were an outward expression of the struggle
going on within, to strike down, and then
to keep down, the stubborn passions of the
natural heart.

XXXIII.

Watching for Souls.

THE evil effects of Sir Lacy's residence at
the Hall were soon seen in the village school.
Franks found that his boys became less regular in attendance, and less respectful in manner. He more than once, when giving a serious reproof, heard, from a distant corner of
the room a whisper, in which " twaddle " and
" donkey's ears " were the only words to be
distinguished. Few of his jovial crew now
ever worked in Wild Rose Hollow; it was
not the fashion to do so. Franks would see
little rustics, instead of engaging in healthful
labor, sauntering about with their hands in

their pockets and smoking. The great ambition of the boys was to get a cigar; and half-used ones, thrown away by Sir Lacy or his rollicking guests, were counted as prizes.

Great was the annoyance of the good old invalid Vicar of Colme, great the vexation of Mr. Leyton, his curate, when it was given out that Sir Lacy would have a cricket-match every Sunday afternoon on his lawn, and treat the boys to strong ale, or, as it was rumored, to something stronger. The vicar and curate held anxious consultations together in the study, where the old minister, feeble and suffering, reclined in his large arm-chair.

"I have written a strong remonstrance to Sir Lacy, as you will see here," said the vicar, handing a letter to his nephew. "I have tried to write as temperately as I could. But would it not be well, Claudius, as you are the baronet's near relation, that you should go and speak to him yourself on the subject? He may be rather careless than actually wicked. We know that

> "'Evil is wrought
> By want of thought
> As well as by want of heart.'"

The young minister shook his head sadly. "I have not the slightest influence with my cousin," he said. "He asked me to dinner once after his arrival at Colme, and I thought it right not to refuse his first invitation. But what I saw at the Hall, and still more what I heard, made me return home sickened and disgusted, and with a resolve that I would never cross the threshold again. It is a misfortune to the whole place that such a man as Sir Lacy Barton should hold the chief position in it."

The curate, who was just beginning to know his flock, and be known by them, to overcome his own painful shyness, and become accustomed to parish work, looked overwhelmed by the new and unexpected difficulties which had started up before him.

" My dear boy," said the old vicar, in his fatherly way, " this will be a sifting time in the village; but we must not forget that temptation itself is turned into a cause of rejoicing to those who in God's strength overcome it. Were there no battle, where would be the victory? It is *when the enemy comes in like a flood* that *the Spirit of the Lord shall lift up a banner* against him. Let the danger to our flock make us but more watchful, more vigilant, more earnest in prayer. God is above all, and even sinners are made unconscious instruments in his hands for working good that they intend not. Is it not written, *Surely the wrath of man shall praise thee, and the remainder of wrath shalt thou restrain* "?

" One comfort is that we have Ned Franks to look after the school," observed Mr. Leyton. " He has such an energy and intelligence, his heart is so thoroughly in his work, and then his piety is so sincere, that his influence is always for good."

" Such men as Ned Franks are indeed *the salt of the earth*," said the vicar. " The Christian's calling is, not only himself to be, through God's grace, purified, but to become a means of preserving all over whom his influence extends from the corruption of sin. No man can live merely unto himself; the effect of his example is ever silently working on others ; it is a talent entrusted to him, for which he will, at the last day, render an account."

" For one like Barton how fearful an account ! " cried the curate.

"He needs our prayers," said the vicar.

The letter of Mr. Curtis was sent to the Hall; Sir Lacy was at the billiard-table when he received it. He tore it open, glanced at its contents, then, laughing, twisted the paper round and round, and used it to light his cigar.

"Since the good parson's squeamish about Sunday cricketing," he said, "we'll have a little cock-fighting instead to please him."

The vicar was so much annoyed at this attempt to draw away his people from church, and make them violate the sanctity of the day set apart for worship, that all the entreaties of his wife, backed by the orders of the doctor, were scarcely sufficient, as Norah told her uncle, to prevent him from having himself carried up to the pulpit on the following Sunday (as he could not have walked up the steps), to preach on the Fourth Commandment. Very unwillingly the good old pastor gave up to his curate the work which he had not the bodily strength to perform. He felt like a wounded veteran standard-bearer, when obliged to resign into the hands of the young recruit at his side the banner which he would fain have defended himself to the

last.   Never before had bodily infirmity been
so painful a trial to the vicar.   He was
rather grieved than surprised to hear how
empty the benches had been at afternoon service, though Claudius Leyton had exerted
his utmost efforts in the morning sermon to
warn, to convince, to persuade.

"I should have been utterly disheartened,"
said the weary curate to his uncle on the Sunday evening, "had not Nancy Sands been
seated just before me, looking so quiet, at-
tentive, and earnest.   When I remember
what she was, and see what she is, I feel that
I dare never despair."

"*Oh, rest in the Lord, wait patiently for
him, and he shall give thee thy heart's desire*," repeated the vicar.

Difficulties were however to thicken, and
trials to increase.   An incident occurred on
the following day which caused great excitement through the village of Colme.

XXXIV.

Put to the Question.

Persis sat with her work in her hand by her open window in the little room over that in which the school was assembled below. Pleasant to her ear was the hum of voices rising from beneath, for it told her that her husband was, as usual, opening the day by devotion, and her busy needle stopped, and she silently joined in the Lord's prayer repeated by many young voices.

Persis was then about to set to her work again, when, chancing to glance out of the window, her attention was drawn to three gentlemen walking along the road, each smoking a cigar. Though Mrs. Franks had not before seen the baronet, who never appeared at church, she instantly recognized him as the central person in the group, by the description which she had heard of him. There was no mistaking the short, thick figure, the face where the color lay in patches of purplish red, and the hat cocked a good deal upon one side, over a mass of sandy-colored hair. Sir

Lacy's companions were a young lawyer and a medical student, neither of whom looked as if they would be likely to do much credit to their respective professions.

Persis Franks dropped her work on her knees, instinctively clasped her hands, and drew back a little from the window, while keeping her eyes anxiously fixed upon the unwelcome strangers.

"I hope and trust that they'll pass by the school without entering it," she said to herself, while the sound of their coarse laughter grew louder as they drew nearer.

The hopes of Franks's wife were not realized. The three men were evidently on their way to the school. Persis could catch a few of their words, — something about badgering and baiting, and putting the fellow to the question.

Hot as was that July morning, Persis grew cold and trembled, and for the first time let her baby cry in his cradle for at least two minutes before she went to see what her darling wanted. She had a terrible misgiving that nothing good could come of the visit of those three men who had just disappeared under the porch. Earnestly Persis prayed that her husband might be able to command his temper under any provocation, and so defeat the malice of one whom she could not but regard as an enemy.

Franks, upon every Monday morning, as soon as prayers were ended, questioned his boys on the subject of the sermon heard on the preceding day. This was his invariable custom, and he found it to be followed by two good results : it made the boys listen more attentively to the sermon, and it enabled him to explain to them in his simple, homely way, whatever had been too hard for them to understand. The addresses of the young curate, unlike those of the vicar, were often above the comprehension of some of his ignorant hearers.

Franks, upon this particular Monday morning, had just begun his questioning with the words, " Now, Sims, what was the text ? " when there was a murmur of " Sir Lacy, Sir Lacy," heard through the school-room, and every eye was turned towards the door through which the three gentlemen were entering.

It must be owned that to Franks the visitors were extremely unwelcome, and especially at that time. The influence of the baronet was already working for evil amongst the Colme boys, and he was but too likely, not only to take offence at the subject of the sermon, but to try to turn into ridicule any religious instruction that he might hear. There was some stiffness in the air of the schoolmaster as he received the lord of the manor.

"Go on, go on, just as if I were not here," said the baronet, replacing the cigar which he had taken out of his mouth for a moment; and Franks felt that for the sake of his boys he must go on. His pupils must see in him no cringing fear of man overcoming the fear of God. Had he changed his regular custom on account of the baronet's presence, he would have shown himself unfit to train boys to do their duty faithfully and fearlessly in the face of all the world.

"What was the text of the sermon?" repeated Ned Franks, addressing himself again to young Sims.

But if the one-armed school-master preserved his presence of mind, the scholar certainly did not do so also. Sims, the same boy who had had his ear twitched by Sir Lacy in Wild Rose Hollow, looked with an uneasy, frightened expression, not at his questioner, but at the formidable visitor who was standing with his hands behind his back to listen. The boy began to stammer forth, "Remember the — the," and then stopped short, not daring to finish the verse.

Sir Lacy Barton burst out laughing at his evident confusion. "A precious bright scholar you!" he exclaimed. "If you'd been questioned as to whether Sharpspur or Redcomb had the best of it yesterday, you'd have answered him a deal quicker;" and the baronet wound up his sentence with a loud oath, such as had never been heard before within the walls of that school-room.

Franks felt that the honor of his Master, the welfare of his pupils, forbade him to pass over in silence, on account of the rank of the offender, what in the case of any one else would have called forth instant and stern rebuke. "*Thou shalt not take the name of the Lord thy God in vain*," he said, in a tone not loud but clear, which, in the breathless silence kept by the awe-struck boys, was heard distinctly in the farthest corner of the room; and, as he spoke the message of God, the master fixed his eyes calmly and fearlessly upon the profane young man, who quailed and blanched under their gaze. The effect upon the astonished boys was greater than would have been produced by the most eloquent sermon against swearing. They saw that in Franks they had a leader who would not only bid them wage war against vice in every shape, but who would himself head the charge, and expose himself freely in the conflict.

Badham, the lawyer, came to the assistance of the discomfited Barton. He had a supercilious, sarcastic manner, almost more disgusting to Franks than the coarseness of Sir Lacy himself.

"You are well up in the commandments, I perceive, my good friend," he observed, addressing himself to the school-master, "and no doubt your knowledge on all other parts of education is equally deep. May I ask in what college you have studied?" Badham winked at the baronet as he asked the question.

"I was never at college," replied Ned Franks; "I was brought up at a village school, but left it early to go to sea."

"But of course you have read and studied a good deal since, or you would hardly have been placed by the late Sir Lacy Barton in the position which you now hold."

Ned Franks flushed. He felt as if he were being put upon his trial, and before judges determined beforehand to condemn him. "I have not great book-learning," he replied; "but Mr. Curtis recommended me to Sir Lacy as one who could fulfil the duties of school-master here."

"But the present Sir Lacy takes such a fatherly interest in the school which his ancestors founded," said the lawyer, winking again at the baronet, "that he wishes to judge for himself as to the competency of one entrusted with such a responsible charge as yours. He has desired me to ask you a few educational questions, to which, I have not the slightest doubt, you will give a prompt and able reply."

"I do not think this the time or place for such an examination," said the school-master, whose countenance was glowing with indignation at the insidious proposal. "I will wait upon Sir Lacy at the Hall at any hour that he may choose to appoint."

"No time or place like the present!" cried the baronet, who had a keen relish in the "baiting and badgering" of the school-master in the presence of his pupils. "As I'm the patron of this school, I've a good right, I take it, to see that the teacher isn't a blockhead or a dunce."

And then, at a sign from him, the flippant lawyer began to aim a shower of questions, like a flight of arrows, against the unfortunate school-master, — questions ingeniously contrived to perplex and puzzle even one who had received a better education than had fallen to the lot of Ned Franks. At every query to which no reply was or could be given by him who had passed his youth at sea, the baronet burst out into an insulting laugh, which was echoed by the medical student; as if the ignorance of Franks regarding Neri and Bianchi, Palleschi and Piagnone, the respective styles of French, German, and Dutch infidel writers, and the names of female favorites of Bourbon kings, was as absurd as if he had been unable to repeat the multiplication-table. Certainly, Sir Lacy could not have himself answered one of the questions. But what of that? One needs no deep study to learn how to laugh; and it was rare fun to him to humble and degrade

the teacher before all his pupils. Franks
was more annoyed by the titter from some of
his scholars, which now followed the gentlemen's uproarious mirth, than he was by the
more direct insults of the strangers. That
his "jovial crew," that a single boy amongst
them, should be mean enough to join in the
laugh against him, was almost more than his
spirit could endure.

*I am purposed that my mouth shall not
transgress*, had been the text which Franks
had chosen on that morning for his meditation
during the day. Sorely he needed it now.
As he stood silent before his persecutor, with
flushed cheek and flashing eye, again and
again he repeated that text to himself, to
keep in the burning words that were rising
to his tongue. He had spoken out boldly
when the insult was against his Master; there
was the more need that he should show self-
command when the attack was personal to
himself.

"You don't mean us to conclude," said
Badham at last, "that you have never so
much as heard of all these well known matters before?"

"Sir," replied Franks, as calmly as he

could, though his tone betrayed some emotion, " my work is to train village lads for usefulness here and happiness hereafter; and I do not suppose that farm-lads will be the less suited for either the one or the other because they can't give the names of Italian factions or of the favorites of French kings."

Badham shrugged his shoulders, the baronet and the medical student shrugged theirs, to express their utter contempt for such a very ridiculous observation. The baronet was the first to break the silence which followed, which he did by addressing himself to Badham.

" What say you to our master here, — you who have all kinds of learning at the ends of your fingers, — is he fit to be a teacher of boys ?"

" About as fit as to be a performer on a lady's grand piano," said the lawyer.

" While he remains here, the motto of the school had better be, 'Where ignorance is bliss 'tis folly to be wise,'" observed the medical student.

" It was a shame for Mr. Curtis to recommend such a fellow to my father," said Sir Lacy. " You see how unfit he is for the place."

"Utterly unfit!" cried the lawyer.

"Disgracefully incompetent!" chimed in the student.

"I suppose," said Sir Lacy, in his insolent manner, "that school-masters, like footmen, expect their masters to give a month's warning. What day is this?—the sixth of July. Well, on the sixth of August you will bundle yourself off, my fine fellow, and I'll take precious good care not to consult the old parson as to whom your successor should be. He might, in his wisdom, recommend some saint from the Idiot Asylum!" and with another laugh at this brilliant joke, which was echoed by his two companions, but by none of the boys, who stood aghast at the sudden dismissal of their master, Sir Lacy sauntered out of the school-room, accompanied by the lawyer and medical student.

There were a few moments of silence after they had left, during which the ticking of the large school-clock sounded almost painfully loud. It was broken by Ned Franks himself, who, turning towards his class, resumed the interrupted thread of the morning studies by asking Sims for the third time the question, "What was the text of yesterday's sermon?"

XXXV.

Village Talk.

VERY uneasy had Persis felt while Sir Lacy was in the school-room; very anxiously she watched the porch, in hopes of seeing him and his visitors quit it. She could hear from beneath the sound of laughter; but it was laughter which raised in her soul a very opposite feeling to that of mirth. She listened intently; but her baby was fretful from cutting teeth, and his crying soon drowned every other noise. Persis fondled him in her arms, and hushed him on her bosom, and just as she had succeeded in quieting the child, saw, to her relief, the three strangers issue from under the porch. She did not, however, like their looks, still less the laughter which followed words of which she could not catch the exact meaning, but which she was certain had none which was good. Persis watched the three men till they disappeared down a turn in the road, and then heaved a long, anxious sigh. Lessons were evidently going on as usual below,—Persis knew *that* from the hum of voices from the school-room. She had to wait in restless expectation till the school broke up for an hour's recess, and she saw the stream of boys come issuing forth from the porch.

Their grave yet excited looks frightened the wife yet more. That something remarkable had happened was written on every young face, as the boys thronged together in knots of three or four, all seeming far more eager to speak than to listen. But Persis was not much longer to be kept in suspense; she knew the step of her husband; she saw him enter, looking paler than she had ever seen him before. Franks seated himself beside his wife, put his arm round her, and drew her tenderly towards him, unwilling to inflict pain, scarcely knowing how to break the news that he was a ruined man. Persis had guessed the truth before Franks said, in a tone which he vainly tried to make cheerful, " Well, sweetheart, you and I will have to set out on our travels together."

But when Ned gave his wife a more detailed account of what had occurred; when he told of the absurd questions, the mocking laughter, the insolent taunts which had made his blood boil, even natural anxiety concerning his future prospects was swallowed up for the time in passionate indignation. "I longed to strike him," exclaimed the late sailor, "and I had to chain even my tongue! Wife — wife — it is no easy matter to endure, or to forgive insults and injuries such as that man has heaped upon me! To hold me up to the contempt of my own boys, — that was the most intolerable wrong of all! I actually heard Sam Barker and Peter Core tittering behind me, the little sneaking— But your fire-ships are bearing down upon me full sail; I must not trust myself to speak on these matters, — I must try not to let my mind brood over them, — would that I could drive the whole scene out of my memory forever!"

Persis did not, as most wives would have done, stir up her husband's wrath to a blaze, and heap on it the fuel of her own grief, fears, and regrets. She tried in her gentle, loving way to make him look beyond second causes, to see that the trial — bitter as it was — was sent in wisdom and love, and that man could inflict no real injury except by drawing into sin. Persis did not say much, but she looked bright and hopeful, to keep up the spirits of her husband. If they were to leave their happy home at Colme, their pleasant occupation in the village, it might be because God had provided for them something better still, some wider field of usefulness in which they might humbly serve him. They were spared to one another, and their darling was left to them still. "Whilst I have you and our boy," cried Persis, as she rested her head on her husband's shoulder, "I feel that I could be contented in a hovel, or in a prison."

The news that Ned Franks, the one-armed school-master, had been dismissed by Sir Lacy, spread like wildfire through Colme. The tidings were received with almost universal regret and indignation, for both Ned and Persis were great favorites in the village. Mrs. Fuddles of the "Chequers," indeed, observed, as she wiped the dust from a bottle of whiskey, "I guess that Sir Lacy knows what he's about. It aint likely that a sailor that's been spending his life in mopping up decks should know much about hedication." But the publican's wife was almost the only person who did not regret the disgrace of the Frankses. Bat Bell, the miller, declared that to send off an honest fellow like Franks from the school was like damming up a mill-stream; and that everything would come to a dead lock,—while his little girl cried as if her heart would break, and wished that that wicked Sir Lacy never had come to make every one unhappy. Ben Stone the carpenter, on his bed of sickness, heard the news with less than his usual placid calmness.

"Sir Lacy," he observed to his wife, " is like the idiot who sawed at the branch on which he was seated. If he goes on with this kind of work he'll come down with a crash one of these days, though I shan't live to see it," added the invalid, whose increasing weakness warned him that his hours were numbered.

I will not say that the Clerk of Colme looked grave and solemn when he carried the tidings to his wife, for he never looked otherwise, except on the very rarest occasions; but his solemnity and melancholy were of a shade so much more intensely black than usual, that his Nancy exclaimed, as soon as she saw him, "Why, John Sands, has any one been murdered to-day?"

But when she heard that Ned Franks had

been dismissed,—dismissed in disgrace as incompetent and ignorant,—the wrath of the clerk's wife blazed up with a sudden fierceness that showed that the old shrewish spirit was not quite dead in her yet. As her torrent of indignation poured forth like lava-streams from a volcano, John Sands scarcely knew whether he was glad or sorry to be so forcibly reminded of the Nancy of former days. Nancy was certain that the school would go to rack and ruin; they would never, never again see the like of Ned Franks and his wife!

But perhaps in no place did the news cause deeper regret than in the vicarage. Norah was almost overwhelmed by the sudden blow, and her letter to Sophy Claymore, informing her of what had happened, was wet with the young girl's tears. Mr. Curtis lay awake half the night, meditating over a second letter to Sir Lacy (which was—when written and sent—to meet with just the same fate as the first), and the invalid had, in consequence, a relapse of fever in the morning. Claudius Leyton, the young curate, broke through his resolution,—never again to enter the Hall, and, like a man on a forlorn hope, set out to

endeavor to move and persuade his cousin to
recall his hasty words. The nervous shyness of the curate was not lessened by his
being handed into a room full of rollicking
revellers ; a room which in ancient days had
been used as a chapel, but which was reeking,
even at that early hour, with the fumes of to-
bacco and the odor of spirits. It need scarcely
be added that the visit of the young clergyman was as unsuccessful as regarded its object, as it was to himself painful and disgusting.
The baronet, laughing, said to his cousin,
" My dear fellow, you have come a day
too late for the fair. I have already written
up to my friend, Dick Sharpey, — you know
Dick, — all the world knows him as the luck-
iest card-player in London. I've bid him look
out for a cute fellow who can teach the clods
in the day, and be my billiard-marker at
night.   That's what I call killing two birds
with one stone, ha ! ha ! ha ! "

It was with a heavy heart that the curate
again turned his back on the Hall, not surprised, though grieved, at the utter failure of
his mission.

Mrs. Curtis, a very practical as well as kind
woman, directed her efforts to writing to

friends in various quarters to try by their means to procure some other situation for Franks before he should quit the one which at present he held. As Ned would have nothing to fall back upon except his very trifling pension as a disabled sailor, Mrs. Curtis knew that, unless he could procure some work, he and his family would be reduced to absolute want. She also quietly set on foot a subscription to raise a little fund to supply his immediate need and the expenses of removal to some new home, perhaps at a distance. "It is only right," said the vicar's wife, and her husband warmly seconded her proposal, "that a testimonial should be given, on his departure from Colme, to a school-master who has for years so faithfully performed his duties, and who has won the good will and respect of all whose approbation is worth having." Ned Franks and his wife knew nothing of this secret subscription. The most active agent in collecting it was Nancy Sands, who went from cottage to cottage gathering the pence given with willing hearts by the children, and the little offerings freely bestowed even by the old tenants of the almshouses in Wild Rose Hol-

low.   Had the power of the villagers to give
been equal to their will, Ned would have been
the wealthiest man in Colme ; but it needs a
great weight in copper to make up a single
sovereign's worth, and even the vicar, whose
charity never left him a full purse, was unable to contribute largely, though he gave with
all his heart.

XXXVI.

A Struggle.

Two, three, almost four weeks passed,
every week bringing fresh disappointments to
Franks and his wife.   The vicar sent over to
them every morning the advertisement sheet
of the *Times;* and anxiously were the col-
umns of the paper searched and searched
over again each day, and many were the letters written by Ned, or by Persis to his dic-
tation, to take advantage of what they fondly
hoped might be openings to some new sphere
of work.   But few of these letters brought
any reply, and there was not one of an
encouraging nature.   Ned always frankly

stated the facts that he had passed no regular examination, and that he had lost his left arm; and one or other of these disqualifications seemed ever to bar his way to obtaining any employment.

Isaacs had exerted himself greatly in his friend's behalf in London, but hitherto without any success.. He thought that the chance of Ned's making his way would be greater were he himself on the spot, and sent a pressing invitation in the name of Sophy to the family of the Frankses. It was arranged that Ned, Persis, and their baby should travel up to London on the succeeding Thursday, the day on which their dear home must be given up to a stranger.

The new school-master had already arrived at the Hall, and was constantly showing himself in the village. He even made his appearance at church, where, on the first Sunday in August, the vicar had come to return thanks for recovery after his long and dangerous illness. The irreverent manner of the school-master-elect, who looked like — what he was — a low sharper, likely to teach the boys little but how to play, or to cheat at cards, made a very painful impression, not only on the vicar and curate, but upon all who cared for religion or morality in the parish.

A very sad Sunday was that to Ned and Persis. Even under happier circumstances, the thought that it would be their last at Colme would have sufficed to throw a shade over the brightest prospects. All their happy wedded life had been spent in the place. There seemed to be dear associations connected with every cottage, nay, almost with every tree. The friends who were dearest to them, the children whom they had taught, the pastor whom they revered, all, all must be left behind. Would they ever see them again? And what darkness hung over the future! Would Franks, a one-armed man, succeed in earning enough to support a wife and child? And if not, what distress might be before them! And all this wrecking of peace, this breaking up of one of the happiest of homes, was the work of the wanton malice of one unprincipled man!

On the Sunday evening, Ned Franks, usually so cheerful and brave in spirit, was over-powered by deeper depression than he had ever experienced since he had first met with

Persis. He sat gloomy and silent in the darkening twilight, with his hand pressed over his eyes. Persis had just placed her babe in his cradle, and drawing forward a footstool, she now seated herself upon it, at the feet of her husband. She longed to give comfort, yet scarcely ventured to speak, and at last, feeling that the words of the Lord were far more likely to soothe a troubled spirit than any of her own, she repeated very softly, "*Peace I leave with you, my peace I give unto you.*"

"If I had only that," said Franks, sadly, as he removed his hand from his eyes, "I should care less for the troubles that have come upon us thus. Do you know me so little, Persis, as to think that I'm so downhearted just because we're in a few days to be turned out of our home, or because we've been disappointed in these letters from London? I do not say that I do not feel these things, but I should be a coward if I could not bear them, and a fool if I'd expected that troubles never would come." Then, suddenly appearing to change the subject of conversation, Ned abruptly asked, "Did you hear what

Mr. Leyton said to me this afternoon when we had just come out of church?"

"No, I was speaking to Nancy Sands."

"He said, 'Poor Stone is now sinking fast. The vicar himself is going to administer the communion to him — I fear for the last time — to-morrow evening at six. Stone told me that he hoped that you and your wife would come over and partake of the Lord's Supper with him, as he owes more to you than to any one else upon earth!'"

"And what did you reply, Ned?" asked Persis.

"Nothing. Mr. Leyton noticed Nancy Sands at that moment, and turned to ask her a question, and, as you know, you and I then walked home."

"Surely," observed Persis, "it will be a satisfaction to us both — once more — in this dear, dear place — to" — She dared not go on, lest her voice should betray her distress at leaving the village.

"How can I share the feast of love," exclaimed Ned Franks, bitterly, "when my heart is full of hatred! I've been searching and examining myself ever since Mr. Leyton spoke, and I *dare not* go to the Lord's table!"   The school-master rose from his seat, and began pacing up and down the room while continuing to speak.   " 'To be in charity with all men,'—that is absolutely needful; without that I should but profane the holiest service.   I can't shut my eyes to the truth, I can't deceive my own heart,— I do hate and detest Sir Lacy, more for what he *is* than for what he has done!   So I must keep away—like an outcast—from the feast to which I am so lovingly invited; I must not share it with my poor dying friend, or the pastor whom I reverence, though, by keeping away, I shall own before all the village that I know myself to be unworthy to join in Christian communion.   And if I am unfit to partake of the holy supper, I am also unfit to die, unfit to appear in the presence of my God!   O Persis!" exclaimed the agitated man, throwing himself again on his chair, "people talk well of me, think well of me — much too well; tell me that I've helped them on their way to heaven; but what will it profit me if, after preaching to others, I myself should be a castaway!"

"God forbid!" exclaimed Persis.   "But, Ned dearest, surely it is not the entrance of

sin into the soul, but the harboring it there,
that makes us unfit for heaven, or unworthy
to receive the means of grace."

"I *do* harbor malice and hatred," muttered
Franks.

"But you would turn them out this moment if you could."

"I can't; whenever I think of Sir Lacy"—

"Oh, think of him only when you're on
your knees!" cried Persis. "Ned, I share
your temptation, I feel what you feel, — not
quite so warmly perhaps, but just as deeply.
Let us kneel down together now; let us confess our sin, our heart sin, to our heavenly
Father; let us together ask of him that Holy
Spirit that can cast out the 'strong man
armed,' and keep him out; and make us
ready to forgive even as we have been forgiven!"

The husband and wife knelt down side by
side, and silently poured out their confession
of sin and prayer for help unto Him who
could himself pardon his murderers. Night
darkened around as they prayed; and with
the night came a rush of refreshing rain after
the fervent heat of the long summer day.

When Franks arose from his knees his manner was calmer and more subdued.

"Persis," he said, after he had resumed his seat, "God has been showing me my weakness. I cannot by myself subdue the fierce passions within; but he can, and he will send his Spirit, even as he sends his rain from heaven to quench the fire, and calm the proud, resentful spirit! I have made one resolution, — and may God help me to keep it! — never, if possible, even to name Sir Lacy, except in my prayers. Yes, Persis, you and I will not harbor malice and hatred as guests, but resist them as foes; and, to gain strength for the struggle, you and I will to-morrow seek the Lord in his own ordinance by the bedside of our poor dying friend."

XXXVII.

The Sudden Summons.

On the following morning Franks started before breakfast for a spot called Cliff Farm, to make arrangements with the owner of the place for the loan of his cart to carry the school-master's family, and what little luggage they possessed, to the station on the succeeding Thursday. The errand was not a pleasant one, but Franks had no longer the heavy weight on his heart which had oppressed him so long as he felt that, not being in charity with man, he could not be at peace with his God. Franks could now look calmly up at the clear blue sky, flecked with rosy morning clouds, with a spirit in harmony with the tranquil, holy beauty of nature.

Cliff Farm owed its name to its position. It stood on very high ground, and was approached by a road steep enough to try the breath and mettle of any horse drawing a conveyance. On one side, not a hundred yards to the right of the farm-house, there was an abrupt fall of the ground, forming a sheer perpendicular descent of some fifty or sixty feet, down which tumbled a light sparkling cascade. It was the joyous leap of the young stream which, not a mile lower down, turned the wheel of the mill, after winding its way past the village of Colme. The brook, rushing with a pleasant gurgling sound over its rocky bed, added to the charm of the spot, which was one of the loveliest in the county. Franks had often bent his steps towards Cliff Farm, and stood on the edge of that steep, rocky bank, to enjoy the extensive view which it commanded.

And there the school-master now lingered to gaze, perhaps for the last time, from that point on the beautiful landscape before him. There lay beneath him the village of Colme, the ivy-mantled church in which he had been married to Persis, and to which they had brought their first-born babe to offer him unto the Lord. There was the dear little school-house, at once the scene of Franks's earliest labors, and the home in which he had known more of pure happiness than falls to the lot of most men, even during the longest life. The eye of the school-master wandered along the high-road leading towards the town; his gaze lingered on the cottage of Nancy Sands; never would he remember that dwelling and its inmates but with feelings of thankful joy. Then the glance of Franks fell on the chimneys of Stone's house; trees intervening hid the rest of the building from his view; there the one-armed sailor had sought faithfully, and not unsuccessfully, to open blinded eyes to the truth. Farther on—how well Franks knew its position!—lay the wooded dell in which Persis had dwelt when he wooed her, and where he had first met with Isaacs, then an unconverted Jew,—now, partly through his words, his prayers, his example, a consistent Christian believer. The little stream plunging over the cliff, which was almost at the feet of Ned Franks, was the same from which—by the mill in that same wooded dell—he had drawn the drowning Nancy at the imminent peril of his life. The pines on yon eastern hill looked down, as the school-master well knew, on the almshouses nestling in Wild Rose Hollow. How greatly would he be missed there! If that thought was sad, it also was sweet. There would be many a tear shed by aged eyes in those cottages which he had labored so hard to repair. Ned sighed to think that his work there must be left unfinished.

Still farther on roved the eye of Franks. On another hill, girdled with woods, stood the Hall; he could see its upper windows glancing in the light of the morning sun.

"O God! Thy blessing may yet rest on that dark place—as it seems to us," said the school-master half aloud. "Thou sendest

thy sunshine to all, so may none be shut out
from thy grace. It seems to me at this moment as if I could forgive from my soul even
Sir Lacy Barton."

As Ned pursued his meditations, suddenly
he was startled by a cry of "Stop him!
stop him!" from behind, with the sound of
the clattering hoofs of a horse rushing on in
wild, frantic career down the steep slope just
above the spot on which Franks was standing. Turning quickly round, he beheld a
black hunter dashing towards him at a furious
speed, which its rider, tugging at the rein,
tried in vein to check, as his horse was carrying him direct towards the cliff and — unless
it were possible to stop his career — to inev-
itable destruction! Franks had but an instant to calculate chances, to recognize the
rider, to resolve to try to save him by catching at the rein as the maddened hunter rushed
like a whirlwind by! Franks made the attempt, but failed, and was struck to the earth
with violence! The hand of no single man
would have sufficed to stop the furious and
powerful animal which the baronet rode.
Ned instantly sprang to his feet, and, as he
did so, saw the fearful plunge over the cliff,

and heard the wild cry for help from one beyond all human help. Then followed a terrible crash below !

"He's lost !" exclaimed the owner of Cliff Farm, who came panting up to the spot, followed by one of his men, who had also witnessed the frightful catastrophe, and Ned's gallant though fruitless effort to avert it.

"Let's make our way down without a moment's delay !" cried Ned; "he may be living still !"

The three men, Franks the foremost of the party, with all speed clambered to the bottom of the cliff, at a place where a little roughness in the ground, and a few bushes to hold by, enabled them to manage the descent. I will not dwell on the fearful sight which awaited them. The black horse lay dead, the rider apparently dying. Franks took the lead in doing all that could be done for the sufferer. One messenger was sent off to the Hall, another to the town for a surgeon. There was no difficulty in finding messengers, for country people, who had seen the horse when it first started off, now came running to the scene of the disaster.

With all the tenderness that he could have

shown to his dearest friend, Ned helped to place the crushed and senseless Sir Lacy upon a shutter, and to carry him by a steep path which wound up the cliff at a little distance from the cascade, to the shelter of Cliff Farm. Franks did not quit him till his own people, summoned hastily from the Hall, were around him, and amongst them the school-master-elect. Then, as he could be of no farther use, Ned Franks, thoughtful and grave, returned to his home. He found his pupils already assembled. Of course the tidings of the accident to Sir Lacy Barton were on every one's lips, and the boys awaited from their master an account of all that had happened, perhaps with such comments as what they deemed a judgment upon a wicked man might call forth from their teacher.

But Franks was not one to condemn a poor sinner already under the chastening of Heaven, nor to gratify private malice under the pretence of enforcing a lesson. He was much more grave and serious than usual, but avoided making any allusion to the fate of his persecutor, though the awful scene which he had witnessed was the uppermost thought in his mind. It was a relief to Franks, when, study-time being over, his pupils dispersed, and he was able to go to his own quiet room, where Persis was anxiously awaiting him. She, of course, like every one else in Colme, knew what had occurred, and knew, also, that the baronet had by this time been conveyed to the Hall, where he lay in a very critical state.

"Persis, how thankful I am that God had enabled me to forgive that man," said Ned Franks to his wife as they met. "Poor fellow! poor fellow! had he wronged me far more than he has done, I could feel nothing but pity for him now. Let us pray that God may spare him yet for a new and a better life."

The day wore on, and Franks and Persis did not fail at the appointed time to go to the cottage of Stone; a neighbor taking care of their baby during the short time of their absence. Glorious was that evening in August! The fields were dotted with golden sheaves, where the summer harvest of joy was following the early sowing in tears. Mr. Curtis, the venerable vicar, himself raised from what had been likely to prove a death-bed, came to administer the Holy Supper to a dying, penitent man. While the pastor had been a prisoner to his own room, as had for many months been the case, he had been constantly visiting in thought the dwellings of his flock; if he could not preach to them, he could pray for them. There were two of his parishioners whose cases had then lain particularly heavy on the mind of the good old man, Nancy Sands and Ben Stone. At the beginning of the year they had been the two in all the village who might have been pointed out, from their appearance, as giving promise of long life; the brawny carpenter, jovial and hearty, and the clerk's wife with her strongly built form, muscular arms, and loud voice. They were also the two about whose spiritual state their pastor had felt most concern. Nancy, a slave to violent passions, furious temper, and a craving for drink. Stone, free from all the sevices, yet, in his self-righteousness and blindness of heart, almost as far from the kingdom of heaven as the neighbor whom he despised. Almost at the same time the two had been stricken down, the one by a terrible accident, the other by sudden illness. Affliction had come to both the Pharisee and the publican. One had been raised and restored, though maimed, to her home; the other was never to quit his cottage till carried forth in his coffin. But mercy had visited each, and, as they met to attend the solemn service together, both penitents could say in the words of the Psalmist, *It is good for me that I have been afflicted.*

This was the first time that Nancy had been a communicant; she had never before dared to approach the table of the Lord. Stone, on the contrary, had attended regularly, at stated times in the year; but with him, until now, the service had been but an empty form, only tending to increase the blindness of his conscience, by leading him to think that he had fulfilled all righteousness, when he made thus open profession of faith, without one spark of its living reality. At that time Ben Stone would have scouted the idea of Nancy Sands, whom he deemed the worst woman in Colme, being permitted to enter his cottage on an occasion so solemn, to show that she shared his faith and his hopes, and might share his happiness in the mansions above. Yet there were they now together, Pharisee and publican, both brought to the foot of the cross; the once despised drunk ard meekly giving God thanks that she was not what she once had been, and the Pharisee, not raising up so much as his eyes unto heaven, but silently uttering the prayer, *God be merciful to me a sinner!*

Often had Persis and her husband joined in the holy service, but never had they felt heaven nearer to them, and the Christian's hope sweeter, than they did in Stone's cottage on that bright August eve. They saw the saving power of the gospel in the two penitents before them, the one rescued from the rock of self-righteousness, the other from the whirlpool of intemperance. The little flock gathered together in that peaceful home seemed an emblem of that blessed band, who, through God's mercy and grace, shall, after life's troubles and tossings, reach in safety the heavenly shore.

As the Frankses returned, after the solemn meeting by the sick-bed of Stone, a rich, golden glow was over the sky, and a deep stillness in the air; heaven seemed to be all brightness, and earth all peace. Then came a sound, solemn at all times, but especially so at that hour, the measured tolling of the church-bells for a departed soul. It was the first announcement to those who had met in Stone's cottage that the unhappy Sir Lacy had been called to his last account.

Yes, the bells that had been silent on his arrival at his ancestral home, now, with slow and mournful peal, announced his departure. Soon would a dark and narrow home receive the mortal remains of the late possessor of thousands of acres. Had power, wealth, and high station been a blessing or a curse to him who had not indeed *buried* his talents, but made them an instrument of evil? The profane tongue was now silenced; the hand that had rattled the dice, the brain once so busy with evil designs, the heart that had been a den of wickedness, now lay lifeless and cold. The baronet's spirit had passed from earth, and left no sweet memories behind. Another and a far better man would now bear his title and rule in his Hall, and dispense happiness as widely as the late lord of the manor had tried to spread the contagion of evil. Every toll of the solemn bell, which pealed through the calm evening air, seemed, with a voice more impressive than that of man, to repeat the warning, *He that being often reproved, hardeneth his neck, shall*

XXXVIII.

Conclusion.

FRANKS and his wife received a message from Mr. Curtis, on the following morning, to desire them to come to the vicarage at one. At their accustomed time of assembling for study, the boys of Colme flocked to their school-house, full of expectation and excitement, the congratulations beaming in their eyes which their lips did not venture to utter; for something in their master's manner told them that they must not speak to him of any change in his prospects likely to be caused by the baronet's death. The boys, who were rejoicing in the assurance that they would keep their "dear old Ned Franks," since there was a new baronet now, could hardly settle to business or attend to their tasks. Had not their teacher found it quite as difficult to do so himself, he would have had to reprove or correct half his pupils for the most ridiculous blunders. There was also an unusual amount of nodding, whispering, and smiling, which Ned Franks for once tried in vain to repress. The boys had never seemed to care so little for addition or multiplication, or found it so impossible to master a column of spelling. "He'll never leave us, not he;" "Won't the curate be glad to keep him!" "That fellow with the sly look, who was to have been our master, will have to take himself off sharp, like a beaten dog!" "Won't we have jolly days now, and won't we work double hard at Wild Rose Hollow!" Such were the eager whispers which passed from mouth to mouth. It must be owned that Franks seemed to be an inefficient schoolmaster on that day, and had very inattentive pupils.

Lesson time was over at last, and punctual to their appointment, the Frankses appeared at the vicarage just as the church clock struck one. The boys, instead of dispersing as usual, had followed them, like an escort, as far as the garden gate. Norah, with a beaming countenance, was waiting at the door to usher them in. The young maiden had double cause for her joy, for her mistress had received a letter that morning from Mrs. Lowndes, mentioning that the confession of Martha, her late house-maid, that she had taken the lost sovereign which had accidentally dropped on the floor, had entirely cleared Norah from all suspicion of theft. Mrs. Lowndes expressed her satisfaction that Norah had succeeded in getting a place, and gave her testimony that, except in one unhappy act of deception into which she had been drawn, a more truthful and faithful servant than Norah she never had known. Norah had not at this moment time to tell the Frankses of this letter, which had been a great relief to her affectionate heart, but her pleasure was seen in her looks. She ushered her uncle and his wife into the study, and then would herself have retired, but her mistress, with a kindly smile, beckoned her to remain. Never had she been more readily obeyed.

In the vicar's study were collected several of the villagers of Colme, looking on with curiosity and interest. Sands, the clerk, unusually placid and serene in his mien, stood by the side of his wife, whose dark eyes expressed pleasure mingled with something like triumph. The sturdy miller was also present, holding by the hand his little Bessie, who looked brimming over with joy.

Mr. Curtis, who was seated in his large arm-chair, shook hands with the school-master, and then Persis received first from her pastor, and then from his wife, the same kindly greeting. Had there been any doubt before on the subject, the manner of Mr. and Mrs. Curtis, and the smiles of the villagers present, would have assured the Frankses that they were summoned to hear good news. The pastor when he spoke was listened to in respectful silence.

"I have been requested, Franks, by Mr.— I mean Sir Claudius — to express to you his hope that you will continue, and *long* continue," there was a strong emphasis on the word long, "to instruct the boys of our village school. He has had, during the time that he has been curate at Colme (as I have had during a much longer period), the opportunity of seeing how faithfully, zealously, and successfully you have performed the duties of your office. To no one could we more gladly, more confidently, entrust the charge of our boys."

Ned Franks bowed and colored at the

praise; Persis exchanged a glance of pleasure with Norah.

"And I have another pleasant office to perform," continued the old vicar, turning to receive from the hand of his wife a well filled crimson purse which had lain on the study table. When we were afraid that we were going to lose you, that you and your good wife were about to leave Colme, a little subscription was set on foot, to procure a testimonial to be given at parting to those who have earned the respect — I may say the affection — of those amongst whom they have dwelt."

"They have — they have," murmured Nancy, and little Bessie squeezed tightly the hand of her father to express *her* silent assent.

"We are happily to keep you with us in Colme," continued the vicar; "but our friends" — here he turned smilingly towards the parishioners who represented the subscribers, — "our friends will not lose the opportunity of offering the *present*, though we all unite in hoping that the *parting* may be very far off."

Ned Franks, by whom this tribute of regard from his neighbors had been altogether unexpected, was taken by surprise, and looked more confused and embarrassed than if he had been receiving a reproof instead of a present.

"No—indeed, sir—I am very thankful—grateful to you—to all—but I could not,"—he stammered forth, shrinking from touching the proffered purse. "Pray, let the money be returned to the subscribers. I feel, from my heart I feel, their great kindness all the same as if I availed myself of it."

"They won't touch it, not a penny of it!" exclaimed Nancy, who was standing behind the vicar's chair. "I went round to every one this morning. You must take the purse, Ned Franks, if it be but to throw it away!"

John Sands, who had a high sense of decorum, looked aghast at his wife thus venturing "to put in her word" in the vicar's own study; but the clerk only attempted to stop her by a faintly murmured "My dear!"

"No, indeed, I will never throw away money so kindly, so generously given," said Franks. "Pray, sir," he continued, addressing Mr. Curtis, "let the contents of the purse go towards repairing the almshouses in Wild Rose Hollow. I and my wife have everything that we need, and I think that I can answer for Persis that this is the way in which she would best like the money to be spent."

There was a little murmur through the circle of villagers, in which admiration of the sailor's generosity was mingled with something like dissatisfaction at his giving everything away. Nancy said, in a very audible whisper, "They could have had their trip to the sea-side." Mrs. Curtis, who had hitherto remained a silent though interested spectator, now spoke.

"Perhaps all parties will be gratified by a compromise," said the lady; " let half of the contents of the purse be contributed by Franks to the object for which he has pleaded and worked so hard, and let him satisfy his friends here by using the other half for a little holiday-trip for himself and his wife, when his pupils for a time give up their studies for gleaning."

The proposal of the lady gave universal satisfaction, and when Ned Franks and his happy wife had quitted the vicar's house, the loud ringing, joyous cheer which greeted them from the boys who had been waiting outside went as warm to their hearts as the praise of their pastor, and the practical token of the loving esteem of their neighbors.

When the sound of cheers had died away, and all the shaking of hands and exchange of words of kindness were over at last, Franks and his wife, thankful and happy, turned towards their own home, whilst neighbors and boys dispersed to theirs. For several minutes neither husband nor wife spoke a word; perhaps each understood too well what was passing in the mind of the other for any words to be needful. At length the silence was broken by Ned.

"Persis," he said, with emotion, "I think I'm more humbled than exalted by all this kindness, and all this praise. How our friends judge by the outside! It is God alone who reads the heart. How little they guess what a struggle with evil was going on here," Ned laid his hand on his breast, " and that not forty-eight hours since!"

" God gave you the victory," said Persis, softly.

" He helped me in the hour of temptation," said Franks; " and when the enemy of souls takes advantage of my weakness, and sends his fire-ships again to set this impatient spirit in a blaze, may I be enabled to be watchful and vigilant, and steer my onward course in the safe track left by Him who was *meek and lowly in heart!*"

My little story is almost ended. I shall not linger over any description of the well-earned holiday-trip, which was greatly enjoyed by Franks and his wife. The almshouses in Wild Rose Hollow were put in most perfect repair before winter, and each one had a beautiful porch. The work of Ned and his "jovial crew" was helped forward by the ready purse of the new baronet. Sir Claudius never forgot that he was the minister of the gospel, as well as the lord of the manor.

I will but give a short glimpse of the party of village boys gathered together on the following Christmas day in the school-room, not for study, but to partake of a substantial feast provided for them by Sir Claudius. The large room was richly decked out with wreaths of bay and holly, bunches of mistle-toe, and sprigs of laurel. Even blind Sophy had helped to form the garlands; for the long-cherished wish of Benoni had been grat-ified at last, and Isaacs had brought him and his adopted sister to spend their Christmas at Colme. The preparations for the banquet had been made by Persis, with Norah and Nancy Sands as her cheerful assistants, while Benoni, proud of the charge, had insisted on taking care of the baby.

"What a different Christmas this is from my last!" thought Nancy, with a humbling recollection of having made the last anniversary of her Lord's birth an occasion for plunging into mad and sinful excess! Such memories but deepened her thankfulness to Him who had snatched her from the whirlpool of destruction.

"What a different Christmas this is from the last!" observed Benoni, looking up with a glad smile into the face of Persis, his first friend in Colme, and still the one most tenderly loved. "Last Christmas we were in London, and there was such a yellow fog that we could not see to read without a candle, and we had no candle to light! and we should have stood shivering round the fire, only there was no fire to stand round! And when we came home from church, we were hungry enough for our Christmas dinner, only," the boy added, with a laugh, "dry bread and cold tea didn't look much like Christmas fare!"

"You must have had a sad time of suffering, then, dear Benoni!"

"It would have been sad indeed, except that the Lord was with us in our trouble, as he is now in our joy!"

"Ah! my boy," said Ned Franks, who had overheard the last observation, "that is the secret of having life's voyage a safe and a happy one. It is when the Master is with us that we are guided through the rocks and the shoals, and kept from running aground. It is having the Master with us that turns the storm into a calm, so that the winds and waves are still. And so, when the children of God reach the heavenly shore, it will only be because the Master was with them, and hath brought them at last, through his power and his love, unto their desired haven."

THE END.